The Red Room

MODERN KOREAN FICTION

Bruce Fulton, General Editor

TREES ON A SLOPE
Hwang Sun-wŏn

THE DWARF
Cho Se-hŭi

THE RED ROOM: STORIES OF TRAUMA
IN CONTEMPORARY KOREA
Bruce and Ju-Chan Fulton, translators

THE
RED ROOM

Stories of Trauma in Contemporary Korea

Translated by Bruce and Ju-Chan Fulton

Foreword by Bruce Cumings

University of Hawai'i Press

Honolulu

This book has been published with the assistance of the
Sunshik Min Endowment for the Advancement of Korean
Literature, Korea Institute, Harvard University.

Printed in the United States of America
14 13 12 11 10 09   6 5 4 3 2 1

Library of Congress Cataloging-in-Publication Data
The red room : stories of trauma in contemporary Korea / translated by Bruce
and Ju-Chan Fulton ; foreword by Bruce Cumings.
    p. cm. — (Modern Korean fiction)
Includes bibliographical references.
ISBN 978-0-8248-3326-8 (hardcover : alk. paper) — ISBN 978-0-8248-3397-8
(pbk. : alk. paper)
    1. Korean fiction—20th century—Translations into English. I. Fulton, Bruce.
II. Fulton, Ju-Chan. III. Pak, Won-so, 1925– Puch'onim kunch'o. English. IV. O,
Chong-hui Param ui nok. English. V. Im, Ch'or-u, 1954– Pulgun pang. English. VI.
Title: Puch'onim kunch'o. VII. Title: Param ui nok. VIII. Title: Pulgun pang.
    PL984.E8R44 2009
    895.7'14—dc22
                                        2009020882

An earlier version of "In the Realm of the Buddha" was published in Koreana
10:2 (Summer 1996); an earlier version of "Spirit in the Wind" was published in
Acta Koreana 11:2 (June 2008).

Designed by University of Hawai'i Press production staff

Printed by The Maple-Vail Book Manufacturing Group

Contents

Foreword _____

BRUCE CUMINGS

The Korean War was clearly a war, but what kind? The official view
insists it was a war of aggression, with all blame going to the Russians
and the North Koreans. According to this point of view, the war began
on June 25, 1950, when the North invaded the South, an open-and-
shut case of aggression. Still, there is a nagging point: Koreans invaded
Korea. What do we make of that? A different view, expressed as early
as 1950, holds that the unilateral American decision in 1945 to divide
Korea at the 38th parallel was "the invitation to such a conflict as has
in fact arisen":

> In the American Civil War the Americans would never have tolerated for
> a single moment the setting up of an imaginery [sic] line between the
> forces of North and South, and there can be no doubt as to what would
> have been their re-action if the British had intervened in force on behalf
> of the South. This parallel is a close one because in America the conflict
> was not merely between two groups of Americans, but was between two
> conflicting economic systems as is the case in Korea.[1]

I agree: the essential nature of this war, the thing we need to know
first, is that it was a civil war, a war fought by Koreans, for Korean

goals. Koreans know this war in their bones as a fratricidal conflict, something that is etched into the stories that they tell in this wonderful collection.

War Is a Stern Teacher

The Korean War, like the U.S. Civil War, had a long gestation and occurred primarily because of issues internal to Korea. That is the basic reason it has never ended. The civil conflict began not in 1950 but in 1945 with the partition of this ancient nation as World War II ended. Only this conception can account for the one hundred thousand lives lost in the South before June 1950 and the continuance of the conflict down to the present, in spite of assumptions that Moscow's puppets in Pyongyang would surely collapse after the USSR itself met oblivion in 1991. It is therefore instructive to see what Thucydides, the first philosopher of war, had to say about civil war. "War is a stern teacher," perhaps the most famous line from his *History of the Peloponnesian War,* comes from the civil war in Corcyra:

> War is a stern teacher. So revolutions broke out in city after city. . . . What used to be described as a thoughtless act of aggression was now regarded as the courage one would expect to find in a party member; to think of the future and wait was merely another way of saying one was a coward; any idea of moderation was just an attempt to disguise one's unmanly character; ability to understand a question from all sides meant that one was totally unfitted for action. Fanatical enthusiasm was the mark of a real man, and to plot against an enemy behind his back was perfectly legitimate self-defense. Anyone who held violent opinions could always be trusted, and anyone who objected to them became a suspect.[2]

This passage is a mnemonic for "Korea." It fits the Korean civil war with no necessity to dot "i's" or cross "t's," and it explains the continuing blight from that war on the Korean mind. To understand the Korean War "from all sides" is still to go to jail in the North and to risk oblivion in the now (and finally) democratic South. The passage also fits the American Civil War, by far the most devastating of all American wars to Americans, but one that happened long enough ago that most Americans have no idea what it means to have warfare sweeping back and forth across the national territory or to have brother pitted against brother.

Now that South Koreans are free to write about this war—its origins, its nature, its consequences—we see that an entire population was traumatized by one of the most violent and intense wars of the twentieth century. No one knows for sure how many Koreans died from 1950 to 1953, but most experts accept a figure of about 2 million for the North, which had a prewar population of about 8 million, and around 1 million for the South, which had about 15 million. (Another 1 million Chinese died.) This makes Korean suffering comparable to the other two worst-case situations of the last century, Poland and the Soviet Union in World War II (the Soviet side lost about 27 million people). These are extraordinary figures, but much of the loss came from the U.S. aerial bombardment of North Korea. All told the North lost perhaps one-quarter of its population.

This episode of bombardment, now very well documented, left barely a modern building standing in the cities, which were much more urban and industrial than comparable cities in, say, North Vietnam. I think many of the odd and repellent aspects of contemporary North Korea bear some relationship to this nation's suffering from a terrible collective form of war trauma. When I first visited there in 1981, the bombing was the first thing my guides and handlers brought up to me. Is it possible for an entire nation to have post-traumatic stress disorder?

South Korean fiction seems to suggest that it is. Just about every Korean lost a family member in the war, and some 10 million Koreans still have kinfolk in either the North or the South that they have not seen since 1953. Pak Wan-sŏ's brilliant career, as Bruce Fulton points out, is a matter of working through war trauma for the rest of her life. Im Ch'ŏr-u comes from a region of Korea doubly and triply traumatized: the Chŏlla provinces in the southwest. Here in the early 1890s a major peasant rebellion broke out that the old Korean regime and the Japanese put down with ruthless force. A second major rebellion erupted under the U.S. Occupation in the fall of 1946, an unknown number died when the North's army swept through in July 1950, and tens of thousands more died when the South Korean forces of order retook this region and lashed out in retribution against real or imagined collaborators with the North. Thirty years later came the Kwangju Massacre, which shook the nation to its roots and spawned an entire generation of young people who not only hated and rebelled against the military dictatorship, but also reviled the United States for its continuing support of these same militarists.

For Pak Wan-sŏ, it goes without saying that this long-running con-flict was a civil war, an internecine struggle between brethren. "The eyes that had seen" that war later averted their gaze from it; forgetting was salutary; living was in the here and now—better grab up some real estate bargains and get on with life. But this forgetting is also a result of trauma, and Americans, too, need to ask themselves why they call this major war "forgotten." Was it ever really *known*? Most Americans know nothing about the horrific civilian losses in the North and would bridle even at the suggestion that somehow they victimized North Korea. Is it not symbolic that in the late David Halberstam's recent book about the war, *The Coldest Winter*, he can name only two South Koreans in the entire book? A wife wanders away from her husband in O Chŏng-hŭi's story, searching for something—herself, her past—for she was one of Korea's hundreds of thousands of war orphans (fully one hundred thousand of them were adopted by Americans). She feels rootless, a vagrant, even though she is ensconced within a family. What would crack her "hard shell of oblivion"? Truths suddenly emerge from an unknown past to unnerve a child. Im Ch'ŏr-u's character remembers the experience of water torture, and today we Americans read this with a new recognition: that's what we do, too, to prisoners held in Guantanamo. There, ironi-cally, Americans even read North Korean torture manuals from a sixty-year-old war for pointers. No one really escapes a cataclysm like this, Pak suggests. All have bloody faces in their dreams and cold sweats when they wake in the wee hours of the morning—even Americans.

Restorative Truths

What is truth? The Truth and Reconciliation Commission in South Africa defined that vexing term in four ways: factual or forensic truth, personal or narrative truth, social or "dialogue" truth, and healing or restorative truth. Book after book has appeared in South Korea in the past two decades, full of revelations about the nature of the Korean War and the horrible suffering of the Korean people. Survivors have pressed their case against all odds for years.[3] Forensic evidence has also turned up with nauseating regularity, as the Korean Truth and Reconciliation Commission (established during President Roh Moo-hyun's term) disinters the bodies of thousands of political massacre victims. These forensic and eyewitness truths establish lies and misrepresentations at all levels, perpetrated for half a century, especially by officials in Washington.[4] But they also (in the South African commission's words) "reduce the number of lies that can be circulated unchallenged in public discourse."

The stories in this collection, the restorative truths told by the courageous survivors and living victims of the Korean War, and the many new articles and books examining this war from all sides that have appeared in South Korea, are fruits of the popular struggle for democracy in Korea; this surge of civil society is also a surge of suppressed information and would never have been possible during the long decades of dictatorship before 1988. This Korean outpouring is also, however, akin to what writers like Ambrose Bierce did for Americans in the aftermath of their own civil conflict, penning poignant stories that captured the terrible truths of fratricidal war. Now it is high time to take the personal truths of the victims and survivors and turn them into a restorative truth, a requiem for the "forgotten war" that might finally achieve the peaceful reconciliation that the two

Koreas have been denied since we first etched a line at the 38th parallel in August 1945.

Notes

1. Public Record Office, London, Foreign Office file 317, piece no. 83008, Stokes to Bevin, December 2, 1950.
2. Thucydides, *History of the Peloponnesian War*, trans. Rex Warner (New York: Penguin Books, 1954), p. 147.
3. For example, Mrs. Chŏn Ch'un-ja, twelve years old at the time of the Nogŭn-ni massacre, who witnessed American soldiers "play[ing] with our lives like boys playing with flies." *New York Times*, September 30, 1999, p. A16.
4. The massacre of some four thousand political prisoners by South Korean police in July 1950 in Taejŏn was blamed entirely on North Koreans in the official U.S. military history of the war authored by the late Roy Appleman: *South to the Naktong, North to the Yalu* (Washington, D.C.: Center of Military History, U.S. Army, 1961).

In the Realm of the Buddha

PAK WAN-SŎ

The candles were 120 *wŏn* a box and the longevity incense 100. I decided to play dumb. I produced 200 *wŏn*, then snapped my purse shut.

"That'll be another twenty *wŏn*, please."

"Really, mister, these candles go for a hundred everywhere else."

I put on the straight face I wore when I bargained down the price of a pike mackerel by 5 *wŏn* or bought 20 *wŏn* worth of bean sprouts and haggled an extra handful. Then I produced my Coy Innocent Look for the man and tucked the candles and incense in Mother's shopping bag.

"Sweetie." Mother nudged me aside. "These aren't for bargaining." She hoisted her skirts, produced two 10-*wŏn* coins from the large pocket of her bloomers, and politely presented them to the man, bowing a couple of times for good measure.

And this was the woman who would have put me to shame had we been in a bargaining situation.

I don't think she was bothered so much by what she considered my stinginess. Rather she seemed to think it represented a lack of devotion to the Buddha on my part, and I sensed she feared the consequences.

We left the shop, and all the while we walked, Mother's face was clouded and solemn. The solemn part seemed mostly an act, and I thought she was overdoing it. Have you ever seen parents teaching games to their kindergartners? They look so earnest and their expressions are so exaggerated. Well, that was how she won me over, and I found myself adopting her solemnness.

Some time ago she had sweet-talked me into tagging along with her to see a shaman man, and I realized now that she'd put on that air of solemn majesty then too. Ptoo! The thought of that man made me spit, and then spit again, as if the street was that fellow's face. I shuddered.

I was already regretting my decision to accompany Mother to the temple. But by then we had arrived.

Mother had told me it was a historic temple, occupied only by nuns during its three hundred–plus years, and she guessed it was second to none in our country in terms of the number of female believers who came to visit. Still it was much larger than I had expected. It resembled a fortress more than a temple, dwarfing the clustered dwellings outside. The ponderous two-story concrete structure with its tile roof, neither Korean nor Western in style, separated the homes from the temple compound, which it enclosed on three sides like a fence. Viewed from the homes, the temple had the severe quality of bare, unornamented concrete. And it possessed an uncertain dignity combined with the absurd incongruity of a traditional tile roof resting on two stories of concrete.

And yet the dharma hall looming directly above us at the top of a flight of stone steps as soon as we entered the compound was a gratifying sight, with the beautiful multicolored patterns that emblazoned its woodwork and especially the wooden construction that exemplified the temple style. Mother bowed toward the hall, her palms together.

When we entered the compound I was puzzled to see that the inside was altogether different from the concrete building I had seen outside. What had looked so cloistered and conspiratorial out there was surprisingly bright and open in here. There were no walls to speak of, only the gleaming glass of sliding doors that opened onto a succession of rooms with laminated paper flooring that were as spacious as the VIP rooms in a fancy restaurant. The largest of these looked as big as two grade-school classrooms. Arrayed before it was an endless line of rubber shoes, and from inside there rang the invocations of the faithful:

Homage to the greatly compassionate Avalokitesvara,
I vow that I will soon gain the eye of wisdom.
Homage to the greatly compassionate Avalokitesvara,
I vow that I will quickly ferry across all sentient beings.
Homage to the greatly compassionate Avalokitesvara,
I vow that I will soon gain skillful expedients.[1]

To my delight I recognized these chants. In fact, I was so used to hearing them, I felt I just might be able to follow along.

It so happened that I awoke every day from my shallow sleep to the sound of these chants, which issued without fail from Mother's room during dawn's gray twilight. It was early, too early to make breakfast for the children. I didn't mind the chanting, though I constantly feared it would wake my husband. Perhaps I had tried somehow to draw a day's security from her chants.

And it was because of Mother's chanting that I could readily write down "Buddhist" in the religion section of the children's home-life survey given out by the school. This was a good thing because the children hated having a lot of "None" responses appear.

Inside the spacious room was a long table and chairs covered with seat cushions. Across the table from one another sat the faithful, shoulder to shoulder, the young on one side and the old on the other. I was reminded of a wedding hall, where one side of the aisle is male and the other female. I was about to find a seat with the young people when Mother took my hand and led me before an image of the Buddha.

"Do your bows—the offering comes first."

Backed by a garish mural, the Buddha sat on a silk cushion inside a glass cabinet similar to a show window. Thus bedecked, the likeness looked worldly and fake, not so different from the Buddhas in the

---

1. Translation by Robert E. Buswell, Jr., from his book *The Zen Monastic Experience* (Princeton, N.J.: Princeton University Press, 1992), 237; reprinted by permission of the author.

display cases of the Buddhist supply shops clustered along the fourth block down Chongno.

On the wide altar in front of the cabinet sat more stainless steel candlesticks than I could count. Every one of them was lit, the motionless flames resembling tiny light bulbs. None of the candle holders was empty, so Mother lit one of the candles we had bought, extinguished someone else's with her fingertips, and replaced it with ours. Everyone else seemed to have done the same, judging from all the candles lying neglected among the candlesticks with only their wicks singed.

Directly in front of the cabinet's glass window was a slightly higher altar containing a basket heaped with 100- and 500-*wŏn* notes. I fished a 500-*wŏn* bill from my purse and added it to the pile. This seemed a bit dear because I also had some 100s, but I regretted having upset Mother over the 20 *wŏn* for the candles and wanted this time to please her. Well, you can imagine my surprise when she blanched at the sight of that 500 *wŏn*, plunged a hand fearlessly into the pile, rummaged about, and extracted four 100-*wŏn* notes.

"I'm sorry—I should have said something," she tsk-tsked. "I guess I forgot to ask you to bring some small bills. I hope you didn't think this would be the only offering. By and by we'll have to go up to the dharma hall, and then the Seven Stars shrine, and after that the Mountain Spirit's shrine. So hurry up and do your bows."

I did just that, mortified by Mother and the four 100-*wŏn* notes. Many of the faithful were sitting on the floor reciting prayers. Many others were performing bows, and there I was stem to stern with the woman in front of me and bottom to forehead with the woman behind.

Still I bowed, and then again, and yet again. I had no alternative. My legs grew sore, but on I went. It was like being in a cheering section: dare I act independently when everyone around me was in passionate motion?

"All right, let's sit down for a bit."

Mother sounded satisfied. And I was delighted. Delighted at being able to take a break, delighted at having made Mother feel fulfilled again. I made a motion to join the young people sitting on the floor, but Mother insisted I sit beside her—that part of the floor didn't look heated, she said.

The faithful kept coming, kept extinguishing the candles of others and lighting their own, and among the chanting worshipers already seated there were also those who jumped up to replace others' candles with their own; all of them, each and every one, bowed and bowed again, placing their palms together over and over, then bowed some more, and with each prostration, bottoms wide as kneading boards shot up toward the ceiling and the backs of the long skirts parted like curtains to reveal synthetic slips, Tetron slips, wool slips.

Bluish smoke rose from the longevity incense packed into the brazier-sized stainless steel burner and filled the spacious room. The thick fog irritated my throat, and my chest tightened in reaction to the turbid air. But I managed to bear up. Most of the chanting was done by the older believers, who lacked the energy to bow as fervently as the others: *"Namora tanadara yaya namagalyak parogije saebaraya morisadabaya mahasadabaya mahagaro nigaya om salbabayesu. . . ."* This was another chant I heard every morning, and I could follow along. But I found it as unintelligible as a magician's abracadabra.

I had once asked Mother the meaning of this chant. But she skillfully parried the question, saying, "Why fuss over the meaning?" And then she told me a story: There once was a man who went off to battle. His wife worried day and night for his welfare, and when she came to her wit's end she sought out a Buddhist master who lived high in the mountains and asked what service she might perform to ensure her husband's safety. The master bade her call out "Homage to Amitabha Buddha" with all her heart, day in and day out, morning, noon, and night. The woman returned home calling out, "Homage to Amitabha Buddha," but as soon as she crossed the stream at the entrance to her village, she forgot the words. She racked her memory, but nothing came to mind. She then sought out a learned man in the village and begged him to teach her the forgotten invocation. Though this man was learned, he was also a lewd-minded rascal, and instead of the prayer he taught her the worst obscenities imaginable. The woman chanted these vulgar words at all hours, and the villagers scorned her as a madwoman crazy for her man after her enforced separation. But the woman continued chanting with all her heart, then chanted some more. In the end her husband returned home alive. More than once he had escaped the jaws of death, and this could only be accounted for by the providence of the Buddha.

The meaning of the words was superficial; the devotion and belief they inspired were the essence. This was Mother's point.

But I couldn't shake the habit of wanting to understand the meaning of these invocations and through my limited knowledge to comprehend Buddhism and the Buddhist mind. In point of fact my knowledge of Buddhism was not only sparse but also extremely basic—the kind everyone learned at school. Worse still, it was half-baked and was accompanied by no faith whatsoever.

In short, I was trying to look at Buddhism with the same amount of knowledge I had of Jesus or Muhammad—enough knowledge, that is, to earn me a score of 50 out of 100 on a test. It was like looking at something through glasses worn on the tip of one's nose.

And so I found it obnoxious that the dharma hall in this temple compound existed side by side with a Daoist Seven Stars shrine and a Mountain Spirit's shrine. But for Mother, the more deities there were to look after us, whether the Buddha or the Daoist spirits, the more grateful and awed she felt.

The Seven Stars shrine appeared to date back before Mother became a believer at the temple. The Mountain Spirit's shrine was newly built on top of a rock wall above the dharma hall, its construction funded with large-scale donations by the faithful. At the time, Mother had kept trying to read my feelings on the matter until finally I grew embarrassed. She had ended up practically begging me for money to make a donation. I told her I didn't see what a Mountain Spirit's shrine was doing at a Buddhist temple. They were a bunch of fakes, those so-called nuns; they were bogus through and through. I called them every name I could think of, then refused Mother a single *wŏn*. And not only that. I had a hunch she couldn't abide not giving, and so I brazenly interfered with the housekeeping, which I had pretty much entrusted to her, going to extremes to make sure not one copper leaked out in the form of a donation.

This amounted to a terrible insult to Mother. But she held up to my mistreatment: "Here we go again—temper, temper," was all she said. I sensed she had found a way to make a donation. Sure enough, I discovered one day that she was no longer wearing the gold ring I had given her on the occasion of her sixtieth-birthday celebration.

Mother was all too familiar with my tantrums. I had a very short fuse and managed to lose my temper for any reason or none at all. Mother tended to me in my ill humor as a nurse would a patient.

The smoke from the incense was awful. It hurt to swallow. Still I remained patient and kept my eyes respectfully closed, and when all the faithful rose, I followed suit, heaving a sigh of relief that the ceremony appeared to be over.

But no—the next moment I realized it was probably just beginning. There appeared an elderly monk in a crimson cloak, his hair and even his eyebrows white with age, supporting himself with a knobby walking stick. He sat down in a chair that had stood apart and unoccupied since our arrival. He was followed by several nuns, who bowed first to the Buddha and then to the monk before seating themselves in a row directly across from him, their backs to the door.

"He's giving a lecture," Mother whispered in my ear. "He came all the way just for that."

The audience of believers bowed in unison to the monk, over and over, as if they would never stop. And then the monk gently closed his eyes and began to chant. The nuns did likewise and the audience too, now seated.

But some of the younger women continued to worship the image in the display case, lighting candles and incense and performing bows. An older nun begged them to be seated and to please stop lighting incense, which clogged the throat and made recitation difficult. But the women were oblivious; like shamans in a trance, they continued their compulsive, undulating bows.

In the meantime the lecture had commenced. The monk explained how the Lord Buddha had achieved deliverance from worldly desires and obtained true freedom, then spread the truth. But for the most part, using simple language, the monk focused on the miracles the Lord Buddha had performed—taming a gigantic viper so it would curl

up in a monk's wooden rice bowl; rending asunder the raging waves
of a fearsome flood and occupying dry land; and so on. I found it interesting enough, but since there was no mention of the suffering the
Lord Buddha had undergone before his deliverance or of the wandering he finally put an end to, it was inevitably a ho-hum subject.

I'm too old to have much interest in that sort of story.

More interesting than the lecture was the sight of the young women
still frantically performing their bows. They drew grand arches in
the air with their outspread arms, brought their hands together at the
chest, then prostrated themselves on their knees, and for every woman
who placed her palms reverently against the floor, there was one who
rested the sides of her hands on the floor and curled her palms inward
like a fence and another who placed the backs of her hands on the floor
and reached out in supplication toward the Buddha. For all of them the
bowing itself was an act of ecstasy.

The Buddha had said, "The person who has achieved true enlight-
enment, the person who has found deliverance from worldly desires,
is the very person whom it is suitable to worship." And so it was quite
proper to come to a temple to bow—isn't that why we use the same
word, *chŏl,* for temples and for bowing?

But something about these women didn't sit right with me. They
venerated the Buddha as one who had obtained deliverance from
various worldly concerns, attachments, and forms of greed. They
worshiped him so earnestly, and yet the more absorbed they were in
bowing, the more their prostrations smacked of a gross, profane
materialism. Just like the glossy, sticky beads of sweat bubbling from
my pores at the height of the dog days.

I gradually grew weary of sitting, weary of the lecture, weary of
watching the others bow, and I began to squirm, to yawn audibly, to
play with the clasp of my purse, to gnaw on my fingernails. And then
I heard the older women beside me chatting in low voices:

"Those gals must have legs of steel—look at them; they don't
give up."

"Maybe this year we'll see quite a few make it to a thousand again."

"More than last year, I'll bet. Remember the ones who were bragging about their thousand bows and how their husbands' businesses took off last year? Their families are still swimming in money, from what I hear."

"And so they're bowing like crazy this year too. Damned if these old legs of mine are anywhere near that strong, no matter how good the money is."

"I'll say. Maybe it would be different, venerable sister, if our old men could give us a nice massage. Heeheehee."

"Is that what those hens said—they get a massage from the old man?"

"Venerable sister, didn't you hear them bragging about it? They pray to the Buddha for good fortune, then go home and pretend their legs are killing them. Hubby gets into a tizzy and stays up all night massaging them."

"Filthy women."

"So you pray early in January, do your thousand bows, and you get good fortune the rest of the year—is that the idea?"

"Well, look who's changing her mind—that's what a husband will do for you."

"Who's going to pray for a husband that's got one foot in the grave? I'm talking about my son—nothing ever turns out right for him, and it frustrates me so."

"Venerable sister, I've got an idea. There's a temple, I think it's up in Ui-dong, where they've got a stone Buddha that does miracles you wouldn't believe. Make one wish—just one—and he always listens. We ought to go there."

"Well, why not? Seems to me I heard the same thing somewhere."

"Now don't fly off half cocked, you two. You know how far away it is? You're better off doing your thousand bows right here. That place is for rich folks with cars—they toss around money like Kleenex there."

"It's no different here—on Buddha's birthday last year the shaved heads had more money than they knew what to do with. They stuffed it into a straw sack like cabbage leaves, stomped it down, then hauled it off to the bank."

"No. . . ."

"Give me a reason why not, venerable sister. This is business we're talking about—and when it comes to balance sheets, you're not going to find a merchant who does as well as the folks who deal in the Buddha or Jesus. Why don't we set up a temple ourselves, damn it?"

"Now where are you going to get the money? You have a hard enough time with the offering."

When I heard them giggle, I had to remind myself it was old women I was listening to. They turned to bragging about the clothes and jewelry their daughters and daughters-in-law had given them. And then the subject changed to so-and-so, whose seventieth-birthday celebration was coming up, and to such-and-such, whose grandson was taking a wife—it was one thing after another and there was no end to it.

The old monk's lecture seemed close to an end when suddenly his low voice exploded in a roar: Everything was being consumed in the fires of greed, of anger, of sorrow, suffering, and fear!

But even if he was correct and none of these women dared contradict him in the least, these were empty words spoken mostly for effect. Better if he had shouted that the incense was burning, and the candles, and our throats.—Weren't these the more immediate issues that would have drawn a response from us?

The smoke from the incense was awful. I could no longer put up with the burning sensation in my throat.

I rose, threaded my way among the elderly women, and escaped through a side door to the veranda. I crossed the wooden floor to the railing, then located my shoes in the array on the shoe ledge below and put them on. Ah, much better! I opened my mouth wide, drank in the air, and gave myself up to a sneezing fit.

Before I knew it, Mother had joined me. She silently read my mood.

"Is it all right if I go home, Mother? I'm getting chilly, and I'm afraid I'll catch cold. You take your time, though."

"Go home without doing the ceremony? Listen to you!"

"Gosh, of course. What's gotten into me?" I said like an idiot. I even giggled.

Today, early January by the lunar calendar, was the propitious date selected by the temple to offer a service for good fortune. It was also the twenty-second anniversary of my father's death. Twenty-two years ... and yet today was the first time we were formally honoring his memory, and this temple Mother frequented was the place. It would be a day of deep emotion for Mother, for there was a story behind our disregard of that observance until now, as well as behind our decision to hold it, and here again it seemed I had added to her feelings of regret.

"You little mischief. I was afraid you were running off again like you did at the shaman man's, so I hurried out after you."

Mother was so thankful I hadn't run off that she overlooked my indifference to the observance we would hold today. I felt sorry to see her this way.

"How long do we have to wait around?" I mumbled between sneezes.

"Well, until they finish the service—it should be over soon. But I can ask the nun who's taking care of us if we can start now. You stay right here—I'll be back."

"Where are they keeping the memorial tablets? I can wait there— it's too cold here."

"Go by yourself? You don't want to do that. I'll be right back."

True to her word, she was back in a jiffy. It pained me to see this woman so wound up.

The memorial tablets were kept in a chamber beneath the dharma hall. From the outside the hall appeared to be a one-story structure reached by a flight of stone steps, but a door set back from the steps led to that chamber, and so for all intents and purposes the hall was the upper floor of a two-story building.

Mother clutched my hand. She still labored under the misconception that I had run off from the shaman man's house because our visit had proved a shock to me, and now I sensed she was afraid the ceremony for Father would pose a similar shock. To ease her fears I smiled sheepishly and allowed myself to sneeze some more.

Three walls of the somber, desolate, wooden-floored room were covered with memorial tablets and photographs of the deceased. Those of Father and Brother were among them, side by side, resting on a bed of white-paper lotus blossoms.

I had never seen the photographs before. I knew of no photos that large of our departed family members and guessed Mother had arranged for enlargements to be made at a photo shop. But the photos were overly touched up, and I wouldn't have recognized them had Mother not pointed them out. Their features had been altered only enough to give their skin the color of thick makeup and to remove their expressions; as a result they looked idiotic. And the age difference between father and son had been erased, so that the only thing you'd notice was their resemblance to each other. I, who took after Mother a great deal, now wore her sad and solemn expression as I stood facing them. And this was how our family of two decades ago gathered together now. I felt no emotion whatsoever.

The offertory table soon arrived. We placed it before Father's tablet, and a young nun began chanting, accompanying herself with a wooden clacker. The table was shabby, the invocation clumsy.

Mother mumbled a needless excuse: "I begged them to keep it simple. After all, it's the heart that counts."

My only response was a faint smile. Mother had me light the candles and incense and pour the offertory water, and then we both performed the bows. I did four, then withdrew, head down. Mother took longer, drawing out each of her four bows. There was an earnest, gentle charm to the way she bent over, and she prostrated herself long enough to seem asleep before rising. She did the same for the photograph of Brother, for whom no table or offertory food was provided. Her back was narrow, her shoulders emaciated, her white bun no larger than a baby's fist. Here too, faced with the wretched irony of having to prostrate herself before her own son's memorial tablet, Mother could only bow her head submissively.

Through Mother's silent but heartfelt movement I painfully felt how long and how severely their two deaths had obstructed our daily lives and how fervently she was pleading to be released from that obstruction. It was a silent cry, an inarticulate struggle. And I now realized that I actually did feel something.

Ours had been a close-knit family, and we were satisfied with what we had. Father and son, mother and daughter. And then suddenly father and son had died in turn. Their deaths were horrifying. Even now, more than twenty years later, their awful appearance in death had yet to relax its grip on mother and daughter.

For a time after the outbreak of the civil war Brother was in high spirits. He was already involved in the leftist movement and had gotten himself into enough scrapes that there was never a dull moment. So I could understand his animation. And we sensed that Father, who had grown exasperated with Brother, was inclined to be indulgent since the times finally seemed right for his son.

But then Brother abruptly stopped going out. He kept to his room and puffed on cigarettes the whole day through, never bothering to get up. His beard ran riot, and he made no effort to trim it. He didn't try to avoid visitors, but those he met were always upset when they left. The bombing grew worse by the day, but we felt more threatened by the imminent explosion we sensed in Brother's attitude.

One day Brother had a caller, a "comrade" who visited regularly. The visitor was preceded by an armed man. The three of them—Brother, comrade, and gunman—were out in the yard face to face, speaking in an undertone. It was a quiet exchange and sounded tedious enough to put you to sleep. But suddenly Brother shouted, "No, I won't!" "No?" asked the other. "Would you rather die instead?" "I told you, I won't do it!" Life, it seems, can be disposed of with absurd haste. The gunman was for real: he fired. And not just once. A shot to the chest, to the throat, the face, and the forehead.

And then the two visitors were gone. We—father, mother, and sister—had just witnessed a gruesome, obscenely brutal death, and now we had to clean up. He was unrecognizable from the waist up, and remnant by remnant we, his family, gathered flesh, brain matter, and congealed blood without allowing ourselves the mercy of a single scream. Under the circumstances, a death of this kind—a reactionary's death—could not have been more shameful and disgraceful, and so it was not a time for keening and wailing. We engaged someone we trusted and removed all traces, hushing everything up.

With artful composure we devoured his death like wild animals
consuming the afterbirth of their newborns and lapping up the bloody
mess.

Father's behavior gradually turned peculiar. He had no use for the
Reds, but he visited a friend who occupied a high government position,
and we sensed he had groveled and kissed up to this man. He seemed
to make a nuisance of himself tagging after the man and offering to
help him out, and amazingly enough he went so far as to inform on the
son of another friend. We questioned Father's sanity: this was no time
to try to share in the spoils of victory, for by then the Communists
were on the way out.

The balance of power changed, and Father was taken into custody
after complaints were registered by people with grievances against
him. He managed to win his release, but a few days before the January
4, 1951, retreat by the UN forces he was a near-corpse—rotten, stinking, ulcerated, swollen, and broken from beating and frostbite. But
in this hideous condition he somehow clung to life, and while
others fled southward for refuge, he tied us to the capital. And so it
was in desolate Seoul, after the retreat, that Father passed away. His
was a death more awful than Brother's, a scene too dreadful to look
upon. Once again we removed all traces of death. I hate to say this,
but we had developed some skill in dealing with such events.

Even if we had wanted to tell others, at the time there was no one
around to notify. But because it was a shameful humiliation for
Father to have been beaten to death as a Communist, Mother and I
conspired, after Seoul was retaken, to withhold the truth from even
our closest kin. To seal our conspiracy we moved to a different
house.

Many had died during the upheavals of war, but there were many
as well who had disappeared and whose fate was unknown, and so we
let the relatives assume that Father and Brother were missing. This
served a dual purpose, the second being that the two of us, mother
and daughter, would be seen by others as only half as unfortunate as
we actually were since the odds were fifty-fifty that a person declared
"missing" would turn up alive.

And thus we cunningly gulped down the two deaths, and their frightening appearance at death, without batting an eye.

Needless to say, we didn't conduct the usual memorial ceremonies. For they were "missing."

When someone dies, we wail—*"Aigo, aigo!"* If our tears dry, we moisten our eyes with saliva when no one's looking; if we feel drained, we gulp a tonic, and then we wail some more—*"Aigo, aigo!"* For three days we put up with people offering condolences, people playing cards to pass the time, beggars enjoying a free meal; we go through the most complicated formalities—bottomless, endless formalities that flare up in arguments with elders and juniors alike—and we perform the memorial ceremonies on the anniversaries of death and during the holiday festivals. And so we, the survivors, are drained; we get fed up, we grow poor serving the deceased, and as we become sick and tired of it all, we develop an undiluted disgust with everyone else, including the dead person. And then for the first time we, the living, are freed from those who are dead.

But Mother and I had consumed the dead. Clandestinely, treacherously. We bought a house on the outskirts of the city, and I began a life of commuting to support us.

I would return home as the evening sky darkened. Let's suppose I saw a young man in front of me and I admired the back of his head and the way he walked. I was at an age when my heart should have thrilled in sweet expectation of such things. But I was fearful. Fearful that this person ahead of me might swing around, fearful that the face turning toward me would be that very same ruined lump of flesh and blood. I would shudder with a hellish rage and break out in a cold sweat. In this wretched fashion I passed the years before my marriage, years that should have been the brightest, shiniest period of my life. I grew sick and tired of being frightened, of living in fear.

"You ought to get married," Mother said one day. "To a homebody." I agreed at once. A homebody quite suited my fancy. Wouldn't this mean a man who, except to put food on the table for his wife and children, wouldn't resist the society to which he belonged? But at the same time a man who would think twice before getting involved in that society? Sure, a man like that would do. And I felt somehow that by marrying such a man, I would gain revenge on Brother and Father. More than anything else, though, I would marry because my life had worn me out.

I met such a man and married him. I bore a child, and then another child. My desire for children was insatiable. Who knows? I would tell myself. Who knows when we'll have another period of tyranny and madness, a period when the black muzzle of a gun might be leveled at the chest of my child? How could I trust in only two children? Three wasn't enough, no way. Or four. Or five or six. . . . I was frantic to turn out children. I continued to bear them until my husband finally threw up his hands and had a vasectomy.

I had my homebody and a lot of children. But I wasn't happy.

My life had no zest, I wasn't content with it; everything was a pain, I was frustrated; I was sick of it all. The joy of life, my capacity for taking an interest in things, slackened like a spring that's lost its bounce.

The freshness of life was gone. Even the fears that had haunted me before marriage lost their immediacy.

Instead of fearing that their departed souls would return as bloody ghosts in some dark alley, I came to despise those souls. They hadn't become ghosts in the first place; they were stuck somewhere, and they were hopelessly stupid.

The problem, though, was the place those souls were stuck. I always felt them in my innards; they were something indigestible in the pit of my stomach. It was a nasty sensation—a lumpy mass that had re-mained ever since Mother and I had consumed those two deaths, ruin-ing me inside, turning my stomach, and nauseating me—and it didn't dissipate with the passing days.

I reaped what I had sown. For I had consumed them. I had con-fined their departed souls to my innards. And if I didn't purge myself, someday those souls would produce symptoms of something incur-able, the inevitable result being a blockage of my innards. I gradually became aware of something even more curious—that it was not I who kept their souls but in fact their souls who imprisoned me, and that this confinement had isolated me from the various joys of life and the beauty of the world.

I had always considered their deaths mortifying and vexing. But even this attitude changed. What was truly mortifying, I felt, was not my dead brother and father but the fact of my having to witness their deaths. To think I had seen them, those horrible events, at my age, during the brightest and shiniest period of my life, a period of the most piquant fragrance! To think I had been forced to silently consume them! What vexed me, really and truly, was not them but me.

I wanted to free myself of them. To purge myself of the deaths I had consumed. Around this time it became a ritual for me to linger at an unfamiliar street corner, beguiled by a wail emanating from a house in mourning. They wailed themselves hoarse, they indulged in histrionics, and they delivered themselves from the deaths they had experienced. To me that wail was a song of freedom.

Much had changed since the civil war. To eyes that had seen the crucifixions we had undergone then, life was no longer desperate. The eyes that had seen that period, that had seen lives lived foolishly by men like my father and brother, had become magnanimous.

Here was my opportunity. I would wail too, and I would free myself. I made up my mind. And how would I wail? First of all, I would make a clean breast of what I had hidden.

And that's how I broke unilaterally from Mother and our conspiracy.

I took to accosting all and sundry I met and forcing the story upon them: "I'm going to tell you the truth now—about the war—about my father—about my brother." I forced the story upon them, purging the undigested lump that had rested inside me so long. But no one found my secret interesting; no one was keen to listen.

What's the use of a wail no one hears? Don't you need a chief mourner and people offering condolences?

I realized for the first time that a magnanimous view of that period involved such indifference.

There wasn't a single person among my relatives and friends who considered the events of that time of upheaval significant—after all, it was some twenty years ago. They were more interested in whether To-bong or Yŏngdong was the better area for buying up land, in whether private lending or investment in stocks was more profitable. All they thought about was the means to a better life. That's when their interest grew sharp, like an insect's feelers.

Everyone I knew was wealthier than I, but did this give any of them the leisure to listen to my wail? No. In competing for a better house and more advanced artifacts of culture, they had exhausted themselves more than day laborers. Their desires, which made them hungrier than beggars, vastly outreached their possessions.

And so my late-breaking wail turned anticlimactic. Without anyone to offer condolences I was never able to get it all out.

I realized much too late how lonely I would be in my suffering.

The deaths I had consumed continued to strangle my innards, an indigestion, a neurosis that interfered with my daily life. My life continued to be uninteresting, flavorless, tedious, as aggravating as shabby clothing infested with lice, and I wished I could strip it off, scrub and pound it clean.

Now and then I saw a bloody face in my dreams, and oh, did the cold sweat flow! I'd wake up thinking today was going to be another disaster—I wouldn't even give it a chance—and then I'd suddenly get the urge: "I'm going to tell you about the war. . . . The truth is . . . My father . . ."

I wanted to talk about it so much, it was driving me crazy. I still hadn't given up on spilling it out. How could I get them to hear me to the end? How could I capture their interest? Or even their sympathy? When I had nothing better to do, I meticulously composed the story in my mind, trying to roughly suit it to the humor of the person who would deign to listen.

And then one day I found myself writing it down in story form. I wrote in painful spasms of regurgitation, spasms that offered relief.

I was as happy as the barber in the bamboo grove who shouts, "The king has donkey's ears!" But didn't that happiness reach perfection through the ringing echo of his words in the grove? The shout itself was insufficient.

With that in mind I decided to publish the story, and my decision was realized.

Yes, it was my work, but in print I could read it with more objectivity than when I had set my pen to paper, and when I finished reading, there was nothing I could do except shout "It's a lie!" It wasn't so much that I was telling lies rather than facts, but that in fictional form the story didn't ring true. I felt like a punctured balloon.

To a certain extent this failure was probably due to insufficient ability on my part and to my oversensitivity to the tastes of my listeners and the times in which I lived. But the main reason was that I lacked the perspective to fictionalize their deaths or, more precisely, the wherewithal to grasp the entire picture. I was still too closely attached to those two deaths.

All of our experiences, given time and perspective, become distant scenes through which the entire picture is revealed, instead of minor details. But even after some twenty years the two deaths I had witnessed still stuck to me like my own skin, and I couldn't tear myself far enough away to gain an impartial view.

This failure made me gloomy and prompted frequent histrionics to Mother. Mother was my partner in crime in consuming those two deaths, and I wasn't happy that she lived off my husband and me and yet remained mostly content, free of any sense of obligation, and maintained a healthy attitude toward her life. She was also the final outlet for my histrionics. Until then the secret of our complicity had remained with the partners in crime; no mention of the horrible events had escaped the lips of mother or daughter.

Little by little I forced her to listen to my story. My seeing Father in my dreams and my bloody mess of a brother. And the bad luck I had after those dreams.

Mother was more surprised than I'd expected. "People say that once you die, you become a nagging presence—I was afraid of that." She heaved a great sigh. Our hapless lives and bad luck with money; my frequent illnesses; even the failure of my children in the entrance exams for middle school and up—Mother had sensed it was all due to the aggrieved ghosts of those two who had died an ugly death, and indeed this, I believed, had always been an agonizing problem for her, even before I began the histrionics.

"It's been so nerve-wracking for me. You know, I've never had a peaceful day. They died such an awful death, but did we ever bring in a shaman to send them on their way? Did we ever hold a memorial ceremony? Where are they supposed to go, those bitter souls who were never guided to the next world?"

It wasn't just me who had interfered with their departed souls; it was Mother too. And in a completely different manner. For it was around this time that Mother's faith in Buddhism advanced to a higher level. While I struggled to purge myself of their souls as I wrote my story, Mother was a frequent and earnest presence at the temple, where she tried to have them guided to paradise.

But I guess it wasn't enough, because she sought out a shaman known for his efficacy. This man performed a divination and then scheduled a *chinogwi* rite—the ceremony for the restless dead—which Mother had wanted all this time. Proud of achieving the title of Venerable Sister and even having a Buddhist name, Mother felt no compunction, exhibited no hesitation, in simultaneously visiting temple and shaman. My feelings for Mother when she acted like this were equal parts pity and disdain.

I manufactured some excuse or other and tried to beg off attending the *chinogwi* rite. On the surface I laughed off the thought of divinations and *chinogwi* rites, but deep down inside I was scared in a way. It was an absurd fear. Absurd like the gruesome fantasy I had in the years before marriage of seeing a bloody face on the back I admired of a man ahead of me.

To my surprise, though, on the day of the rite Mother somberly insisted that I attend. I actually did have something to do that day but felt compelled to accompany Mother without a peep of protest. I had to obtain the shaman's permission to leave long enough to tend to my business.

I returned just in time to witness the shaman summoning Father's spirit. At the sight of me the shaman hugged me tight and began weeping in a plaintive tone: "*Egugu*, you heartless thing, where have you been? *Egugu,* I keep seeing you. I see you in my dreams, I see you when I'm awake. I can't forget you. Let me touch you one last time, my daughter." He hugged me, rubbed his cheek against mine, fondled me. I smelled something sour—the man reeked of *makkŏlli.* His hands told me he was up to no good: one arm was around my waist and the other pawed my bottom. I pushed him away and ran off. To this day Mother thinks I did so because of the shock of hearing Father's spirit complain.

Observing the wishes of Father conveyed by the shaman, we decided that the least we could do was offer a memorial ceremony for Father and Brother at the temple beginning that year.

"Their spirits must have been so bitter all this time. And oh, how they must have starved: I wouldn't be surprised if they went to other people's memorial ceremonies, bided their time, and had themselves some food—can you imagine a proud man like Father stooping to that? Tsk, tsk. We think we're in no position to hold a ceremony, and yet we never skip a meal—no wonder my rice sometimes feels like thorns going down my throat. That shaman was miraculous; he really pinned down the problem. It's a good thing you ran off when you did. You'd have fainted if you'd stayed to the end—you're not very strong. You should have heard Father complain after he possessed him. He was so upset about the way we treated him while he was drifting between this world and the next. 'Your hearts are hard as stone, you two—you're worse than murdering thieves!' Well, everything he was shouting about, we deserve it—serves us right. But the thing I can't believe is how his personality is exactly the same as it was before he died. . . ." On and on she went about her encounter with Father's spirit during the *chinogwi* rite.

‿

Mother offered an endless series of bows, then bowed some more, each prostration as earnest and ardent as the last. "Why don't we stop now?" After several such suggestions by the nun, Mother finally finished. The offertory table presently returned as a meal table. I was hungry and ate copiously. I added rice to my radish soup, and while munching on fried kelp, I mixed a variety of vegetables with the rice remaining in my bowl and shoveled it down with gusto. Mother seemed drained the way she merely sipped at her broth. Her letdown after the long-awaited ceremony seemed to have left her no energy to eat. Perhaps she had saved up all her strength until today so she could perform the ceremony, and now that it was finished, she looked weak enough to collapse at the tap of a finger.

But instead of going home, she followed her original plan of taking me to the dharma hall, the Seven Stars shrine, and the Mountain Spirit shrine, where she had me perform bows and make offerings. For some reason I reined in my repulsion toward those two shrines and my scorn toward their mishmash of religion and shamanism. Hell, what is it with you!—I got mad at myself for being so meek. The best I could do was try the sneezing routine again, but even that didn't work out the way I wanted.

I overdid the bowing and ended up rubber-legged and dizzy.

"You must be tired, Mother."

She produced a tender smile. "It's all right."

"Shall we take a cab home?"

"Goodness, no—you've already spent too much, haven't you?"

I hailed a taxi and practically forced her in before sitting down beside her.

"Thank you," she said, taking my hand, "for being a good daughter today. Now don't forget the ceremony for your brother this summer."

"I won't, as long as you come along and show me how it's done."

"All right, if I'm still around—you can't be sure with us old folks. But don't you forget, eh?"

I merely smiled.

"I'm serious—when the dead go to paradise, that's when the living find peace. I can die now with no regrets. I've taken care of what was weighing me down night and day."

She lay her head against my shoulder and closed her eyes. And stayed like that. She's asleep, I told myself. Her small head, free of weight, rested softly against me; her gnarled hand gently held mine.

For whatever reason the taxi frequently had to brake, causing

Mother's head to lurch forward dangerously and upsetting my stomach and making me gag. As I forced down the sour, offensive stuff that rose to my mouth I was reminded of the various vegetables I had eaten at the temple, and I found myself wanting never again to taste a single one of them. And everything that had happened at the temple—the Buddhist ceremony for good fortune; the Buddha seated on the silk cushion with the garish mural in the background and the offertory basket full of paper money almost close enough for him to hold; the women's frantic, trancelike bows; the ridiculous waste of candles and incense and the acrid smoke; the chattering of the "venerable sisters"; the cornerstones and pillars of the Seven Stars and Mountain Spirit shrines inscribed with the names of donors in sizes corresponding to the amount of the donation; the inimitably crude hodgepodge of religion and shamanism—gave expression in yet another disgusting belch. I found it no less nauseating than my experience at that shaman's. At least I had found no mishmash there.

We entered our neighborhood of unpaved streets and the taxi began an indescribable rattling. Worse still, the driver overreacted by spitting out a litany of curse words and driving roughly. The winter scene of our desolate, impoverished neighborhood framed by the window bounced all over.

From its perch on my shoulder Mother's head slid slowly down my chest silently, weightlessly, almost imperceptibly, like a silk scarf come undone.

I made her comfortable in my arms. Was it possible to sleep so deeply? She looked as tranquil and innocent as a baby. She must have been exhausted, but above all her mind was now at ease, and this was the reason she had slipped into a sleep that seemed almost comatose. She really was like a baby. As I held my poor mother, I felt something like compassion soar up from deep inside me, as if I were the mother and she the daughter. And as I held her, a thought suddenly occurred: What a sad, sad thing karma is to make us live out our present life to the end.

If not for the faint warmth of her soft, coarse hands and the feeble pulse from her wrist, I would have thought that Mother, as I held her to my chest, was dying then and there. And then it struck me: the dead can truly look this lovely in death! This peace, this innocence—before I knew it my heart was pounding. Someday—yes, someday won't that be the lovely, sleeplike face Mother will show me in death? That will be something I can watch. I know what a blessing a lovely death will be. Because I know what a tenacious curse an ugly death is. Well now, I had better stop my histrionics to Mother. So she can die in peace.

And that was the first time I had ever thought of a person's death with not an ounce of loathing. Far from loathing, couldn't I think of it as a wellspring of ecstasy, however unfilial that might seem? In Mother's death I would see a clue to the loosening of, and my freedom from, that which had bound me for so long.

Spirit on the Wind

O Chŏng-hŭi

One

Dinner was over, the meal table back in the kitchen. No more dishes clattering, no more water running from the faucet. But where was my wife?

As I lay on my side in our living room watching the news, a pillow wedged under my arm, the soft footsteps from the veranda and then the opening and closing of the wardrobe drawers offered the only proof of her existence.

She's back. In the past this realization had either put me at ease or else made me feel that yet another crisis was looming. But not anymore.

Five days ago my wife had returned from her latest disappearance.

The week she was away my mother-in-law had looked after us. She had worn a hangdog look, as if she wanted to hide somewhere.

"I've given up," she told me the last night she was with us. "You can get rid of her for all I care—it's up to you."

And home she went in a flurry, late though it was, just as my wife was returning.

But I had realized, before my mother-in-law spoke up, that I finally had to make a decision.

"What are you doing, crawling back here? Are you supposed to be living here or what?"

Why couldn't I have thrown her out and barred the gate? That way I could have avoided the sight of our boy waking up and clinging to his mom. But when I saw her out there, head drooping, fumbling in the dark with the buttons of her worn-out, shapeless coat, and when I recalled how hesitant and apprehensive I had felt as I heard her pace outside the wall for the longest time, my resolve drained.

She had seemed better after Sŭng-il was born, but this year she had already left home three times. By now I no longer felt compelled to ask where she'd gone. Pressing the issue almost invariably brought the same answer: "Just around, here and there." Was it really possible, I would ask myself, that she didn't specifically remember where she'd been? Making a decision would have been much easier if I'd been able to convince myself she had gone on a binge gambling at flower cards or was caught up in a dance craze or had joined one of those singles tours where men and women pair up on the bus. But her responses to me rang true, and there seemed little she could add to them.

My older sister's husband had a suggestion: preempt her by taking her on a couple of trips every year.

But that would have demanded more than I had left to give her. My patience with her was wearing thin.

My father, when he was a young husband, had knocked about much of the time, until on one of his wanderings he had died. In the meantime my dispirited mother had looked after the house and raised us. But I couldn't be like my mother.

Ask anybody on the street, I told myself—they'll tell you. My wife usually gets her own way, she takes off for no good reason—what other man would put up with it?

I felt myself boiling over again, and before I knew it, I had jerked myself to a sitting position.

Sŭng-il probably thought I was going to explode. "Daddy, the tunnel fell down," he whined. "Can you make it again?" He'd been crawling in and out of my upraised knees, pretending to be a train.

"Sure."

I gazed at the boy, at the receding chin and the slender body, in both of which he resembled my wife more than me. Five years old, he was already used to his mom's frequent absences, and he didn't complain about having to sleep next to his grandmother or daddy.

For the life of me I couldn't figure out what it was with my wife.

And there she came, drifting silently into the living room. The sweep of her clothing brought with it a cold, refreshing draft that by contrast left the stagnant air feeling disgustingly stuffy. She sat down at her vanity and began applying cream.

"Open the window, will you?"

She rose and flung the curtain aside. The window slid open with a rattle.

The curtain fluttered and cold air washed in. The rush of the wind drowned out the television and beat against my ears. With every gust I could hear the singing of the power lines not far away.

"Did I tell you to open it all the way?" I carped.

Sŭng-il looked back and forth at the two of us in wide-eyed alarm. "Why the loud voice?"

She closed the window a hand's width, then gazed outside a moment, as if something in the thick gloom had caught her eye.

Her face, reflected on the dark surface of the glass, looked like a film negative.

The wind—winter's last gasp—grew louder. The weatherman had just appeared on TV to inform us we were in for blustery weather but the spring flowers would bloom all the same.

The wind singing madly—was that what she was seeking in the dark distance?

Sŭng-il tugged at her skirt with the same anxious look.

"Mommy, sit down!"

She gently stroked his hair and squatted near my feet. Then she pulled the newspaper toward her and with her other hand groped along the floor the way she always did for her cigarettes. She lit up, the match flame bending toward the cigarette. Her eyes had remained fixed on the newspaper, but nothing seemed to register. She looked at the TV listings on page 12 and then the city page. She scanned the large headlines, then leafed backward to the front page before turning to the ads. A wisp of smoke from the neglected cigarette in her left hand floated toward the fluorescent light in the ceiling. More than half the cigarette was now ash, a whitish curl poised to drop.

Bad habit. I glared spitefully at the back of her shoulders, which seemed more hunched and narrow than usual.

Her eyes, still glued to the paper, were squinting because of the smoke. She was reading the notices for missing people. "Kim So-and-So, age 46, 300,000 *wŏn* reward." "Please come back; everything's forgotten. The children can't wait to see you." "Yi Such-and-Such, age 30, female, left home, last seen wearing a purple sweater and a long, flower-print skirt, mentally deranged."

Idiots!

Those notices always left me with a bitter taste—because they reminded me all too vividly of the notice I myself had thought of placing the first time she had left: "Ch'oe Ŭn-su, female, age 28, 5'2", short hair, delicate build. Notification requested from anyone knowing the whereabouts of the above. Generous reward."

Six years ago, miserable and heartbroken, I had jotted this down in my appointment book.

She looked drawn during these few days she'd been home. The fluorescent light exaggerated her protruding cheekbones, making her face look haggard and rigid. Her hair was hacked short as always—she wasn't one to worry about hairstyles—exposing the wrinkles in the nape of her too-thick neck. That neck was the only fleshy part of her. But fleshy didn't necessarily mean healthy-looking. Instead the short hair made her head seem unbalanced, giving her an odd, unwholesome appearance overall.

I'd once seen a cosmetics ad warning women not to neglect their neck, for a thickening neck was a sign of aging in married women. If I hadn't come across that ad, I probably wouldn't have cared about her neck. As I considered this, it occurred to me that my wife was thirty-four.

"Here I am, turning gray already."

She always sounded dejected when she said this. Last year, I guess it was, she had taken to plucking out her white hairs in front of the mirror.

My wife crushed out her cigarette. Maybe she felt my gaze.

A cross shape had been scored in the surface of the filter. It was her habit, whenever she was mulling over something, to press down on the filter with her fingernail.

"Do you ever wonder what I do while you're at the bank?" she had occasionally asked me early in our marriage.

I had to admit that I'd never given much thought to what women did during the day. After the man left the house, the woman did the dishes, cleaned up, did the wash, flipped through the paper or a magazine, or listened to women's radio programs— light classical music, anecdotes and chitchat about home life, whatever— then planned dinner and went to the market. That was the best I could come up with for a day in the life of my wife.

When I returned home at the end of the day, the house always seemed clean. But on closer inspection I could make out ash streaks on the floors and the veranda, and it wasn't unusual for me to come across a cigarette butt in the bathroom or the coal shed or on the kitchen floor. And then there were the butts in the ashtray, the filters etched by her fingernail with the familiar cross mark or a circular pattern that resembled a wheel.

Her smoking depressed me more than it angered me. I found it distasteful. The cigarette holes in her clothing, in seat cushions, in the tablecloth—it was difficult for me to treat such carelessness lightly.

"Anyone drop by today?"

"No—why do you ask?"

There was suspicion in her tone.

Well, it really was a silly question.

Her social network was strangely limited, and she was her widowed mother's only child. So visits with her friends and relatives were rare. It was the same after our marriage.

Our first meeting had been arranged by others, and during our brief courtship I was never introduced to any of her friends. I fell to wondering if she was ashamed of her friends, if maybe she felt they weren't presentable. Or perhaps, cautious by nature, she was acting out of consideration for me, since I was a bit introverted. This seemed a more likely explanation. Then again it may have been the possessiveness of the one in love, who wanted no one to come between us. I was comfortable with these interpretations.

At first her closed lifestyle was difficult for me to understand. But I soon grew used to it, and gradually I became thankful for the narrow confines of her world.

Women tend to go around together, trying to make themselves useful, jabbering nonstop, but all they end up doing is making waves, and 90 percent of the time they have nothing to show for their efforts. This is how most men see it, and I'm not exactly in a position to disagree since I'm basically a standard-issue sort of fellow myself, but I will say that if women start dissecting you, you can bet they'll find fault with you more often than they praise you.

So instead of hanging around with friends and neighbors and getting involved in petty complications, why not give our life a touch of elegance through pursuits that made use of her major? That was my own unspoken wish at least.

My wife had gone to art school. She said she'd majored in Western art, and when we first met, she was working as a designer for a publisher of children's books.

Her skin was clear, her eyes large, and she seemed good-natured. That was about all there was to her. Nothing else really caught my eye, and she didn't put on airs. I'd have to confess that much of what attracted me to this woman, who struck me as quite ordinary otherwise, was her having been to art school.

"Since your concentration was in painting, do you think you'll continue to paint?" I had asked her the first time we met.

"When you're as mediocre as I am, you might as well not paint at all."

She smiled faintly, perhaps deprecatingly, making me wonder if she had been born with meager talent, had found her artistic goals only half realized, and had opted for the obscurity of the working life.

"It seems to me painting would make a great pastime," I said. "And besides, for a woman...," I hastily added.

Back when I was in middle school and high school in a small city in the countryside, I had secretly envied the students in art class who went around with their easels and sketch boxes, just like I had once wished I had tuberculosis, which I considered an affliction of geniuses. As far as my own experience with painting is concerned, about all I can remember is a tulip I tried to copy from our first-grade art primer. It was shown planted in a vase, and my version looked hopelessly one-dimensional. And so it seemed positively elegant to me that she had actually majored in painting. Which is not to say that I had my hopes set on my wife becoming a successful painter.

When the subject of painters comes up, I automatically think back to the biographies of van Gogh and Gauguin that I've read. I've always found it inconceivable that the tragic lives of these two men were filled with such passion, ardor, and madness. And so I tell myself that if painting is an activity that demands strong individuality, to the extent that the artist might discard children or family like a pair of old shoes, then it's fine if one isn't an artist. To me, the second son of a widowed mother who for the past ten years had kept a hole-in-the-wall shop back home, a bank teller without much experience who was clearly destined only to plod upward step by step to department head—at best—before retiring, the art major my future wife had selected seemed part of a lifestyle I could never attain, that I didn't dare try to incorporate into my own life, that I could scarcely even consider as a complement to it.

As long as we intended to hang something from the empty walls of our home, why not my wife's paintings rather than some reproduction? And after we had provided ourselves with a roomy house, it would be nice to see my wife set up her easel in our garden in June, with the roses in full bloom, smell the paints she stirred up, and watch her at work.

So there you have it. I was a run-of-the-mill middle-class type who hankered after a taste of the artistic in his life.

But there wasn't a single brush among the items she brought to our marriage.

I could never figure out why she smoked so much when she was alone. People, unless they're chronic smokers, usually smoke because they're worried or anxious. Of course, she emptied the ashtray when she cleaned house in the morning, but why did she smoke the way she did during the five or six hours from lunchtime till I returned for dinner? Even if it was a habit, she smoked so much it was sickening. What could possibly have led to a habit like that?

Whenever she saw my eyes travel to that heaped-up ashtray, she grew flustered, picked it up, hand cupped over it as if to conceal it, and hurried out.

Apart from that one alarming habit, there was nothing about her that I could really find fault with. The house was always tidy, and everything was nice and neat and right where it ought to be.

Back in the days when we had rented a house, she planted lettuce and scallions off in the corner of the yard. When the lettuce grew big and fresh and green and opened up, she'd pick a handful and serve it with dinner. She got a kick out of that.

During the bus ride home I'd think of my wife and our room. They reminded me of a single light flickering in darkness at the far reaches of a cold, gloomy, and barren plain. I felt for the first time I was casting anchor after a long, destitute, and lonely life.

My wife was a woman of few words, but her body was gentle as water and warm. I could scarcely believe I was embracing that body, which at times was so gentle, so flawlessly yielding. After dinner I'd lie with my head in her lap and play with the gentle bulge of her chest through her clothing, suddenly aware that the air in our room, warm and languid like spring fever, harbored something fuzzy and insubstantial. Was it anxiety? Coldness? I would have to remind myself that this vague sensation was merely a fiction implanted in me by the common wisdom that notions such as eternal love and eternal happiness were unreliable, that life was cruel and realistic.

Done getting Sŭng-il into his pajamas, my wife again groped along the floor and located her cigarettes.

She was looking in the direction of the television but didn't seem to be watching.

I fretted—how could I divert her gaze, which seemed to have drifted to some distant place? Oddly, nothing came to mind.

From where I lay diagonally across the floor, I reached out and turned the channel. My wife's eyes were fixed on the screen. One of her hands rested on the boy's head; the other held a cigarette.

That image resurrected my cold feelings toward her, the agitation, the impatience, the ambivalences that had congealed, then hardened, that had settled to the depths of my being since that first time she had left, finally to clarify into utter rage.

We'd been married about six months. I had returned from work and as usual had pressed the bell at our front gate and called out to her a couple of times. Actually this was unnecessary because by then she could pick out my footsteps from the foot traffic passing down the alley in front of the house. When I realized no one was responding, I gently rattled the gate. The single panel opened partway; the crossbar hadn't been drawn.

The house was silent.

Had she gone to market? Was she asleep? But 7 p.m. on an early-winter day was too early to be in bed and too late to be shopping at the market. She had always been home when I returned from work. And there, neatly arranged in the entryway, were her slippers with the flowery beads.

"Ŭn-su—Ŭn-su, where are you?"

Feeling oddly hesitant, I called her name, and when she didn't appear, I ventured onto the veranda. I searched the house, opening each door in turn and looking inside—the kitchen, the bathroom, the storage areas, the coal shed. My wife was gone.

The house was spotless—not a speck of dust, and the ashtray had been emptied and cleaned. The bedding had been laid out on the warm part of the floor, and the patchwork quilt felt nice and toasty. But the chill of a vacant house was all around—a lack of warmth, an emptiness.

I knew my wife's habits. I knew she rarely visited the neighbors. But

I went next door anyway and knocked on the gate. The middle-aged woman who lived there appeared with a steaming ladle—she must have been serving dinner.

"The young lady?" The woman shook her head. "No, she's not here. Haven't seen her face all day. I think I heard her doing the wash, though."

I hadn't expected much in the way of information from my neighbor, but even so I could only look down in silent dejection to conceal my disappointment.

The dusk gradually settling along the ground began to climb the house, making it appear squat and lonely, as if it were shrinking.

It never occurred to me to change out of my work clothes. Instead, helplessly anxious, I paced the house looking in desk drawers, kitchen cabinets, even the small compartment in the back of the wall clock.

If something urgent had come up, the least she could have done was leave a note—but there was nothing.

As night set in and the wind rose, the laundry on the line began to freeze, and soon there was a stiff but lifelike fluttering of whitish arms and legs.

At nightfall my anxiety became a hunch and then a conviction: my wife had met with an accident or else someone had buried her alive.

Though there was no sign of forced entry, I searched the house inside and out with a flashlight. I was so distracted I didn't realize the radio had been left on. This fact finally registered when I went back inside and realized it was time to turn on the lights.

The only places she could conceivably have gone were the home where her mother lived by herself and my older sister's home in Kwangmyŏng-ni, all the way across Seoul from the suburban area where we lived. I paced and fidgeted almost till ten, then ran outside and staked out the pay phone on the street. As I had suspected, she wasn't at her mother's or my sister's.

Her mother mentioned a number of places, but without conviction: "There's no reason she would have gone there. . . ." Nonetheless, I tried them all, the telephone consuming the ten coins I'd exchanged for a hundred *wŏn*. I hadn't a clue to her whereabouts. I waited till 4 a.m.

and the end of curfew, then roamed the city hospital, which handled bodies awaiting claim by next of kin, and the general hospital emergency room. I was asked to describe her appearance. This was embarrassing. I thought of my wife in such terms as *delicate* and *lovable* and I found it difficult to talk objectively about her as if she were some other woman. During our six months of marriage I had become deeply attached to my wife, and the image of her that had developed in my mind could only be described by the simplest of feelings.

As I gave first one statement and then another, I gradually succeeded in putting my emotions into words, feeling as I did that I was stripping off successive layers of clothing, and by the third or fourth day of her absence I was able to speak of her as a missing person: "Ch'oe Ŭn-su, female, age 28, 5'2", short hair, slender build. Distinguishing features: pale complexion, mung-bean-sized wart behind left ear. . . ."

Rereading this entry among the rolls of the missing, I had to wonder if these features truly represented the reality that was my wife.

But my state of mind was of no consequence. The double-sided, ruled form for reporting missing persons lacked categories in which I could note my love for my wife, the home life we had established, the dreams we had planted in the domestic web we had joined hands to weave, the anxiety and impatience I now felt.

At the bank I occupied my seat at the teller's window but found it impossible to focus on the business at hand. I listened constantly for the telephone behind me, kept glancing back at it, but when it actually rang—and it was rarely silent—my blood ran cold because my scanty powers of reasoning could not advance beyond the notion of "sudden accident." By then I could admit to the possibility that she had left home, and I tried to recall her appearance the morning she had disappeared. I retraced our relationship back to the time we began seeing each other, trying to uncover a motive for her disappearance. But I could find no thread from which to draw inferences.

We had experienced occasional differences of opinion regarding the arrangement of the furniture or the interior decoration, and I frequently found myself peeved when she dished me up a steaming bowl of freshly cooked rice while she herself ate unwarmed leftover rice or scorched leavings from the bottom of the pot.

Five days before, she had seen me off to work at the front gate. And as always she had momentarily detained me by asking, almost as an afterthought, if I would be coming home late.

"Twenty-eight is kind of late for a woman to get married," my sister had said when the sixth day had passed with no news. She examined me out of the corner of her eye, gauging my reaction. "Haven't you ever wondered about her past? Do you suppose there's another man?" The implication was that such a possibility was not exactly unheard of.

And there you had my sister—the mind-set of a woman whose life revolved about weekly magazines and TV dramas! Infidelity was a frequent occurrence in this world, but it had never occurred to me that my wife might be unfaithful.

Next it was my brother-in-law's pet theory: "Maybe she's pregnant. Pregnant women have these crying jags and fits of hysteria for no reason at all. They get so thin-skinned and irritable—I've never been able to understand it."

I shook my head. It was out of the question. My wife and I had agreed that we wouldn't have children for the time being.

My mother-in-law arrived to look after the house and me. But her presence offered me no strength or comfort. Deep sleep eluded me. Every time I dropped off for a moment, an image would appear: my wife dumped in a weed patch on a remote hillside.

"Was there a place where the two of you used to go when you were seeing each other?" asked loan officer Kim, who had recently entered his seventh year of marriage. "Maybe the place where you first met or where you kissed for the first time? It's hard to understand, but women have a sentimental streak. It's probably a waste of time, but why not go there and see?"

I had to admit it was plausible.

I had made no effort to conceal my wife's disappearance, assuming all along that she had met with an accident and dismissing the possibility of a family problem, and so it was a matter of public knowledge in my department at the bank. The instant I told my coworkers, they tried to remember if they had seen anything in the papers on the day in question or the following morning about the discovery of someone who had died an unnatural death. All the next week, when no such hideous news appeared, they spoke sympathetically to me and steered me toward the belief that my wife's departure was due to a domestic problem or to some personal matter. But to me those possibilities were just as dreadful as the notion that she had had an accident or had simply left home of her own free will.

After all was said and done, I decided to look for her at our honeymoon site, a well-known seaside resort. What else could I do? Getting there normally involved three hours on an express bus, followed by a transfer to a local bus. I took a taxi instead of the local bus.

Visible among a grove of small pines was the roof of the hotel where we had spent our first night. I held out little expectation of finding my wife there.

My nerves had been spent during the past week, and I was physically exhausted. My body was telling me to give up on her. My hopes were so low that when I saw my wife's name in the guest register it almost didn't click.

"Ch'oe Ŭn-su? Isn't this the one?"

The room clerk had to point it out to me. Her familiar handwriting finally registered, and I nodded, stunned. My vision blurred. I felt as if I had been hammered over the head.

Next to her name in the guest register was entered the very date she had left home.

"Room 306," said the clerk. "But if you don't mind, sir, could I ask what business you have with the guest? We're not supposed to give out this information."

"She's my wife," I snapped. I could imagine all the possibilities my response would arouse in the clerk's filthy imagination, and they filled me with shame.

"Oh! Would you like me to ring her? Oops, that won't work! She left a little while ago—but she said she wouldn't be gone long. Heavens, it's been cold, but she's always out by the water! Seems preoccupied with something."

Unadorned curiosity shown in the eyes of this fellow, who was so given to speaking in exclamations. Probably got bored just sitting there at the front desk at this slack time of year.

I tossed my cigarette on the floor, crushed it out, and turned my back on him. Maybe his curiosity was superficial and he was merely inquisitive or trying to be friendly, but I was in no mood for it. I must have looked like a cuckold, a dumb cluck looking for his wife, who had run off after a fight. I suppose that hotel was a place where you could witness practically anything imaginable.

"She took her room key with her—would you like to go upstairs? To tell you the truth, we've been a little worried! First, she's a young woman, and she's been staying longer than we thought she would. . . ."

The guy kept trying to pry information out of me.

"Forget it," I barked. "I'll wait here."

I had absolutely no interest in waiting in a hotel room while my wife was out. And I didn't want to give anyone—not my wife, not this fellow—the impression that I was lying in wait for her.

Now that I knew she was alive, I felt betrayed more than relieved. A fierce, bare-knuckled rage surged inside me.

"Why not wait in the restaurant? You can order a hot drink and . . ."

I turned away before he was finished, pushed open the door, and went out. Slowly I walked down the shallow flight of steps that led to the beach.

My gaze had been focused on the hotel when I arrived, and I hadn't taken notice of the long gray expanse of sand, devoid of human presence.

I soon discovered high-heel marks following the shoreline. They looked almost like bird tracks. I traced the line of sharp imprints as they curved along the shore, and when the hotel had become small and distant, I encountered my wife, a spot on the far side of an inlet bordered by rocks, walking slowly toward me.

She was wearing her chestnut-colored half-coat, and the collar was turned up. Legs exposed, skirt fluttering, she looked like a little girl.

I had a mind to slap her, but when I saw how red and frozen her cheeks were, how they'd been chapped by the strong wind, I lost heart and lowered my hand.

She blinked, just as if she were looking at a stranger. Then she lowered her eyes and broke into a strained smile, the kind that turns into weeping at any moment.

I turned back the way I had come. Ahead of me was the line of her high-heel marks along with my footprints. You might have thought we had been taking a walk together.

She scurried after me. In spite of my anger I was utterly confused. There was something awkward and unrecognizable about my wife. I began to feel as if the past week was enough to have sent the previous six months up in smoke.

In the hotel lobby I abandoned attempts at conversation. I sat down and pulled out my pack of cigarettes. It was empty. I crushed it, tossed it aside.

"Unless you have something more to do here, pack up."

I turned to the fellow at the front desk, who had been glancing at us full of curiosity.

"How much do I owe you?"

"Just for today." When I looked at him in surprise, he quickly added, referring very politely to my wife, "She's been paying by the day."

"That's right," my wife finally said. "Every morning I told myself I'd leave." She seemed to be searching for words.

In my wife's cold hand were some seashells that had been polished by the surf and bleached by the sun. A girl's hobby, it nauseated me.

I asked her again to pack, but she hesitated at the foot of the stairs. She seemed to be waiting for me to accompany her. But I was in no mood to enter the room where she had slept for a week, undoubtedly the same room where we had spent our first night as husband and wife. I guess I just didn't feel like giving in to her.

She returned with only her handbag.

"Let's warm up with some coffee or something."

It was well past the lunch hour, but there was plenty of time before the bus left for Seoul, and I expected an explanation before we left.

A few foreign soldiers were sitting around the kerosene stove in the restaurant. Apart from an occasional tropical plant gathering dust, the place had a desolate feel.

I chose a table near some thick indigo drapes that hung heavily, like stage curtains. My back was cold. I guess we were too far from the stove.

My wife remained silent.

Chafing in frustration, I lifted the drapes to steal a look outside. Right before me was the sandy expanse where I had just rendezvoused with my wife. It was early winter, and the ocean was flat and forlorn, a dirty slate gray.

I'd had nothing to eat that day but felt no hunger pangs. I asked the waiter for a wet hand towel and a cup of tea spiked with whiskey. Methodically I wiped between my fingers, biding my time. Before long the hand towel was soiled. My wife produced a handkerchief from her handbag, dampened it, and pushed it in front of me, telling me to clean my face as well. And while she waited for me to finish, she opened up.

"I knew you'd worry. I didn't have any peace of mind either."

It was a good thing she had spoken first. I hesitated before responding.

"Are you by yourself?"

Her dubious expression told me I shouldn't have asked.

"Why? Did you think I came with someone?"

This was an attempt at humor.

"I tried to think of every possibility. A week isn't exactly a short time."

"I believe you—I can tell by your face," she said, her voice trailing off in embarrassment. She looked haggard herself.

The wind kicked up some sand, making everything hazy outside. The sea was no longer visible.

How come you left?! What are you hanging around a place like this for?! Instead of shouting these questions, I made a point of being roundabout: "What have you been doing here?"

"Just . . ."

"Just what?" I barked as a faint smile appeared on her face.

Taken aback, she fumbled for words: "I know you're not going to forgive me. But like I told you, I didn't plan to stay here this long. One day, and that was all—I thought I'd go back home the same night."

She clutched her teacup to steady her trembling hands.

"I know it sounds like an excuse," she quickly added, "but I wanted to come back here just once—to have it just like it was then. . . . I knew the longer I stayed, the harder it would be to go home, but I kept missing the bus."

"Did I do something wrong? Is there something I don't know about that's worrying you?"

"No." She shook her head firmly.

You don't like me anymore—you want to end our marriage, don't you? I really wanted to ask her such questions, but whether out of ego or whether I'd instinctively become defensive because of the hurt I'd suffered—I wasn't at all sure why—I did my utmost to avoid them.

"Have you been sick?" I asked, wondering if she might be pregnant.

She shook her head. "Like I said, I just wanted to come back here. To see if I'd have the same feeling I had then. . . ."

"Were you afraid I'd say no if you told me? It's not that far here—we could have come together."

I tried to draw her out, but it seemed she really had nothing to hide. There was no denying I was frustrated by the persuasiveness of what she said—that she had merely felt like coming here.

She asked for a cigarette. By force of habit I reached into my suit pocket, then remembered I'd thrown away my empty pack. I called the waiter.

"It's all right—don't bother," said my wife.

And that's when she began to cry. Tears streamed down her cheeks; her body shook.

The waiter stiffened and withdrew.

I took her hand. It was small and cold. Gentle affection for her welled up in me.

"Let's go. We'd better get your things and call a taxi—we ought to be able to catch the last bus."

As we left the hotel, I turned to look at the small white structure where we had spent two nights on our honeymoon. I had felt awkward and slightly sentimental then. And now, as I felt myself melt to the core of my being at the sight of my wife's outpouring of tears, the knowledge that she had chosen our honeymoon spot as her place of seclusion convinced me I shouldn't make too much of her disappearance, that it was probably just a case of a woman being sentimental. I told myself that women had a childish side, realizing full well that this rationalization was an attempt to cover up my gloomy mood, which was a combination of a fundamental unease, a wounded ego, and feelings of disappointment and degradation.

"Why don't we come back sometime when the weather's a little nicer?" I asked on the bus. She nodded agreeably. I was serious about that. If we could go back there and treat her disappearance as a joke, wouldn't that prove we were a happily domesticated couple?

That night my wife slept the sound sleep of a child who has been scolded and then forgiven, or a child who has returned from an outing. And when I woke from my first deep sleep in a long time, the chopping sound from the cutting board and the footsteps my wife was careful to muffle for my sake seemed suffused with a languid happiness. I had blamed her enough, I decided, stretching out grandly in satisfaction at a night's sleep that was so cozy and sweet.

When I returned home from work that day, there was nothing to indicate that my wife had been absent for a week. My mother-in-law had returned to her home, and our household was neat and clean and warm. The withered flowers in the vase had been replaced by fresh ones.

Nothing was different. We made love most every night, and I thought I was seeing my wife in a new light.

How rare it is in our peaceful everyday life for those who share home and bed to reveal what is deep inside them. And how many different faces a human being wears. Winter passed and spring had just about settled in when my wife left home again.

This time I trembled not in shock but in rage and humiliation.

My "search" consisted of a few phone calls. More precisely I wanted to know if she had in fact gone somewhere, because in a corner of my mind I still entertained the possibility of an "accident."

Three days later she returned. One side of her face looked sunburned. She said she had felt stifled and had left, but without a particular destination in mind. On the sunny ridge of a hill she had taken a nap.

Instead of slapping her, I smashed everything within arm's reach—the radio, the wall clock, the vase—then put my fist through a window. And I broke into tears—the first time I had cried since I could remember.

"Why did you come back? Forget it—I don't want to know. It's not worth living like this."

"I won't do it anymore. It was a mistake. I won't do it again," she sobbed, clinging to me.

Once more my older sister reiterated, carefully yet judgmentally, the plausibility of infidelity on the part of my wife. But I could find no evidence of this. That is, if you limited the meaning of *infidelity* to consorting with a man other than one's husband. I sensed in her no lingering aftermath of lust. Then again, the familiar gentle water of her body was absent, as was the scent of her perfumed soap and the sweet sense of dire urgency that characterizes the love-stricken. There was only fatigue from her journey and the feel of her flaking skin, which seemed irreparably damaged from exposure to a cold drizzle and harsh wind on some street corner.

We resumed the familiar routines of our life. Now and then I'd wake up hung over, head aching, and cut myself with the razor, then scold her for failing to put in a fresh blade for me. Barring special occasions, I went straight home from work on the commuter bus and spent the evening lying on my side leafing through the paper or watching television. My wife, prone on the floor, worked on our budget book, itemizing every last detail, and in red ink updating the records of our installment savings plan and our payments to the mutual loan association.

I noticed nothing different about her, and outwardly there was only the peaceful procession of endless days. Vaguely, though, I began to sense that something intangible and elusive was entrenched in our life and that it was propagating like an amoeba.

One day I looked at the shabby, faded wallpaper of our room and discovered that a dark stain was spreading up from the part I always leaned against.

And one day, as my wife was bent over wiping the floor, her back to me, I noticed that a seam was split in the armpit of her blouse. And I realized that her portions at mealtime had become miserably small. I wondered if the onset of spring had anything to do with this.

I also discovered the sandiness of her neglected skin and the crow's feet crisscrossing beneath her eyes like strands of thread.

As summer set in, my wife left for the third time.

My mother-in-law lost face. "That good-for-nothing deserves to die. They ought to put the leg screws to her," she said in her embarrassment.

I sealed my lips, though I felt like saying that this time I was going to break up with her.

"Mr. Chi, you two ought to have a baby—it's the tie that binds. Even the cruelest woman, once she has a young one under her wing, you can keep her close to home."

Forget it! I silently shot back. I didn't care to have a baby for the sole purpose of tying down my wife. But at any rate, this time I had to lay down the law.

Every time my wife left home, I agonized helplessly, like some plague-ridden old animal, at the images of our life and of the wretched, worthless man that I saw reflected in her eyes. When she returned and our life resumed just as before, our wounds seemed at first glance to have healed. But with her next absence they would open up, deeper and more livid than ever.

Those wounds never really healed. On the surface they may have received balm, but it was all a deception. Like a steady drip of water that undermines a foundation before one realizes it, those wounds had suffused our life, encroaching upon our dreams, our hopes, our trust in each other.

Ten days later my wife slinked back home. The first thing she did was drink water. But she couldn't keep it down. She was pregnant.

She poured body and soul into giving birth and caring for the baby, and her days grew busy and tiring. To my surprise, she seemed more settled. But after the baby's first birthday, when he was just starting to walk by himself, she began leaving home again.

"Worse than an animal!" I spat, pushing her back out the gate after she returned. To my mind, what she had done was abandon our baby. "If you were the least bit humble, you'd realize how sentimental and arrogant you're acting."

In my own way I tried to understand my wife's blue periods. I never went so far as to have her seen by a specialist, but I did try to analyze her from various angles.

Her response, though, was always the same: "I have these spells—that's all. I just get to wondering, is this how life is supposed to be? Is this how I'm supposed to live?"

How could she talk so irresponsibly, a woman with a baby at her nipple? *"Is this how I'm supposed to live?"* I couldn't believe that a woman in her thirties could be so childish, talking like a teenage girl, not giving a damn about anyone else.

It was a vice, the way she went about leaving home. Or perhaps I should say that my only recourse was to interpret it that way. Such was the extent to which my feelings for my wife had eroded.

People began giving me advice: "Don't keep telling yourself it's just a bad habit. She's ill. She needs to see a psychiatrist."

But still I refused to even consider taking her to a clinic. In my mind, the notion that something had taken possession of her around the time of our marriage, or even earlier, was the least hurtful explanation for her behavior.

ᔆ

My wife quietly gathered her legs beneath her, rose, and left. I next heard her opening the bedding cabinet, then laying out our bedding on the floor in the bedroom.

There was a distinct lull in the sound of the footsteps passing by outside. It was quite late.

Sǔng-il was on his stomach playing with a corner of the blanket spread out on the warmer part of the heated floor. His eyes were full of sleep.

"Why aren't you putting him to bed?" I called. There was an edge to my voice. No answer. The bedroom was dark and still. I noticed light escaping from the kitchen door, which was open a crack.

I slid open the door and heard water gushing from the faucet.

My wife was standing at the sink, her back to me.

I was in such a foul mood that I assumed she had turned on the water full so she wouldn't have to hear my voice.

"What's going on?" I growled. I looked about the kitchen. Except for where the cascading water had splashed around the sink, the kitchen was neat and clean.

The sink began to overflow, but instead of turning off the faucet, she removed the stopper so the water could drain. Her hands played along the indented joint between the sink and the counter. Her narrow, hunched-up shoulders were telling me to leave her alone.

I swallowed hard and deliberately softened my voice: "Why are you doing this?"

"I'll be in right away," she managed to answer in a clotted voice. It was obvious she'd been crying.

I hurled the door shut, returned to the living room, and lit a cigarette. And a second one as soon as I'd smoked the first. Still she didn't appear.

Sǔng-il had fallen asleep on his side. I pulled up the blanket and covered him, then observed his sleeping face. The cheek against the floor was contorted. I wondered what the future held for him.

The hatred and rage boiling inside me gradually diffused into a vague sorrow.

Were we somehow supposed to live like this? And if we were, what sort of life was my wife dreaming of?

I wasn't well-to-do, but I brought home enough money for us to live on; I loved my wife and son, and I treasured the comforts of family life. I was like most people—an ordinary sort—I wasn't cruel by nature, and I was managing to plug along with the obligations that other people in their thirties had to contend with. The blueprint of my life, such as it was, seemed clear enough to me.

One thing I want to make clear: I wasn't the least bit sentimental about life. It was not as if people decided out of their own free will to be born, and death, like life, was simply another aspect of nature. People weren't put on this earth just to achieve something, and in any event I could think of nothing worth pledging a lifetime to achieve.

Other times had demanded revolution, love affairs. Not ours. I lived the way most people lived, and I would likely die the way most people died.

My wife appeared and took Sŭng-il in her arms.

"I'd better put him in the bedroom." Her voice was calm and subdued. She kept her eyes lowered to hide the signs of her tears. "I've made the bed. Are you coming?"

"You go first."

The television stations were off the air. She pulled the plug to turn off the set, then left.

I listened intently to my wife's footsteps. I heard the door to the bedroom open and quickly close. There was no other sound.

An image appeared to me of my wife forever leaving a trace of herself, an eternal trail of smoke, an everlasting shadow. This thought did not strike me as unusual.

At times I was awakened at night by the sensation of my wife's body, surprisingly cold. I was convinced she had come in from outside draped with cold air. If I asked where she had gone, she would say the toilet. Dark and forgotten in sleep, these brief exchanges now came back to life in vivid detail.

When I sat across from my wife at the meal table, I saw in her large eyes the image of a woman no longer young, a woman standing on a dark street gazing vacantly at traffic and people. These days she wasn't sleeping well. A couple of times a night I'd awaken to her faint cries as she struggled through a nightmare. And when she wasn't crying out in her sleep, her breathing was shallow and uneven.

I removed my eyes from the dark television screen and got up.

In the bedroom there was only Sŭng-il, asleep under the still burning light.

The toilet and kitchen were dark. I turned on the light to the veranda but didn't see my wife. I slid open the glass door to the veranda and went outside. I looked in the coal shed and the storage areas and called her name. No response.

The gate was bolted nice and tight.

I went out back and carefully climbed the steps to the roof. Frigid air stole beneath my clothes, making me tremble. The fierce, desolate gusts seemed more unyielding as the night wore on. My teeth chattered.

There on the slab roof stood my wife, a spirit on the swirling wind that rent the dark heavens. Her outline was sharp in spite of the gloom. She looked like something whose interior has been washed out by a fluoroscope.

That outline soon grew fuzzy, as if the surface was being shed. The body itself was about to crumble.

"Ŭn-su!" I tried to shout. What came out was a choked-off scream. "Ŭn-su, what are you doing up there when it's blowing like this?" The wind reduced the sound of my voice to a murmur.

My wife was about to collapse, to be scattered on the wind. I reached for her but my legs refused to move.

My arms, stretched out like those of an actor on stage, grew heavy. I was scared.

Scared of having to give up my wife—or, more accurately, scared of growing comfortable with that notion. And scared of a woman who somehow reckoned it fortunate that our boy now took his mom's absences for granted.

Two

It was nine o'clock in the morning when the Hyewŏn Church bus reached the stop at the bottom of the hill.

Sŭng-il had dawdled while washing up, dawdled while eating, and Ŭn-su tried to hurry him up, almost running down the steep hill. Several times she had to stop and breathe deeply. The wind in her face was taking her breath away.

The bus had made a handful of stops along the way from its starting point at the church. It was half full, and clusters of children's faces were visible through the windows.

Ŭn-su led the boy to the bus, but before he climbed aboard, on impulse she squatted to his level and pulled him close.

Sŭng-il found a seat on the bus. "Bye, Mommy!" He clung to the window and waved. As soon as the door shut, the smiling boy's lips turned down, his face crinkled, and there was another "Bye, Mommy!"—this time a bitter, tearful shriek.

For almost a month this had been the situation every time Sŭng-il was about to part from his mom, and the bitter cry that came with the closing of the bus door pierced Ŭn-su's heart, as if she and the boy were never to see each other again.

When the bus had disappeared into traffic, Ŭn-su turned toward home.

Since the previous month Sŭng-il had been attending the preschool class in the kindergarten operated by the church. Ŭn-su had wondered if it was necessary for the boy to be away from his mother, if he already needed to be in a group setting outside the home during this year prior to entering kindergarten. She voiced this concern gingerly, but Se-jung thought differently: "When a child turns four, he's ready for school."

In the stiffness of his attitude he was clearly criticizing her: "Have you been a good mother?" he seemed to be saying. "How can I trust you to take care of a child when you're always running off?" Ŭn-su could say nothing. She knew that readiness for school, socialization, and the like were relatively minor issues for her husband. She couldn't rid herself of the feeling that his stance on preschool, whether he realized it or not, was a prelude to distancing mother from child.

Every morning Sŭng-il would reluctantly put on his cap with the preschool badge, strap his school bag onto his back, and set out with his mother for the bus stop. Se-jung had drummed it into him that the daily trip to preschool was the boy's duty.

Without father and child the house took on the chaotic appearance of a battlefield. Socks and other items of clothing were spread around like so many layers of sloughed skin where they had been tossed on the veranda or in the living quarters, and toys were scattered about the floor, stabbing the soles of Ŭn-su's feet with practically every step she took. She had closed the windows tightly, but the wind sounded as if it were right beside her ears. It whirled about, making the outside a dusty blur.

Spring was always like this. Whenever she heard the wind, Ŭn-su would nod as if some long-forgotten memory had just then surfaced.

This was the way spring always arrived—the wandering wind and the clouds of dust catching on the bare branches and the power lines, myriad beckoning hands making them tremble like fluttering flags; the unexpected raindrops, delicate and chill, dampening one's hair, promising to calm the winds.

The dusty interior of the house seemed to float dizzily in the sunlight pouring through the glass panels of the south-facing veranda's sliding door. The dust floated in the rays of the sun like shreds of useless thoughts before settling gray over everything. Ŭn-su swept, wiped, and dusted every day, but still the dust streamed in—where, oh where, did it come from?

The bandage around her ring finger was dark with blood, and it was still spreading and drying. She had cut herself peeling scallions that morning. Se-jung was on his way to the bathroom with the morning paper when she had uttered a muffled cry and curled up the one hand in the other.

"What's happened?" he said, glancing at her.

"Nothing—I just nicked my finger."

"Well, if you could just be a little more careful. . . ."

The cut was deep enough for the blood to be running down her other hand and dripping onto her apron. She applied an astringent, then tied a rubber band around the joint below the cut; the flesh above turned deathly blue.

Se-jung frowned and said nothing more. Rather than being concerned, it was obvious he was displeased at her carelessness. *Can't you pay attention to what you're doing?* Clearly that was what he wanted to say. With his gaze upon her she felt as if she had been discovered flagellating herself. Ŭn-su's face burned with humiliation.

I really ought to start cleaning up, she told herself. Blaming her wandering mind, which was constantly trying to grab onto a gust of the wind rattling the windows, she was gathering up the scattered articles of clothing and putting them away when the telephone rang.

"So, you're home."

"Hello, Mom. What's up?"

"Is everything all right?"

More questions followed: Had Mr. Chi left for work? Was Sŭng-il at preschool? Shouldn't Ŭn-su be making her pepper paste now? How much soybean paste did she have left?

It hadn't been three days since her mother had visited, and to draw out the conversation with these insignificant expressions of concern, plus the all-encompassing questions, clearly suggested she had something difficult to say.

It was as Ŭn-su had suspected. There was a slight pause, perhaps a moment's hesitation on her mother's part, and then in a nonchalant tone, "Did something happen yesterday?"

"Yesterday? No, nothing at all."

Ŭn-su shook her head as she asked herself what she had done the previous day. While Sŭng-il was at preschool, she had dropped by the market—was there something else?

"Well, if you weren't going to come, the least you could have done was call."

"What?"

"The day before yesterday—I guess it was the day after I went over there—I called Mr. Chi at the bank. Told him to bring you and Sŭng-il over for dinner last night. He said fine. So I kept thinking you'd show up any moment—I spent all evening waiting for you. . . . He didn't say anything?"

Ŭn-su searched her mind. Se-jung hadn't said a word about this the previous morning before leaving for work and certainly not the evening before, when he returned from work. When he left home the morning before, she had asked as usual if he would be late, and he had said no.

"He didn't mention anything to me."

"It must have slipped his mind. Well, I guess it's possible when you see how busy he is at work."

Her mother's subdued sigh carried distinctly over the line.

Preparing drinks and various dishes was the best method her mother could think of to create an atmosphere conducive to reconciliation. Her daughter's many faults caused her always to feel uneasy when she observed the couple, prompted her to treat them the way one might handle a cracked dish.

You shouldn't have done it, Mother. He didn't forget. All your preparation was in vain. These words surged up in Ŭn-su's throat, but she suppressed them.

"Now that I have all this food—why don't I bring some over? I'm just one mouth, and it'll take me a while to finish it all."

"What did you make?"

"Not much. Just a few mung-bean cakes, because Sŭng-il's dad likes them, and some of that sticky rice with dates and chestnuts—that's all."

Ŭn-su imagined her mother busy with the cooking, limping along on her arthritic legs.

"Shall I bring some over?" her mother repeated when Ŭn-su didn't answer.

Ŭn-su did some calculating. Sŭng-il and the other preschoolers were supposed to be visiting a botanical garden that day, and so the boy had left with his lunchbox, not to return till three that afternoon. That should give her plenty of time to go to Karhyŏn-dong and back.

"No. I'll drop by instead," she readily replied.

After hanging up, Ŭn-su got busy cleaning the house, wondering

all the while where Se-jung had been when her mother was waiting for
them with the dinner she had prepared. And why hadn't he said anything about her mother's invitation? Her mind was swimming.

The previous evening Se-jung had returned after eleven, dead
drunk; he'd sprawled on his side in the family room and promptly
fallen asleep. As he lay there snoring, breathing short breaths, she
began to undress him. And then she stopped and looked intently at
his face, feeling as if she had never before observed him attentively
and calmly, this man who in recent days in his cold silence had ever
so subtly and gradually been distancing Ŭn-su. With a faint feeling of
shock she herself couldn't understand she stared at the face of a man
about to enter his middle years, a tired face that was beginning to
wear; it was just like looking at her own face in the mirror.

Though he was fast asleep, his relieved expression, drained of all
tension, couldn't conceal that which rose from the depths of his unconscious—the residue of his boredom with life, his flagging desire
for her. "I smell like money. You can't imagine how strong that smell
is." She still remembered how he used to wash his hands over and over
again as soon as he got home from the bank.

She pulled the quilt up to his shoulders, which left his feet sticking
out from the other end. Something about the sight of bare feet gave rise
in Ŭn-su to a queer sensation, as if she were witness to stark, humble
nakedness. Se-jung's protruding feet were large, with prominent bones
and little flesh. She gathered those feet to her bosom. Sadness, she had
to call it—though it bordered on grief—calmly filled her heart to its
depths. Was this it? Was this the measure of their six years together?

While adjusting his pillow she cradled Se-jung's head in her arms.
As he habitually did in his sleep, he embraced her shoulders.

She gently released him, tucked the quilt over him, and went out to
the veranda. She slid open the glass door and drank in the cold air. The
clock struck twelve.

The bolt to the front gate—Ŭn-su remembered having slid it firmly
shut after Se-jung had tottered in, but she checked it again anyway.

The air was distinctly colder now that it was night, and the stars,
clusters of pinpricks in the sky, twinkled in lonely desolation. Ŭn-su

gathered her clothing snugly about her, as if trying to restrain an impulse she couldn't get rid of, a malevolent spirit nesting in her heart. What was this anxiety that kept beckoning her away? She opened her eyes wide and peered into the far reaches of the darkness for the unfamiliar street corners, thoroughfares, rooms that remained vivid in her memory, that she had seen in her wanderings after escaping from home.

"I wonder if you have the post horse curse. You're like an untamed pony the way you roam about free as the wind—it's no wonder you got lost all those times."

She had certainly heard that often enough from her mother while growing up. The thing was, Ŭn-su had no memory of those times she had gotten lost. Did this mean that instead of memories there remained only sensations of a part of her life that had been buried fast and deep like a rock ever since her early years, which themselves she could not remember? Was this the reason for her wandering searches, her anxiety? Her mother had tried in her own way to offer Ŭn-su every protection. Around the time Ŭn-su graduated from grade school, her father had succumbed to illness. Her mother proceeded to sell off the family estate in the port city where they had lived, then moved with Ŭn-su to Seoul. She had virtually cut the two of them off from family and relatives, doing no calling on others, wanting to keep Ŭn-su from being seen, spoken of, or heard of by the relatives. Already the previous summer Ŭn-su had learned the reason for this: she had been taken in by her mother and shared not a drop of blood with her. There had been a cousin, a year older than Ŭn-su, who often came over to play, and one day, when the two girls were playing with dolls, they got into an argument. For her age Ŭn-su was as tough and unyielding a child as you could find, not a whiner, and the cousin found herself grabbed by the hair and held fast. "You're a beggar!" the cousin shouted. "A hand-me-down! Mommy said so! I'm not gonna treat you like a little sister anymore! And don't you call me Big Sister anymore!" As Ŭn-su stared at her, wide-eyed in surprise, the cousin began wailing. Greater than the pain of her hair being pulled was her fear at having let slip these words the elders had made her promise never to repeat. Ŭn-su released the handful of hair, spat in her weeping cousin's face, and walked out of the house. A young child's intuition is a frightening thing. Not for a moment did Ŭn-su doubt the truth of her cousin's words, for she had at once connected them, albeit vaguely, with the resistant coldness she occasionally felt from her mother (which the mother clearly was not even conscious of), whose affection and intimacy were otherwise un-limited, a coldness that prevented Ŭn-su from impulsively running to her arms; with the opaque mood of dissatisfaction Ŭn-su had in-stinctively perceived in their home; and with the mixture of curiosity and compassion with which visiting relatives regarded her. And with this realization there came a single consuming thought: *This is not my home.*

Late that night Ŭn-su's mother had found her in a vacant boat moored a short distance away. She never did learn the reason for her disappearance, Ŭn-su's cousin having gone straight home after blurt-ing the terrible secret and Ŭn-su for her part keeping a tenacious silence.

This is not my home. The idea hardened in Ŭn-su's mind. *This is not my room. This food I'm eating doesn't belong to me.* Such thoughts gave rise in turn to a constant belief that everything about her was temporary.

The wild girl whose face more often than not bore the marks of other children's fingernails gradually became quiet and docile. Her mother thought it amazing: "Well, they say when a child is ready to get some sense, it can happen in a day."

But now and then Ŭn-su would lie awake and, unlike a young child, cover herself with her quilt to hide the sound of her weeping. *Who am I? And who are the people who gave birth to me, then abandoned me?*

It was as if part of her early childhood had been jettisoned from her memory. Attempting to recall that lost part felt like trying to dig up a hard rock buried in the deepest recesses of her heart.

A flight of steep wooden steps leading up into darkness and a pair of small black rubber shoes all by themselves in a yard bleached with sunlight—this was her earliest memory.

Ŭn-su figured she had been four or five at the time. Everything before that seemed hidden behind a dark curtain; none of it had surfaced in her mind. At odd moments she would be caught off guard by the arrival of an unanticipated but familiar mood, and something like the tip of a massive iceberg would rise indistinctly in her mind. But this feeling was so faint and feeble that if her mind so much as reached out to capture it, it would retreat whence it emerged, a shapeless, formless thing. The memory of the black rubber shoes in the sunny yard was linked specifically to the Japanese-style house in the port city where she had lived until the family moved to Seoul.

The resentment, the hatred, the loneliness that dwelled in the mind of the child weeping beneath the quilt died out with the passing years, leaving only the remnants of her anxious quest for identity to be stirred up and given wing by the slightest breath of wind.

At one point during puberty Ŭn-su had dwelled on the mysterious possibility that she was the fruit of a sad but beautiful love affair between her prematurely deceased father and some woman, and she had indulged in romance-novel fantasies about unrealized love. Even so, it was not until she decided to marry Se-jung that she had finally raised the issue of the circumstances of her birth with her mother.

Se-jung had left after being introduced to her mother, who by then was tipsy from the homemade wine set out for the occasion.

"Who am I? I mean, whose child am I?" Ŭn-su had asked, looking her mother straight in the eye.

Instantly the flush of liquor had left her mother's face. "When did you find out? And who did you hear it from?" She had pressed Ŭn-su, matter-of-fact yet flustered.

"I knew before Father passed away. And then suddenly he was gone, and I remember all this hush-hush about a rolling stone knocking other stones out of the way."

To Ŭn-su's sheepish smile her mother had sighed with a dispirited expression, as if on the verge of collapse.

"Since you already know, I guess it's no use lying to you anymore. And since we've come this far together, the truth shouldn't do much harm."

Unlike her moist and reddened eyes, her mother's tone was dry and bleak. She began to pour herself some wine, hand trembling notice-ably. But ultimately it was Ŭn-su who felt vaguely as if she were sink-ing, sinking.

"Were you trying to keep me in the dark all this time?"

Ŭn-su took the kettle of wine from her mother and filled her shot glass to the brim.

"I didn't see any particular signs of trouble when you were grow-ing up, so I thought to myself that the critical moment had passed, and I felt easier. Of course, it was never my idea to keep it from you forever—can you imagine what it's like to have to cover up something all these years? But when you didn't say anything or show any out-ward signs, I just went along thinking, well, if she doesn't know by the time she graduates from grade school, then maybe I'll just wait till middle school, and then it was maybe just till college—it always made me anxious and I kept putting it off. I figured you were going to find out someday, and I thought that marriage and children would help you sink some solid roots, and then you wouldn't be so concerned about whether I was your birth mother or not. But since it's out in the open now, it makes no sense to try to hide anything. To be honest, I was afraid that from the day you learned the truth, I might have to drop out of your life forever. . . . I tried in my own way to raise you as if nothing was different, but I suppose you bore a grudge whether I knew it or not."

Ŭn-su gently shook her head. "It's not true. No one could have done better for me."

Well, then, why bring it out in the open now? the violently trembling hand silently questioned her. *Why not continue as before, not showing what you knew and what you didn't know?*

But for Ŭn-su that was no longer possible. It was time she rid herself of that stray feeling that had occupied her since who knows when, the feeling that this wasn't her home. She was tired of wandering, tired of feeling that the home in which she was living was temporary. Her mar-riage should be a sowing of seeds, a sinking of new roots, and not a transplanting of herself.

"Bring some more wine, will you? I'm going to need it."

Her mother accepted the refilled kettle and filled Ŭn-su's shot glass.

"You came to us during the war," she began. "You must have been about four then. You certainly weren't the only child who lost her parents in the war. It's terrible to experience; war is—hell is the only word for it. And your father who passed away was a friend of your birth father. I'd been married six years and couldn't conceive, but even if I'd had my own children, I couldn't have ignored your situation—parents lost in the war, a child left alone, and on top of that the offspring of a friend. Your father who passed away felt exactly the same."

Her mother said nothing about what kind of people her natural parents had been or how they had died.

"Where were you living then?"

"In that two-floor Japanese-style house we had before we moved here to Seoul."

But there had been nothing like a courtyard full of sunshine at that house. So where, then, did it come from, that large, sun-bleached courtyard, which remained vivid in her earliest memory, and that pair of black rubber shoes lying all alone within it?

"That's all I can say. You probably know better than me about the time you've been with us. . . . Mr. Chi will find out someday—don't bother telling him now. . . . I can't imagine it being an issue between you, but you never know."

Her mother had continued to drink but offered nothing more.

Ŭn-su had never believed she was simply a war orphan. But where had she come from? The stars? Had she sprouted up all by herself from the far ends of the earth? What had she been hoping to hear in what her mother had left unsaid? And how was it that Se-jung seemed not to know that Ŭn-su had been adopted? As a matter of course Ŭn-su had been recorded in the family register as her adoptive parents' own child, but the more likely reason was that her mother had kept mum to Se-jung, despite her ordeal every time Ŭn-su left home.

When she had decided to ask her mother who she actually was and where she had come from, she knew she would sooner or later have to inform Se-jung, and to her this decision meant that she had carried out her intention to look squarely at the world and her life, to draw herself up and confront them. In fact, though, she had never told him, precisely because to do so would have been to plant yet another seed of prejudice in the mind of this timid, good-natured man. To Ŭn-su this was not an excuse. In the face of the simple truth that, as her mother had said, Ŭn-su was not the only child to have lost her parents in the war, wasn't it babyish, all this business about her tragic fate? After all, she plainly recognized that the present couldn't compensate for the past, couldn't become an excuse for, or protection against, the reality of the past. But this orphan mentality of hers, her wanderings from home, as if she had been pushed out unexpectedly, as if she had been caught by the unseen wind—were they merely the contrivances of a person who could no longer endure the reality of her life and its mix of ennui and fever?

Ŭn-su made quick work of the housecleaning, then put on her makeup. To conceal the mottled discolorations that had spread from beneath her eyes to the tops of her cheekbones, like dust that had escaped the mop, she applied a thick coat of powder and then rouge. What to wear? She selected a bright, showy lavender suit. To Ŭn-su dark colors on a spring day were like the curtains of a house in mourning.

A thick coat of lipstick and a quick check to make sure the ashtray was spotless, the drawers shut, and everything in its place, and she was off. Seeing the key into her handbag, she pulled the front gate shut. The clank of the latch jolted her.

At once Ŭn-su scolded herself for her habit of connecting all the trivial, normal feelings of her daily existence into something ominous. Every time she left on a short outing, certain she would return in an hour or two, the shutting of the gate behind her always sounded hard and cold, as if it were pushing her out.

That morning it had been windy as usual when Ŭn-su had led Sŭng-il by the hand down the hill to the bus stop. The boy had shut his eyes against the wind.

"Mommy, why does the wind blow? I wish it didn't do that."

Ŭn-su turned and walked backward in front of Sŭng-il to shield him.

"The wind is a lot of lonely people calling and waving to each other."

There weren't many buses to Karhyŏn-dong. Ŭn-su paced the bus stop, reading the signs on the buses as they arrived one after another and then departed. Suddenly she felt someone's gaze on her. Insubstantial as a spider web, sticky and deliberate, the gaze prompted Ŭn-su to pat down the back of her hair. She turned to see a man in front of a newsstand staring at her. He was the kind of young man you could often see—mid-twenties, perhaps, off-white windbreaker, bushy hair.

Ŭn-su turned away, but the man continued to fix her with his gaze. A student? A salesman? Someone out of a job?

Uneasy, Ŭn-su stole a close look at herself. Was a button missing? Was something showing? Was the hem of her skirt turned up? She found nothing that should have drawn the man's attention. Maybe a bored man's line of sight had settled on her by chance. And maybe it wasn't so different from the mischief she used to make with a mirror when she was young. From a hiding place she would aim the reflected light from a hand mirror at someone, and in due course the unsuspecting target would first be confused, then gradually grow irritated, and finally be seized with fear.

Ŭn-su wondered if she were experiencing a kind of self-hypnosis. She told herself the man was probably playing a mean-spirited game of watching a woman trapped by his meaningless gaze gradually fall victim to autosuggestion. Whatever it was, she felt bothered by the thick makeup that clung to her face like a mask, and she approached the showcase of a shop near the bus stop. In the outside light the surface of the glass looked dark and deep, as if the window were a well. Imprinted there was the unfamiliar negative of a showily dressed, thickly made up woman, a white, masklike face resembling that of a Kabuki actor. Planted everywhere in this image of the woman's body were bunches of flowers.

Inside the window was a flower shop. Ŭn-su identified roses, freesias, carnations, marigolds, and baby's breath among the leafy potted plants; the rest she didn't know.

And then she felt hot breath on the back of her neck and noticed in the glass the reflection of the young man overlapping hers. Resisting an impulse to leave, she pushed open the glass door and went inside.

For happy occasions or sad, the one essential thing was flowers. Wasn't that why people used them for decoration at weddings and funerals alike? Thinking these thoughts, she bought a bouquet of fragrant freesia.

The young man remained at the show window, staring at Ŭn-su until she emerged with her cellophane-wrapped bouquet. She hoped the flowers would tell the man—and herself—that she had a fixed destination, would give her a more purposeful appearance as she walked. Just then her bus arrived.

As the bus approached the outlying areas of the city, a ghostly blur drew close—the mountains. It was as if the atmosphere had distilled the soil, the sunshine, and the woods into a smoky ether that had settled over them. It was too early for the mountains to be wearing their covering of green, but Ŭn-su recognized the azaleas that grew over the outcrops and colored them dark pink.

Allow me to tether my cow.
beneath the red rock.
Be not embarrassed by what I do:
I'll cut the azaleas and present them to you.[1]

Bathed in a tranquil solitude, feeling as if she were on an endless ride toward the past or the future—it didn't matter which—Ŭn-su watched the mountains draw ever closer until she realized she had missed her stop.

Up close the mountains looked different—the valleys deeper, the ridges more precipitous. On the lower hillsides women were picking wild greens. As Ŭn-su followed a path along one of the ridges, she occasionally looked back at the houses and streets, now distant. Bewitched by the reflection of the mountains in the bus window, she

---

1. "Presenting the Flowers," in _The Book of Korean Poetry: Songs of Shilla and Koryŏ_, trans. Kevin O'Rourke (Iowa City: University of Iowa Press, 2006), p. 15; reprinted by permission.

had ridden past her stop in the market area, continuing on to the final stop. Well, she could always make a quick stop at her mother's on the way home. The freesia in their cellophane wrapper, grown in a hothouse, drooped and withered before the sun and wind.

The mountains were still but for the occasional cry of a cuckoo. It wasn't time for the neighborhood children to be returning from school or for inveterate morning hikers to be returning from the mineral springs. Gaining the high point of the ridge, Ŭn-su no longer saw the women picking wild greens either. What caught her eye instead were the neglected burial mounds, their sod coverings peeled away by the sun, the exposed earth worn and broken by rough feet.

Ŭn-su sat down next to one of the mounds, on a soft covering of withered vines and dried grass from the previous year. She removed her shoes and stretched her legs. Her feet, released from the confinement of the narrow shoes, breathed in relief.

She lit a cigarette. An airplane flew far above, a silver bird. Empty of thoughts, enjoying the inarticulate realization that a place such as this was peace itself, Ŭn-su watched as the sharp line of the contrail thinned out, as if dissolving in water, and disappeared.

Figures appeared, flickering in and out of sight as they descended the hillside across the valley, the large outcrops making it difficult for Ŭn-su to pick out the path they were following. Each was shouldering a sack and carrying a walking stick that looked like it might have been fashioned from a branch. As they came down toward the valley floor, they made constant use of the sticks to beat their way through the bare scrub. Crossing the valley, they turned up toward the rear of the burial mounds and approached Ŭn-su.

"How's about a cigarette, Missus?"

Ŭn-su looked up and saw three men in reservists' uniforms, each with an azalea sprig stuck into his upper jacket pocket and cap. Without a word she passed her pack to a tall man with an outstretched hand.

"Much obliged. And while you're at it, could you give us a light?"

The tall man lowered his sack and plopped down on the ground.

"I've got matches," said a short, thin man. "All this tightwad carries around with him is his mouth." He tossed a box of matches to the tall man, then took a cigarette himself from the pack.

The third man, still standing, took a swig from the ample bottle of *soju* he carried, then opened his sack, took a handful of azaleas, popped them into his mouth, slowly mashed them, and spat. The ruminating lips were moist with the vivid purple, as if he had been eating the flowers all along. Ŭn-su recalled the people she would see in springtime who sold azaleas out of a sack or from a large basin that they carried from door to door on their heads. She crushed out her cigarette underfoot, then covered the butt with grass so the smear of lipstick on the crumpled filter wouldn't show.

"Does the Missus live around here?" asked the tall man, who had been staring at Ŭn-su all along. He leaned toward her, as if to move closer.

"No—just out for some fresh air."

"Don't look to me like the Missus came to offer up a drink to this lonely grave out of the goodness of her heart. . . . And when I look at you sitting there with your legs stretched out, I'll bet you have a story to tell—loneliness, heartbreak—how about it? Am I right?"

The short, thin man glanced at Ŭn-su's bare feet and produced a giggle that seemed to catch in his throat.

Flustered by the man's gaze, Ŭn-su hurriedly located her shoes and put them back on.

The men avidly helped themselves to another cigarette each.

In their thirties? Their swarthy faces, their hands tanned and coarse from rough work, the reservists' uniforms that looked like their work clothes—these made it difficult for Ŭn-su to guess their ages.

"Do you sell them at the market?" Ŭn-su tried to sound as nonchalant as possible to cover up the anxiety rising inside her.

"Yeah, flowers in spring, snakes in summer—whatever comes our way."

The men looked at one another and chuckled as they passed the bottle around, their gulping of the *soju* sounding unnaturally loud to Ŭn-su. About a third of the bottle remained. The stillness of the mountains, so peaceful to Ŭn-su earlier, was suddenly unbearable, the odd daytime silence stifling her—even the birds seemed to have stopped calling. Ŭn-su gathered her bag and bouquet and rose.

"You aren't going to leave without a little chitchat on this fine day, are you? Seems like the Missus don't have much she can do with herself and no place to rush off to. The day's still young—how about some friendly conversation with us? Now there's an idea, eh?"

"I have to go. The flowers are so nice; I just came up for a few minutes to have a look," said Ŭn-su with a smile. Her mouth felt drier and drier.

"Just the flowers?" said the pudgy man with the purple lips, still standing and gazing at the distant mountains as *soju* dribbled from his mouth. "Nice to have a sweetheart too. Enjoyed the smoke. But what are we going to do—this is all we got to offer in return. Don't you want a sip?" He shoved the bottle in Ŭn-su's face.

Ŭn-su flinched and took a step backward, eyes widening.

The tall man casually pocketed her pack of cigarettes.

"Not so fast—the ferryman gives you a free ride and you go and steal his goods. Uh-uh, got to return them to their owner. You got to watch yourself—give you an inch and you take a mile."

The short man snatched the pack of cigarettes from the other and placed it in Ŭn-su's hand. His coarse, clammy hand seized hers and held it for a moment.

"No, no, help yourself—it's all right."

"Hey, the Missus is all right! Knew it all along—what did I tell you?"

Chuckling, he put the cigarettes into his own pocket.

Ŭn-su scurried back to the ridge top, stumbling over stumps that poked out of the ground. Where was the path? Behind her she could faintly hear the men's hushed voices and chuckling.

Far below was the very end of the neighborhood where the bus had taken her. The women picking wild greens along the ridge seemed to have disappeared. Time had stopped in midday in the stillness of these desolate mountains, where not even a shadow flickered. Ŭn-su felt a cold, primeval terror.

From behind her the sound of confident footsteps. Ŭn-su whirled

about. The men were just steps away from her. Their sacks had been
left behind. Purple Lips still had the bottle of *soju*. Ŭn-su forced a
smile—or at least she told herself she had to smile.

"Well, I got up here somehow, and now I can't find my way down."

She could hear how ridiculously high and pinched her voice
sounded.

The men were not smiling.

All those women picking wild greens—where were they hiding?

With the gazes of the men tightening about her like a net, Ŭn-su instinctively retreated, looking around for the women, who had vanished
like apparitions. Would anyone hear if she shouted? The men stood
arrayed before her in a half circle, a foot apart, blocking her way. Faces
flushed with drink, they had the composure of hunters certain that
they have captured their prey. Ŭn-su heard children singing, the sound
carrying past along the ridge.

"What are you doing? I have to go," Ŭn-su said in a strangled voice.
Backpedaling, she stumbled against a rock, or maybe it was a stump,
and fell helplessly backward. As she tumbled to the ground, she hastily drew her skirt down. *You've got to do better than that!* But the dam-
age had been done—all had been revealed. One more humiliation.
Wretchedly she looked up. Even if she were to screen herself with the
bouquet, hadn't she been naked in the eyes of that man at the newsstand? Wasn't she naked in the eyes of the man chewing the azalea
blossoms?

The men drew nearer. And as the half circle tightened, the deep valley they had crossed was pushed into the background. She was a pris-
oner inside a triangle, trapped in a bottleneck. Hidden from the foot of
the mountains, she would not be easily seen here.

The man with the *soju* bottle shoved her back onto the ground with
its covering of dried grass.

"Why are you doing this? What are you going to do?" she shouted
impotently, overwhelmed by a mix of terror and outrage.

"What are we going to do? You'll see," he muttered, passing the
bottle back to the tall man. And then Ŭn-su felt two hands take hold of
her jacket in a commanding grip. The buttons ripped loose; the jacket

was spread wide. Ŭn-su tried to struggle free with her legs but succeeded only in irritating the man, who took off her shoes and flung them aside. Then he put a hand over her mouth and drove his knees down onto her legs. If she confronted her terror head on, it would go away, wouldn't it? The large, moist, purple lips loomed huge and close, a hand pulled her skirt up. All this time Ŭn-su had been gripping the bouquet of freesias, and now, with all her strength, she swiped at the man's face with it. The man smirked.

The reek of liquor fresh on his lips, the smell of crushed azalea blossoms, the nicotine stink of the filthy hand covering her mouth—whatever it was, Ŭn-su felt suffocated.

"Easy now. Nobody comes up here. We could kill you and no one would ever know. So if you want to go back home in one piece, be a good little Missus and do like we tell you."

"We just want to have a little fun, and you're already broken in, so one more time's not going to hurt, is it?"

The tall man, keeping watch over the entrance to the valley, finished off the *soju*, then with a cackle tossed the empty bottle far below.

The short, thin man was urinating, his back to the others.

Footsteps sounded in the valley below. Disembodied voices carried close.

The tall man, hands folded behind his back, scanned the valley and shouted, "Hey! Do you know where you're going? There's snakes around here—snakes that bite!"

The voices and footsteps faded into the distance.

The sun shone in Ŭn-su's eyes. The azaleas on the outcrops filled her vision.

Rough and hurried, the man's hands searched her tense body. She wished she could make herself smaller, wished the other body would go away. She turned her head aside, shuddering at the feel of that body, at its unfamiliar smell. There she was, skirt hitched up, naked from the waist down, pinned to the ground by the man's midsection. *Why can't I faint?* Was she supposed to keep her eyes and ears wide open, to etch this scene in her memory? She felt like she was falling, lower, ever lower, pulled by a heavy weight. How far down was the bottom?

She closed her eyes. But the sunlight still blinded her, the azaleas on the outcrops were still a vivid violet. She imagined what she must look like spread out in the sunlight—a frog awaiting dissection, still conscious, its four limbs pinned to the sides, still flapping about. But the strange thing was this: shining through from the furthest depths of her memory, like a shard of porcelain resting in water, was her earliest recollection—a pair of black rubber shoes lying in sunlight so strong it seemed about to jump.

The man removed himself from Ŭn-su, and the tall man who had been standing guard approached, his belt buckle clinking as he unfastened it.

And then the third man.

"Pathetic, stupid broad! Unless you're fixing to die, you don't wander around a place like this by yourself."

Ŭn-su thought she could hear them whistling as they went down the hillside. Even after their footsteps had died out, she remained hunched up where she was. What had happened to her? If not for the ripped jacket and its missing buttons, if not for the sticky mess in her sodden panties, she would have thought it all a dream or something out of a movie. She couldn't remember the men's faces. The only things that came to mind were the azalea sprigs in the hats and pockets and the moist, purple lips.

The mountain twilight was spreading, thickening. What time could it be? It must have been past the time for Sŭng-il to return home. Her watch was nowhere to be seen—had the band snapped? The wind rattled the bare branches of the scrub trees. Was a thirty-four-year-old woman supposed to cry if she was stripped naked in broad daylight and gang-raped? No, the right to cry after being raped was reserved for girls who didn't know any better. She watched vacantly as dusk rose like fog from the deep valleys and crept toward her, a formless, darkening gloom.

Ŭn-su climbed the slope until she reached the alley to their house. The way felt long and distant. Evening arrives early in spring and soon becomes night. A streetlight shone at every bend in the alley, softening the thickening gloom beyond.

She kept stopping to lean against one of the dark walls and heave a great sigh.

"Why, it's Sŭng-il's mom—where have you been all this time?"

The question made Ŭn-su feel as if someone were shaking her.

There before her was her next-door neighbor, kerosene container in hand.

With a noncommittal utterance Ŭn-su moved out of range of the streetlight and straightened her clothing, concealing the front of her jacket where the buttons were missing.

"You'd better get home." But even after she said this the woman continued to block the alley, scrutinizing Ŭn-su with a most inquisitive expression until Ŭn-su realized that she had something to say.

"If you're going off somewhere, the least you can do is let us know. Now when was it . . . a little past lunchtime, I guess, we heard little Sŭng-il calling for you outside your gate. I didn't pay any attention— thought you were taking a nap—but after another ten minutes or so I heard him banging on your gate and no answer! Well, I tried to talk him into coming inside, telling him maybe you ran out to the market and we'd hear you when you came back. But he said he'd wait at the gate for you. Well, I couldn't keep pestering him all day long, so I told him he could come inside anytime he wanted—we'd leave the gate un-locked. But these little kids are stubborn as oxen, aren't they? I was all ready for dinner except for the fixings for side dishes, and I headed out for the store. And there he was, all this time, sitting back against your gate, nodding off. The poor little kid, I felt so sorry for him. . . . Mommy had something to do and she's late, but she'll be back be-fore dark, and I told him to go on inside, but all he did was shake his head. Some people might think it's amazing that a youngster can wait so long for his mom without crying, but to me it was scary. By now, women up and down the alley were outside trying to talk some sense into him—we'll give you something good to eat, and you can play and watch TV with the big kids; your mom will come looking for you. No matter what they said, he just wouldn't listen. Looked like he was ready to sit there all night long. But then a little while ago his dad came home—we let him go up on the terrace where we keep our soy sauce crocks, so he could climb over the wall into your yard. He unlatched the gate and carried Sŭng-il inside. Good thing he came straight home from work. . . ."

The woman's words rung stridently in Ŭn-su's ears.

Ŭn-su turned away. Aware of the woman's searching gaze, she withdrew from the lamplight, conscious of every step she took.

Except for the family room, the house was dark. No sound of the television even. Propping herself against the wall, she stood on tiptoe and gazed at the brightness shining from the family room, so close beyond their tiny yard that she could almost reach out and touch it. Now and then she could hear Sŭng-il's uncomprehending voice and Se-jung responding in a low murmur.

Her hand shaking, Ŭn-su found the doorbell and pressed it. At the dull, abbreviated sound of the bell, her hand jerked away from the button.

The window to the family room opened and Se-jung's face appeared.

"Who is it?"

"It's me, Ŭn-su."

The window banged shut. The curtains were drawn, and the light from the room, dimmer now, seemed more distant to Ŭn-su.

"Who was that, Dad? Huh?"

"Nobody. It was next door. Now go to sleep."

Se-jung's reply carried loudly over the wall. Was he raising his voice on purpose?

Her energy spent, Ŭn-su clung to the gate and desperately pressed the buzzer.

Someone's outline briefly flickered at a window next door, then disappeared. The window of the family room remained shut. Suddenly the television was on, blaring throughout the empty alley. Probably to keep Sŭng-il from hearing her.

Where had Sŭng-il curled up to entertain himself while waiting for her all afternoon? Ŭn-su sank in a heap against the gatepost. Any sound from inside was drowned out by the blaring of the television, which to her ears seemed building for an explosion.

The woman next door trotted by with her kerosene can, failing to notice Ŭn-su hunkered down in the shadow of the gate. The footsteps of passersby continued to sound. Before long the footsteps of those returning home would cease, and only the gloom and the secretive stillness of the deepening night would remain.

Ŭn-su shuddered. All over her face, everywhere on the insides of her legs, she felt tiny goose bumps. What amazed her was that in spite of her sense of helpless frustration, what she felt most vividly now was this physiological sensation of coldness.

Ŭn-su rose and pressed the doorbell twice in quick succession. At some point, the sound of the television had softened.

Some time later the window opened enough for Se-jung to look out toward the gate.

It's me—would you open the gate? But these thoughts remained unspoken.

The window closed. Ŭn-su heard the door to the family room open and then the sliding door of the veranda. A couple of steps and the scuff of sandals, and Se-jung had stepped down into the yard. There he stopped.

Ŭn-su nervously sucked her breath in.

"You still there? Go on back. We can talk during the day."

He spoke in a pronounced undertone, as if trying to suppress the emotions boiling inside him.

Go back?! Back where?! Ŭn-su silently screamed.

"I'm afraid that if I see you"—there was a long pause—"I'll kill you."

"Let me in, please. I'll tell you everything."

"*You*? You mean *you* have something *more* to tell *me*?" he mocked, trying his utmost to control his rage. "Keep your voice down—Sŭng-il's asleep. I want you to go on back; it's late. We need time to think about each other. And let's spare the neighbors the wretched sight of you. I called my mother; she's coming over first thing in the morning, so you don't have to worry about Sŭng-il."

And with that the veranda door slid shut and the family room fell dark.

Three

It was my habit, first thing in the morning, to reach for the newspaper, which was always there beside my pillow, and to ask for water. But my outstretched hand jerked back—a thought had come, had seized me by the scruff, and instinctively I looked next to me.

The cold, faint light of dawn revealed Sŭng-il asleep on his side; he had kicked off his quilt. I drew the quilt over him as I got up, then went to the kitchen and drank a bowl of water.

I tried to remember what I had dreamed about the previous night. On the dinner table in the kitchen was a messy scattering of side dishes and bowls with dried-up bits of rice stuck inside—none of it covered up. And the table on the veranda was just as I had left it—a half-full bottle of *soju*, shot glass, ashtray piled high.

Till late the previous night the restless sound of my wife tiptoeing back and forth outside had kept my ears pricked up; it might as well have been the caterwauling of a cat clawing at the gate. I had sat there with the light out, drinking, sipping.

I opened the veranda curtain, and the dim interior brightened. Day was about to break. When I returned to our room, the sound of the door opening brought a faint cry from Sŭng-il, who was half awake and turning from side to side.

"Mommy, I have to pee!"

As my wife did early every morning, I hoisted Sŭng-il up, draped his arms about my shoulders, and brought the potty near. He urinated and, sleepy again, looked at me with sad, cloudy eyes, then looked about the room. His face crinkled up as if he would burst into tears, but then, realizing his mommy wasn't there, he crawled back under his quilt without a word.

And then, hesitantly: "Is Mommy in the kitchen?"

"No, she's not," I bluntly retorted. And then, to comfort the boy, "In a little while your grandmother's coming up from the countryside. You like Grandmother, don't you?"

I had told her she ought to come up immediately, and sure enough she said she would take the first train in the morning, flustered though she was by my lack of an explanation. She expected to arrive at nine thirty. The clock on the wall chimed—it was six thirty. The sliding door to the yard scraped open, and I stepped outside to fetch the morning paper, which was wedged inside the gate.

I yanked the paper free, then remained standing there. Quietly I opened the gate. She wasn't there. Only the occasional early-bird student passing by. Strange, though—why, after deciding I'd never take her in, did I have this empty feeling inside me, an emptiness like hunger, now that I could actually see she'd left? I felt almost like I'd been betrayed. Yesterday I'd been angry enough to kill her when I got home from work and saw Sŭng-il nodding off outside the gate, but my rage had already cooled, had become an object I could deal with. Did this mean I was hoping she'd cried herself to sleep and was now hunched up outside the gate? Maybe somewhere in the corner of my mind I'd come up with an excuse for her: this wasn't the usual case of her spending several nights away from home, but merely a day's outing that had turned out longer than expected.

If I had slapped her a few times in response to her tearful appeal and broken a few things inside—but then I shook my head vigorously—I couldn't give in to her so easily. I stepped outside the gate with the broom. This was where she had staggered away, drooping and miserable. As if to erase her image, I began sweeping methodically.

I left for work an hour late, after Mother arrived, but I had difficulty focusing. Hadn't I secretly tried to convince myself that the day would come when I would make my wife leave? I asked myself, looking back over the years. Even as I did this, I startled at every ring of the telephone and every time someone called my name.

In between stamping bankbooks for deposits and withdrawals I was in and out of the bathroom, doing nothing more than washing my hands.

The errand girl emptied the ashtray on my desk, saying it was the third time that day. And when one of the tellers saw me drinking one glass of barley water after another, she said, "Goodness, Mr. Chi, you must have had a lot to drink last night." But I wasn't in the mood to respond. What I really wanted to do, once and for all, to these people with the neatly tied neckties who took their places at work untainted by family concerns, personal suffering, or the like was to grab them by the collar—pale, dark, yellow, broad, longish—as they were absorbed in their work and ask, "How would you act if you were in my position?" As always they would extend a modicum of sympathy toward me and nominal forgiveness toward my wife. For the sake of the little boy, they would say, take her in this time, as long as she isn't guilty of something major such as infidelity. Or, if I wasn't going to beat her to death—the ultimate corrective—then I should part ways with her, and the sooner the better.

I wondered where my wife was. At her mother's house in Karhyŏn dong, buried under a quilt? Watching people come and go on a busy street—watching, watching in her absentminded way? Or maybe she was back at our house. Time and again I pulled back my hand as it reached for the telephone and instead had a glass of barley water or sucked on another innocent cigarette.

What was the matter? Mother had asked as soon as she arrived. But one glance at the mess in the kitchen, one look at Sŭng-il still in pajamas, sitting in a sulk at the edge of the veranda, told her everything.

"Grammy's here—everything's all right now. You're hungry, aren't you? Poor little tyke."

She rolled up her sleeves, stepped down into the kitchen, and hurriedly began rinsing rice for cooking.

My wife's wandering tendencies, though I'd never mentioned them to Mother or called her to Seoul like this, had for years now been fodder for conversation in our family, thanks to my older sister.

I wasn't exactly sure whether I was waiting for my wife to return or was dreading facing her. What became clear, though, was that as time went on, there was no longer anything I could do about my feelings of intolerance toward her. This time she had gone too far. But try as I might to convince myself of this, I couldn't shake the nagging realization that I had turned my wife away in the dead of night.

The end of the workday approached, and still no call from my wife—not that I expected it. Instead—and this was entirely unexpected—it was my mother-in-law who appeared at the bank. One of my glances toward the tinted glass door caught her hesitating outside.

My heart sank, and I began trembling to the very ends of my fingers. And when she took a seat in the waiting area, hoping, I presumed, to catch my eye, I pretended I didn't see her. Instead I had a smoke and engaged my coworker at the next desk in some small talk. When she could wait no longer and approached the counter, I rose and manufactured a solicitous expression, as if I'd just then noticed her.

With closing time approaching, the bank was as crowded as the center of an open-air market. The least I could have done was take her to the basement tearoom, but I ended up offering her a seat in the waiting area and sitting down beside her. My mouth was bitter and gritty from all the cigarettes I'd smoked, but again I lit up, more out of habit than anything else.

"You . . . seem to be busy," she ventured sheepishly while fumbling in her handbag.

"It's always like this at closing time."

"So, she's up to her old tricks."

I had to say something, so I adopted a curt, disinterested tone of voice. "Is she staying with you?"

My response gave her the opening she was looking for. The words poured out, words she had come here to tell me, words she had probably mumbled to herself all the while she was trying to work up the courage to walk through the door of the bank.

"No. When she goes off somewhere, she never comes to me. Yesterday she was supposed to drop by and pick up some food—I waited till dark, and when she didn't come, I told myself something had come up and didn't think further about it. But then I had an awful night's sleep, and when I called the house this morning, your good mother answered. When she told me Sŭng-il's mom wasn't there, all the energy drained right out of me. . . . I'm not sure what's best; I can hardly think straight. But if only you'd called, I would have come right over. I wish you hadn't troubled your mother like this."

She looked regretful, resentful even, that in these circumstances I had immediately notified my mother in the countryside.

"Aren't we past the point of trying to cover things up?" I asked.

"It's all my fault. What can I say? Anyhow, it looks like the crazy thing is off somewhere again."

"God only knows. I've been married to her six years now, and I've had it up to here. Am I supposed to send the police out after her? Put an ad in the paper? Set up a lookout post on the street?"

Heads started turning my way in the long line of people paying their utility bills and among the people leafing through the magazines nearby. My agitated voice must have risen.

"I'm going to tell her once and for all to stop it. But just try to re-member, she *is* the boy's mother," she said in a strained voice, seizing my hand.

It was the same old thing, and I was disgusted with it.

"His mother, you say? Show me a devoted mother who acts the way she does," I hissed.

It was all in vain. As unobtrusively as I could, I disengaged my-self from the hot, coarse hand with its dark spots, then deliberately checked my watch.

"All right, you're busy—go back to your work. I'm on my way to your house. Your mother has her store, and I'd like to see that she's back home tomorrow if possible. I'll take care of Sŭng-il until his mom comes back."

She rose.

"That won't be necessary," I said, my tone frigid, looking directly at her. Her old, earth-colored face grew pale. "My younger brother's taking care of the store. Mother will stay with me until we set things straight. When you see Sŭng-il's mom, please have her come see me."

With that I rose, but my mother-in-law was not about to go any-where and said she would wait nearby until it was time for me to go home. Restraining myself, I sent her on her way with the excuse that I had to work that evening since it was the end of the month. The diz-zying whirl of thoughts that had aggravated me all day finally fell into order, and I felt composed—as if the end of a tangled thread I couldn't grasp had come into sight. Peace of mind at witnessing her reaction— her naked anxiety and distress?

I had never thought of myself as being that cold a person. But if anything had hardened, it was my conviction that my family, the family I had cultivated with my own hands, must be safeguarded, made cozy as a bird's nest, solid as a walnut shell. Perhaps my ever increasing mistrust and skepticism toward people and the world had reinforced that conviction and were thickening the wall I had built around myself.

I crumpled the empty cigarette pack and opened my desk drawer. Pens, business cards, pocket calculator, envelopes, and such, all neatly arranged, and beneath them, at the very bottom, several savings account passbooks. I took one of them, a five-year, monthly deposit account that in six months would be worth 5 million *wŏn*. Put that toward the purchase of a home in the fall, along with a loan and the security deposit on our current house, and we could move into a better house. My eyes lingered in turn over each of the last six unstamped squares in the passbook as I tried to order my dizzy jumble of thoughts and define the extent of my obligations toward my wife—practical, ethical, legal.

When, five years earlier, I had suggested putting away money to buy a house, knowing full well the sacrifice this would require, she had responded with childlike delight:

"Instead of buying a house other people have lived in or a newly built house, why don't we build our own house just the way we want it? I'm the kind of person who thinks that the house you live in will become a part of you. I'm not interested in the housing that's going up now. Apartment living's supposed to be comfortable, but who wants the same layout as a million other people? If we build our own house, we can have a lot of rooms. Even if they're like ant tunnels. And for the children, one of the rooms has to be a retreat that's off limits to everyone else, a place for them to go if we get mad or upset. The house doesn't need to be big—just so long as we have a big yard. We can have a round table there, so we can eat or have a drink or read outside when the weather's nice. And we'll grow as many fruit trees as we can—I think the children would prefer fruit trees. You'll probably say it's the kind of thing a girl would dream up, but we'll have a white wooden fence. Green would be good for the roof. I guess that's from reading

Anne of Green Gables in school. Do you know the story? It's about a
homely orphan girl who's poor as a church mouse, and she's taken into
a farmhouse with a green roof and grows up into a beautiful, happy
woman. While I was reading it, I was amazed at what it takes to feel
happiness. I want to build my house with my own two hands, and I
want to live in it for a long time. I'll have a lot of children. I'm small, I
know, but I'll produce them—just watch me. They'll romp around in
the yard, and I'll sit in an easy chair, just sit and sit, like an old woman,
watching them, getting sentimental."

I began filling out a form to close the account.

I knew that regardless of the circumstances, as a husband I was
bound to feel indebted to my wife, but that in spite of psychological obligations, monetary settlements would resolve many worldly matters.

"Why do I have these sad thoughts whenever I see little children?"
Again, my wife. "They say it's the happiest time of life—you're naive
and accepting—but there's something about the innocence of children
romping around so carefree that makes me profoundly sad. I often
think about the children we'll have. But the strange thing is, all I can
see are five- or six-year-olds. It's hard for me to picture having older
children around. Strange, isn't it? I know children are bound to grow
up."

"I'm already imagining a big kid wearing my socks," I'd said. She
was large with Sŭng-il at the time.

For the third time I had to crumple up the form I was trying to fill
out. Either my writing was blurry or I couldn't get a sharp print from
my stamp. I took great pains to get my fourth try right.

Miss Mun, one of the people who handled savings, was about to
leave. Her handbag was on her desk and she was fixing her makeup. I
could have given myself a one-day grace period, but I forced myself to
make up my mind. I pushed the completed form onto her desk.

"Miss Mun, would you take care of this by noon tomorrow?"

Outside the window it was growing dark. Hazy lights sprouted in
the gloom. Night would soon fall, and the lights of the street would
grow warmer, would flourish.

Instead of boarding the waiting commuter bus, I set off in the direction of City Hall. I didn't want to go home in my present state, despite the image I entertained of Sŭng-il and my mother. My mother would be listening intently for the sound of my footsteps outside the front gate, my mother who had difficulty making even a few trips a year to see Sŭng-il, who now would be put to some trouble because she wasn't used to housework. Empty, unhappy, vexed, all I wanted to do was throw a tantrum and get things out of my system, and to hell with what anyone else thought.

The rush hour bustle—more like swimming with the current instead of walking. People bumping shoulders, treading on heels, a human wave flowing down darkening streets. On I walked, didn't matter where. I felt a strange sense of liberation that I could only explain as the result of my awareness of how unhappy I was. From the rear, every woman that passed by resembled my wife. Had I really decided to separate from her? Could I divorce her without feeling she had run away, abandoning a young child on a dark street? Pushed along to God-knows-where by the human tide, I interrogated myself.

My wife was practically night-blind. She'd lived in Seoul almost twenty years, and yet the only streets she knew were the ones to home, school, and work. She was afraid of walking the streets at night, and before our marriage I'd escorted her down quite a few of those streets, telling her I was afraid she'd lose her way on her own—that was my excuse, at any rate. She was always amazed that I knew so many side streets, so many alleys, every bend of them.

Those from back home who had settled in Seoul before me had cautioned me to learn my way around the city to save money, but the fact that I was more familiar with the streets than with anything else about Seoul life was the result of all those lonely years of having to find the cheapest possible room to rent and getting myself ahead on a steady diet of tutoring.

With the deepening of night the human tide swelled. The city was a huge conveyor belt sending numerous vehicles and people speeding on their way. Where did they come from, this flow of people? Weren't we, all of us, like the boys in the legend who were lured by the magician's flute to some unknown place, never to return? Weren't we still being drawn unknowingly by a silent hand toward a gate to the unknown?

Carried by the people past Midopa Department Store to Ch'ungmuro, I found myself falling into an odd sense of unreality and stopping to gaze at the throngs filling the streets.

I felt a sharp reminder from my stomach that I'd skipped lunch. But even if I'd been full, eight in the evening wasn't the time for a miserably depressed man who was pushing forty to be roaming the streets stone cold sober without a clue to where he was going. Instead, it was time for the men who hadn't gone home yet to be longing for a tiny alcohol buzz.

I left the main street for an alley lined with bars.

The bars were filled with smoke from grilled meat and the raucous, boozy voices of customers, who by now occupied almost every seat. I found an empty seat and had myself half a small bottle of *soju* and a plate of grilled octopus. On my empty stomach, before long I was feeling the liquor.

At the charcoal-grill table next to me a man was delivering a high-decibel lecture to his younger companion, who was wiping away with his fists the tears dribbling down his cheeks.

"Hey, that's life. To a strong son-of-a-bitch you're weak, and to a weak son-of-a-bitch you're strong—that's the way the world turns. You think you're the only one who's got a right to gripe? Come on, drink up. Drink your fill and forget everything. 'If somebody's getting you down, then get one-up on him'—remember the song?"

"It's a dirty business, it really is, and I can feel it in my guts I'm so mad. . . ."

I paid up and left. Nine o'clock. I'd have to cross the street to catch a taxi home. But it was an in-between time to be going home, and I was in-between drunk. Sŭng-il was probably dropping off to sleep around now, and Mother would be putting away dinner and listening for my footsteps outside the gate. Maybe my wife had returned. Then again maybe she didn't have the heart for it. If anything, she might be hanging around the dark alley instead. I shook my head stubbornly and walked off. There wasn't a single reason I should go home, but I failed to convince myself of this. In my intoxicated state, the spring evening air felt warm and gentle.

At the bottom of the steps to a pedestrian underpass I stopped to buy a large panda from a peddler woman who had laid out stuffed animals and carved toys on a mat. Seeing her small child crawling around the underpass tooting on a toy bugle, I bought one of those as well.

The woman quickly removed a small toy tank from a pile of boxes, wound it up, and set it rolling along the pavement. Several times the tank rolled over, only to flip itself upright again. I asked the woman to wrap up the tank as well as the bugle.

I tried to remember if I had ever bought Sŭng-il a toy. This job always fell to my wife. The woman wrapped the panda in a sheet of paper and tied it roughly, and I managed to leave with a toy in each pocket and the bear stuck awkwardly in my armpit.

Back on the street, I noticed a small beer hall and pushed open the door. The interior—two rows of tables with dividers between the seatbacks—was long, narrow, and gloomy, like a train compartment. A small group of young men sat near the counter, and I recall a couple, maybe two, who appeared to be romantically involved. There were no other customers.

I ordered two bottles of beer and some dried snacks. The waitress served me, then sat down across the table.

"You can call me Miss Chŏng," she said with a pert bow. "Is it all right if I sit down?"

"That's what the chair's for."

"You must have a companion coming?" she said politely as she poured me a glass of beer. She had long fingers with pale, silver-gray nail polish, and her wrists were unusually slender. It seemed to require an effort just to lift the bottle to pour. Swinging loosely from the upraised wrist was a metal bracelet.

"No, it's just me."

"You don't look too happy."

"Yeah? I wonder why."

"You don't see too many people drinking by themselves."

"Hard-core drinkers do. That way they can really enjoy the taste," I said with a smirk as I filled my empty glass and offered it to her. This brought a smile to her masklike face, expressionless till then behind thick makeup.

"Mister, are those presents for a baby?"

Moving the panda, which was sticking out of its wrapper, she sat down next to me.

"Yeah, but now it occurs to me he's past the age where he'd play with it. I bought a toy bugle and tank too, but the tank's probably the only thing that'll get a reaction out of him."

I took the two toys from my pockets and placed them on the table.

"Well, what a fine dad you are! But do children these days play with bugles?" She put the bugle to her lips and produced a short squeak. "A fine dad and a lonely man there seems to be quite a story here."

The beer bottles were empty; I ordered two more.

"Yeah, a romance novel just waiting to be written."

"I like a lonely looking man. Falling in love with someone like that is the real thing—so I've heard."

"Maybe you're the literary type?"

"Something all girls go through—read books and love loneliness," she giggled.

"Fact of the matter is, I tore down a house today."

Her eyes opened wide in surprise.

"You're one of the people who gets rid of squatters?"

I had to chuckle, and the chuckle sent cigarette smoke streaming into her face.

"It was too good to be torn down, but it turned out to be haunted. Wasn't much I could do except tear it down, foundation posts and all."

The beer bottles on the table multiplied.

"Really, mister, how could you get so depressed over the house of some Kim, Pak, or Yi you'll never see again? They can always build a new one. If something upsets you, you get sloppy drunk, you suffer, and the next morning you get up, and what do you know? All of a sudden yesterday's bother is history. It's so easy for a man."

She filled my glass, giggling with that same masklike smile.

It was after eleven when I left. Drunk to the gills, I still remembered, same as always, to load myself into a taxi with some other men who were hurrying home. Force of habit is a frightening thing. Wasn't it simply a deeply rooted homing instinct that impelled us home by twelve o'clock even though the country no longer had a midnight curfew? How many of those disappearing people were vanishing behind a line of propriety they had drawn for themselves each after his own fashion?

And where was the line of propriety I had drawn with respect to my wife?

I got out of the taxi at the neighborhood alley and relieved myself against someone's wall, gazing up at the moon's halo.

I heard no one else in the alley. "It's too quiet," I mumbled, staggering along the best I could in an elusive, drink-induced loneliness and grief. *Thunk*—something had dropped out of my pocket. The toy bugle the beer hall girl had so carefully placed in my pocket as I left.

Bear wedged in my armpit, I tooted on the bugle. Who was that woman who was always playing a bugle? *Tooooot, toooot.* It was in a movie. Her hair was chopped short, she was a bit slow. A snow-covered road through the woods, and a swindler, a bulky man, leaving the sick woman in bed, leaving a bugle and a few coins at her side before abandoning her. Yeah—that Italian movie. The woman, tiny like a young child, sitting on a blanket in the sun, playing the single tune the man had taught her, then dying. And then a song in a clear, high-pitched voice sung by a tall woman in a scarf hanging laundry in a wind-swept field. These several scenes and the sound of the bugle had survived in my memories. Was that movie supposed to be showing us an angel? The pathos of life?

Her short hair. Her gaping eyes that gave her a look of perpetual surprise, that made her seem seized with fear. *Oh Gelsomina, my sad angel. Oh Gelsomina, where have you gone?* I made a half-hearted attempt to grasp the words and sing, then tried whistling, but the melody of the following stanza eluded me. Again I tooted the bugle. As if rending a thick blanket, the stupid, simple sound of the bugle spread toneless, pitchless, into the darkness.

I was very young the first time I heard a bugle. A circus had arrived

in town, and one of the performers was playing it. I can still hear its
bright tone, a sound so high I thought it would pierce the sky, arriving
suddenly in the still of the surroundings where there had been only the
wind soothing the gathering dusk.

It was a sad, desolate sound. It seemed to come from deep in the
ground of a place we didn't inhabit, from a distant star, chilling my
tiny heart like a constant premonition of sadness, death, parting, casting me into the depths of a sorrow and a fear I couldn't understand.

I reached our house but couldn't bring myself to ring the bell. Like
my wife the previous night, I gazed inside like a stranger, as if peeping
into someone else's house. What had I been like the day before? And
the day before that? And the days previous? I tried to think as
I propped myself against the gatepost. Well, it was all right. Not
everything had been like it was today. Wasn't it like the beer hall girl
had said, and like it had been when I was a boy—that you had a good
night's sleep and when you got up, troubled and painful today had
become yesterday, and a new today lay waiting beside your bed?

When I pressed the bell, Mother would appear momentarily at the
sliding glass door of the veranda, moving sluggishly, as if she were
opening a series of doors, and before long she would stoop over list-
lessly to find her slippers and scuff out toward the gate.

"You're late."

"Yes, I'm a little late. Is Sŭng-il asleep?"

"He nodded off hours ago. Now I want you to cut down on your
drinking, do you hear? You could be a mighty warrior for all I care, but
your health is still going to suffer if you come home dead drunk every
night."

Inside the family room the first thing I did was look intently into
Sŭng-il's face as he lay sleeping on his side. Mother squatted beside me
and hesitantly inspected my appearance.

"No word yet from his mom?" she whispered. She patted Sŭng-il's
hair the way she did with children, then, afraid of waking him, lowered her voice to a murmur.

"The little fellow's so well behaved, I'm simply amazed. In his
little heart he must know something—he hasn't bothered me about

his mom. He didn't once talk back to his grammy. What could be more pitiful, the way his fate is playing out. . . ."

I ignored her mumbling as I removed my socks and then my shirt. What about my wife—had she ever talked back to me? On the whole she was calm and quiet in manner. Had her expression ever revealed the slightest trace of the infernal goblin, or whatever it was, that had permeated her soul?

"I'd like you to get home a little earlier, do you hear? An old woman and a little boy just sitting around looking at each other . . . it gets dark, everyone's gone, a cold wind blows outside, and the house feels more lonely and disturbing, more deserted."

And so, to make things easier for her, I began coming straight home from work.

But not a day went by that I didn't shuffle out in my sandals, whatever the hour, to the mom-and-pop store at the corner of the alley and have myself a bottle of beer before going to bed. I couldn't stand it, couldn't stand the fathomless despair, the grief into which I sank when I heard my boy, so strangely meek and dispirited with waiting for his mom; when I heard Mother's clumsy mumbling as she tried with far-sighted eyes, glasses perched on her nose, to read him to sleep in this house that had fallen into a dreariness deeper than darkness, deeper than night. I couldn't stand it, and I hoped that drinking would offer refreshment, that it would induce raw, basic emotions—rage, hatred, and all the rest.

When Mother inquired discreetly if I'd heard anything about my wife, I answered curtly: "If she comes here, don't bother letting her in; have her come see me at the bank."

Gradually she removed from sight my wife's clothes hanging on the wall. But the dust continued to collect on her vanity, unseen by Mother's dim eyes. Every morning I scrubbed my face with the same damp washcloth and put on a dress shirt washed and ironed by my mother. At breakfast she would place some deboned fish on Sŭng-il's spoon, never failing to say, "There's nothing at that mom-and-pop store worth cooking up, and why is everything so expensive?" Every few days she'd call home and talk to my brother, who was keeping the store. "I was hoping to leave before too long, but I'm stuck here taking care of the house." In fact, my brother and his wife had taken over managing the store some time before and didn't absolutely need Mother's assistance.

By the calendar it was still spring, but it felt like early summer all during this business with my wife. Daytime highs in the low eighties were announced—abnormally warm—and the extreme gap between day and nighttime temperatures had everyone worrying about colds and spring droughts.

One day one of our customers looked me up at the bank—a man named Kim who was a department head somewhere—and we had beef-and-rice soup at a restaurant nearby. When I came outside, chewing on a toothpick, my eyes were drawn to the fountain at the rotary. Beneath the stream of water that looked so refreshing as it shot from the fountain, perched on the stone border of a bed of pansies in three colors looking just like a carpet, was a woman. My wife. _What do I do?_ I felt almost like I'd been assaulted. She sat in profile, blissfully ignoring the "Keep Off" signs, wearing an absentminded expression, oblivious to the glances of passersby. Maybe it was the clothes everyone was wearing during the heat wave these past few days, clothes lighter in color and weight, but in the hot sun her bright lavender suit was to my eye just as odd and alarming as the sight of her sitting there beside the flowerbed.

"What's the matter?" said Kim. "Did you leave something back at the restaurant?"

Without realizing it, I had stopped short to look at her.

"No, it's nothing."

I launched myself forward, as if someone had given me a push.

Back at the office, as I worked, my thoughts whirled constantly about my wife beside the fountain. Well, then, it must have been her that my mother said she saw last night, I told myself. I'd returned late the previous evening, and when Mother let me in, she didn't immediately draw the bolt, even after I'd gone inside, but instead poked her head outside to inspect the dark alley.

And then, "You didn't see her?" she whispered, as if she were tugging on my sleeve. My cloud of intoxication lifted.

"See who? I didn't see anybody."

But I had a hunch it was my wife she meant.

"The woman next door said she saw Sŭng-il's mom in the alley on her way home from the market—about three or four this afternoon. She recognized the woman but turned her back and pretended she hadn't seen her. But the neighbor woman caught up to her, asked her where she'd been all this time. Well, she mumbled something or other that the woman couldn't understand."

During this time, Mother had had frequent contact with the middle-aged woman next door in the course of learning how to use the washing machine and finding her way to the market. They'd exchanged visits and had begun to open up to each other. To see Mother's expression of amazement as she related this incident, you might have thought it was worth clapping about.

"It bothered me to hear this, and I made sure I didn't send Sŭng-il outside. And this evening, when it was pretty much dark, all I could think about was the alley. I had the feeling someone must have been out there, so I took a look. And right then, somebody quickly left the gate. Her back was to me, but I'm sure it was Sŭng-il's mom. I was hopping mad—I've never done anything to her to feel guilty about. . . . These days I don't even want to think about her mother—I'm so disappointed in them. If she finds her daughter's been unfaithful and has a lot of faults, you'd think she'd realize she's lost face and must do something about it. . . . It's been a month now."

All the previous afternoon my wife had been making the rounds of the neighborhood, and when she appeared near the bank, I knew she wanted to see me.

The 3 million *wŏn* from the savings account I'd closed had been transferred to an account of my own. I'd hurriedly closed out that savings account the day after she left, thinking I'd probably see her, but when more than a week passed without any word from her, I had deposited the money.

My expectation of a visit from my wife proved accurate. A little past three in the afternoon she called.

"It's me, Ŭn-su."

Perhaps she was tense, but her voice sounded different—clipped and short, almost like a stranger's. I gulped, momentarily forgot what to say.

"Well, so it is."

"I'm in the basement tearoom—could you come down?"

Her voice was shrill, the words fast, as if she didn't want to hear my response.

"I'm pretty busy now—can you give me another thirty minutes or so?"

"All right. I'll be waiting." Click.

It was a lie: I wasn't so busy that she had to wait thirty minutes. I'd merely blurted that request out of an anxious desire to gain time.

The first thing I did was light a cigarette, and then I set about straightening my desk drawers, which weren't all that messy. Thirty minutes proved to be a long time.

While thinking of my wife waiting in the tearoom, I relieved myself in the bathroom and slowly washed my hands. I withdrew 2 million *wŏn* from my new account, converted it into 4 half-million *wŏn* checks, and slipped them into a white envelope. On my way out I checked my appearance in the mirror beside the entrance, as I always did. My face still had a dirty yellow cast to it, from my latest hangover, but my fresh dress shirt looked clean.

She was sitting at a table with her back to the entrance, easy to spot with the image of her at the fountain still fresh in my mind. Despite the unoccupied tables, the dim red lights and loud music annoyed me and made the tearoom seem crowded. Under the dim lights her lavender outfit had taken on a reddish tint.

After hesitating a moment, I sat down across from her. She half stood up in greeting, then gently eased herself back down. In the briefest instant her face seemed strange and different. And then I noticed—it was her thick makeup. And her hair was cut much shorter, revealing her neck and her protruding ears, lending harshness to her appearance. The makeup must have been meant to take off years and create an air of vitality, but I recognized it at once as a desperate attempt to conceal the coarse, emaciated look of her face.

"It's been a while."

I put my cigarettes on the table and leaned back.

"Shall we go somewhere else? It's too noisy here."

"I have to get back to work."

I had no intention of moving. Instead, I asked our waitress if she'd mind turning down the music.

"Where are you coming from?" I asked, though I was certain she'd spent all morning knocking about the area near the bank. I felt like I had to break the awkward silence, the tension between us.

Head bowed, she was fingering the corner of the table. At my question she looked straight at me.

"I went to the house this morning. Your mother's there."

"Mmm-hmm."

"She said I wasn't to come in; I should see you first."

"That's what I told her."

A faint smile framed her lips. But I could see the throbbing of the bluish blood vessels of her forehead and knew she was trying to suppress her surging emotions.

"I guess you're reasonably comfortable with your mother there."

"Can't complain."

Again we fell into silence. For some time she seemed tentative, a preoccupied expression on her face. The hot drink in front of her remained untouched.

"Is Sŭng-il okay?"

"Mmm-hmm."

"How is he doing in kindergarten?"

"Seems to like it pretty well."

She produced a handkerchief and wiped her forehead. She was sweating profusely, and not because of her clothing, which was too warm for the season. She replaced the handkerchief in her handbag, and then her elbow hit the table with such force that the cup of barley water she'd set precariously near the edge wobbled briefly and then fell to the floor. Crestfallen, she bent to retrieve it.

"Never mind. I'll get it."

As I was returning the cup, my gaze was arrested by the sight of her shoes. She said she'd visited our home, but I wondered if she'd been wandering a long, rugged road, walking every step of the way. For the dusty leather of the heels was scratched and peeling, making them look shabby and worn out. No backsliding, I told myself. Don't get emotional. I quickly turned my eyes away from her shoes. It was like a self-preservation instinct, a defense mechanism, developed over a long period.

"Smoke?"

Seeking the right opportunity to produce the white envelope from my pocket, I pushed the pack of cigarettes toward her.

She shook her head.

"I've done a lot of thinking," I said. "Maybe you too. Going on like this is a painful business for both of us."

I brusquely withdrew the envelope of money and placed it before her.

"And so . . . what's this?" She gazed vacantly at me for a moment and then her face gradually grew pale. She hurriedly took the handkerchief from her handbag and mopped her face. "What is this?" she faltered. "What are you trying to say?"

"Money. I closed out the savings account for the new house. I think we need some time to think about each other without emotions getting involved. To be honest, I don't want to be hurt any more. Don't worry about Sŭng-il. Mother's taking good care of him. This money's for you—I know you don't have any, and this should get you by for the time being. People always need money."

Avoiding the bloodshot eyes that stared unblinking at me, I continued my mumbled speech.

"I feel lousy and helpless not coming up with anything better than this. Now I understand why people say that if you think things over too much, you end up wanting to kill yourself. Anyway, what else can I do? We can't live on like this, can we?"

What I had wanted to say was this: *Will you stop looking at me like that?! You brought it all on yourself! You're not stupid! Didn't it*

*ever occur to you when you were traipsing around so carefree that
things would turn out this way?! The victim, if you want to know the
truth, is me!*

But I had swallowed this torrent of words. What I actually said was
windy, inarticulate, fragmentary, sounding like a clumsy excuse even
to my own ears. Such was my overblown desire to hurt my wife.

"Back to the money—are we talking about . . . alimony?"

It took great effort for her to blurt out *alimony*. Coming from her
lips, the word sent me reeling. For the first time I vividly felt the real
meaning, the weight of that word.

"Don't be so melodramatic. That's not exactly my intention. Let's
just think of it as the best policy for all of us for the time being while
you and I are separated. It's better for you too. It's really unfortunate
things have ended up like this. But I believe in the power of time. As
time goes on, I'm sure we'll come up with a way that will be best for
all of us."

This was the truth. Frankly, I still didn't have the courage to snap
the cords that bound us, thin though they were. I knew there was no
reason to expect I'd be better off in the future even if change came to
my life. On the contrary, it was much easier to imagine my situation
growing worse.

"You sound just like you're laying off someone at work. Perhaps
you've been waiting a long time for this moment."

She produced a bitter smile. Both the smile and her words took
me by surprise, and inwardly I recoiled.

"I think in my own way I've put up with a lot. And I'm sorry to say,
I've reached the limits of my patience. I've been thinking back to
the days we've spent together and wondering how we got to this
point, wondering if the fundamental cause lay with me from the
beginning. But the one thing I've learned is that I don't have the
capacity or the tolerance to understand your actions."

"I know. I understand everything, even without your going to
the trouble of saying all this." She put the white envelope in her
handbag. "How much is it?" And again she flashed me a faint, incom-
prehensible smile.

"Not that much."

"Why don't you go first? Then I'll go."

"Where do you think you'll go—to your mom's?"

She shook her head with a blank expression, as if a fever had erased all her thoughts.

"I don't know yet. I'll have to think about it."

I left her like that. Certain she had fixed me with the glare of someone angry enough to want to pull my hair, I looked back as I paid the cashier, but she was sitting unchanged with her back toward me.

Back at the bank, I stood vacantly beside the windows, having no mind to sit at my desk. About five minutes later my wife appeared in front of the bank. Inside the bank, I was thoroughly concealed by the tinted glass of the window; outside, she was clearly visible.

She stopped at a traffic light, and when the signal changed, she set off across the crosswalk. From behind, as she blended with the crowd, she looked no different from any other woman I might see on the street. A moment later and she'd be indistinguishable among all the people receding into the distance. It would have been the same if I were her.

Like a collection of nameless particles, like the drops of water that make a river, the people filling the afternoon thoroughfare into which my wife had disappeared were flowing along together, looking all alike, all of them wearing on their back an anonymous life.

While my eyes pursued my wife's receding, gradually diminishing outline, the sense of good fortune I secretly felt, that I'd handled a difficult and painful situation without incident, that I'd been able to act coolly toward her from start to finish—all of this disappeared, and I realized that human relations—and moreover that closest of relations, between man and wife—were nothing special, were uncertain, unpredictable. Instead, pain and panic, as if a part of me had departed, gouged at my heart, choked me.

Would the day come when I'd see my wife again? Would the days come when I'd take her in my arms again, that body I knew better, was more accustomed to than my own, that body honest to its desire and submissive to my violations of it? At night she would pillow her head on my arm and talk: "I used to think it was sad sometimes that people had a body. But now I consider the body a source of comfort. I wonder if it isn't the flesh alone that's honest and pure. You can be sure of it, touch it, remember it. Even after one of us closes our eyes for the last time and the substance disappears, the memories of the survivor can bring it alive." And then she'd laugh, sheepish as if she'd said something a girl might. "It's like the words of a popular song. At least that's how it seems when I get to thinking that the business of living is like drifting clouds, like loneliness."

Random fragments of ordinary memories connected with my marriage, the birth of our boy, and his upbringing surfaced, picked at my heart.

I wanted to find my wife among the streaming throng she'd entered; I wanted to pull her back. I wanted to take her by the hair, grab her clothing, pull her, shout: "Where are you going?! Why can't you form an attachment with anyone?! Can't you get down on your knees and beg forgiveness? If the door's locked, you've got to break it down and go in! Why do you hang around your own boy's house like a beggar but you can't go in?!"

But instead of running out and calling "Ŭn-su! Ŭn-su!" I clenched my fists, I gritted my teeth, and I glared at the blurring outline of my wife as she became indistinguishable and disappeared from my sight.

Four

The church bells tolling at daybreak nudged Ŭn-su awake from a troubled dream. She had been waking around the time the bells rang, to sit up as the first light entered her room.

Gazing dispiritedly at the window as the gloom faded to a light blue, Ŭn-su would think about Sŭng-il and Se-jung still asleep as the same dawn arrived. She felt like an amputee experiencing phantom pain in her missing limbs.

"With all the churches around here, there's bound to be a holy racket," her mother would say as churches on high ground joined with churches below in a clamorous medley of bell ringing. "Makes you think this neighborhood is popular with sinners."

Her mother's joke aside, the previous day too the tearful, sighing prayers of ecstasy from the church at the top of the hill hadn't stopped until late at night. Silent prayer would change to low-pitched, whispered murmurings and then to an outcrying of deep aspirations, and finally a round of tearful, ecstatic prayer would ride past on the wind.

Every so often when life took on the smell of a wolf's pelt, it was necessary for a person to have a breath of fresh air. Ŭn-su tried to remember where she had read this.

Ŭn-su opened the window. It was so much brighter outside. Dawn's pale light was washing away before the crimson sprouting of the sun.

She dressed, folded and stacked her bedding, and emerged from her room.

Her mother opened the door of the family room and looked out. Evidently she had been listening for indications of Ŭn-su rising.

"Going out?"

It was the same question she had asked the previous day, and Ŭn-su gave the same answer.

"Just to take in the breeze. I'll be right back."

She opened the front gate.

For the entire month she'd been at her mother's here in Karhyŏn-dong Ŭn-su had felt powerless, unable to lift a finger. Her only activity, if she could call it that, was a morning stroll once around the neighborhood.

She slowly stole out into the alley and was met with the same feeling as always: the alley was too long. And so while she was still partway up the alley she would frequently look behind her, wondering how far she'd come. It was like climbing a steep, serpentine ridgeline and looking back along the way to trace the long line of one's footprints.

A short distance away, at the mouth of the sloping alley, was a procession of three, no, four figures. A *tap-tap-tap* on the cement blocks paving the alley had drawn Ŭn-su's eyes to them, and she realized they were sightless. They were walking toward her with the stride of those who know where they are going, walking sticks tapping in front of their feet. The tips of the sticks were precise feelers, guiding their feet over the pavement, leaving the spaces between the blocks untrodden.

For some strange reason she felt visible to them. She kept to the wall bordering the alley to make way, and as she passed them, she glanced at their faces. To her surprise, the eyes concealed behind the dark glasses were open and clear. Startled, she scurried off on tiptoe, as if chased.

In between her muffled footsteps the *tap-tap-tap* grew distant.

A school for the blind was affiliated with the church at the top of the hill, her mother had told her, and quite a few of the faithful were blind. Ŭn-su had never been there.

With the arrival of summer and early sunup, it wasn't unusual during her stroll to see the blind returning from the sunrise service. But the chilling sensation, the foreboding she had felt that first time she happened upon the group of blind people in their dark glasses in the dim alley from which the gloom hadn't yet cleared—these remained vivid. They had suddenly approached her and, like a hallucination, displaced her usual thoughts.

"The really important things are not visible to the eye. We must try to see those unseen things."

This was what the minister would always say at chapel hour in the mission high school Ŭn-su had attended. This minister had inspired opposition among the students because of the fanatical gleam in his eyes and his revivalist gestures.

Surely it was suffering that constituted the garden of the present life that had to be tilled if one was to achieve eternal life? Every time she met the blind people clutching their hymnbooks and Bibles during her morning walk, the thundering sermons of that minister, long since dim and forgotten, came back to life in her mind, but they also made her think it ironic that it was the blind who sifted through the unseen things. Aren't the things we can see merely an illusory truth? she asked herself.

Beyond the alley was a carrot patch. But this wasn't the season for carrots. Instead, at the sides of the empty, neglected field was a luxuriant tangle of cucumber plants crawling up a series of poles that resembled a fence. Overnight they would grow the width of a hand, turn a deeper green, and the roots would coil and stretch in some unseen place. Once past the carrot patch, she followed the sewer ditch, and where it turned, she saw the tennis courts. Covered by a large Quonset dome, they couldn't be seen from outside, but you could hear the ping of racket against ball and the duller thunk of balls hitting a backboard. The part of the structure Ŭn-su passed by on her walks contained the showers, and around this time she could always hear the rush of water. Beaded with water, the faces of freshly scrubbed young men would briefly appear at the high-set window of the shower room. Occasionally they wolf-whistled at her. She hurried past the Quonset dome and crossed the bridge that spanned the sewer ditch.

Though there was but that one ditch, a difference in the lifestyle and standard of living between the two areas it separated was evident. For there on the far side of the ditch, behind some greenhouses, was a resettlement village.

If you were to walk among the shacks of this village, you could see girls awakened from their dawn slumber squatting on the paths and peeling down their panties, and you could hear the hiss of the night's pent-up urine being released. And it wasn't just young children. Older girls and even old women unhesitatingly bared their nether regions and, drowsy eyes blinking lazily, took pleasure in the act.

Ŭn-su sometimes paused to look at the depressions where they had squatted, at the thin streams of water, and a wild thought struck her: this is the stuff of reality.

Shabby old hags paced the paths, piggybacking peevish young children who hadn't slept long enough. The younger women were in their yards boiling vegetables and getting rice ready to cook on coal-briquette stoves or kerosene burners. During the ten years she'd lived in the neighborhood across the sewer ditch before marrying, Ŭn-su had never visited this village.

Sunshine started to suffuse the haze, and the shacks began to awaken. As Ŭn-su made a circuit of the village, the many places she'd wandered came to mind. In her memory these disparate locations had blended into one, and yet now, as always, she worried that every step she took was leading her yet again to some unknown place.

It was like that whenever she left home. When she heard the roaring wind trying to squirm through the cracks in the tightly shut sliding glass door of the veranda; or when she abruptly put down the wash and with a chill feeling gazed long at the numbingly cold, indigo sky that filled the freshly cleaned window, as if a refreshing wisp of breeze had swept her heart; or when she dropped young Sŭng-il at her mother's house—she could always give the excuse that she was going to the market—Ŭn-su had never thought of anything more than half a day's outing. I'll be back in time to make dinner, she would tell herself, or, at the latest, before Se-jung gets home from work. No evil agency, nothing, could separate her from her boy, her husband, the house she had settled into like a cat. But it was an odd business. In spite of herself, the farther she walked from home, the more she felt pushed along effortlessly, airily, like an endlessly unwinding kite string, like a weight silently sinking into the fathomless deep.

Her boy, her husband, and the minute particulars of everyday life—all of this her present reality—gave way to a vision, blurry and then opaque, of a rootless, vagrant life; her present life was pushed into the background, made illusory, and in the empty space that was left, feelers of memory buried fast in the deepest recesses of her heart would stir almost imperceptibly. And so, like a baby urged to walk who takes one toddling step and then another, consumed with the physical movements, she would go about directionless on unfamiliar streets among people she had never seen before, drawn by a mixture of expec-

tation and apprehension that she would encounter something she had
forgotten.

And then, awakening at night, she would be shocked to find herself
in the squalid room of an inn. When the shock changed to shame and
fear, she would retrace her steps home all in a fluster, as if rewinding
the endlessly unwinding kite string.

She wondered if it were all a dream, a vision of another life, another
place. And wasn't there the merest possibility that she bore in her heart
a fragment of cold, lucid ice or else a faint, feeble flame like the light
of a firefly? Whatever it was that took her by the nape of the neck and
led her away at random times, that steered her outside to flutter along
helplessly before the sighing of the wind—wasn't it somehow a desperate attempt on her part to inhabit a space outside her ordinary life?

Was life something you could start over at the age of thirty-four?
"What are you going to do now? Tell me," her mother had sighed when
she had given Ŭn-su the room she had occupied before her marriage.
As soon as Ŭn-su had returned to the Karhyŏn-dong house, her mother
had notified Se-jung of her whereabouts. Ŭn-su suspected she had visited the bank once or twice as well, but there had been no word from
Se-jung.

"It's not easy for a couple with children to split up and turn their
backs on each other. I think Mr. Chi will get over it eventually. Until
then, why don't you build up some time for good behavior—and don't
you move an inch from this house. Mr. Chi's not a heartless sort. Don't
ever think he's been cruel to you. Just put yourself in his shoes. Show
me a man who likes his woman running off all the time."

Having visited Se-jung a couple of times and doubtless failed to
change his mind, her mother now spoke to her in a caustic and de-
manding tone, each word a small slash in Ŭn-su's soul.

For her part Ŭn-su realized that the trial separation declared by Se-
jung wouldn't be resolved over time. The only by-products of time were
oblivion and resignation. But it was easy for people to say that time
solved everything. Se-jung had said as much when he had handed her
the envelope with the money. As far as he was concerned, didn't that
envelope represent a kind of grace period?

The money from Se-jung was still in her handbag, untouched, even though she had vaguely considered the notion of using it to rent a room if the present situation persisted.

Every night she lay in the darkness of her room, silently twisting and turning as if going through a thresher, anxiously mumbling to herself. *What am I going to do?* Try as she would to shut her ears, out of the darkness she always heard the faint, weak crying of a child. She could clearly see the child waiting in vain, wondering if Mommy would come when he was asleep, wondering if she would be at his bedside when he woke, until finally he sprawled out exhausted across his bedding. Night after night her heart burned from the bitter tears she soundlessly wept as she wondered who the people were who had abandoned her after her birth, as she wondered if Sǔng-il too would end up the same way, living out his life with an unshakable, blazing hatred, and she would pinch her parched, cracked lips together as she made promises to herself over and over.

I'll go back first thing in the morning. If someone's blocking the gate, I'll sweep her aside. If someone takes him out of my arms, I'll put him on my back and we'll fly hundreds, thousands of miles away. I'll go see Se-jung at the bank. I'll return the money, and we'll have ourselves an understanding—period. "You think you can settle things this easily? I don't need the money. I'm coming back to our home. How long did you want this to go on? You said you didn't want to get hurt anymore. I want you to look carefully at what you're saying. I think maybe the reason you gave me is not the whole story. I've heard it said that after a couple live together for a few years they begin to fit each other like well-worn clothing. But every once in a while, when the clothing gets droopy and worn-out, people like to try on new clothes. Harmony and agreement are supposed to be the greatest virtues in marriage, the things that make us most happy, but sometimes when life gets too boring people just want to be by themselves and they're forced to conceal this craving. I'm not blaming you—I'm not. It's my fault, and I pray you'll forgive me. What you don't realize is that I've experienced something no one should have to experience, something so horrible I can't even remember it. But I'm going to make sure I don't remember it—I'll make sure I forget everything. And then that ugly, horrible incident won't be a part of me any longer."

After a few scant spoonfuls of breakfast Ŭn-su busied herself preparing to go out.

"Going somewhere?" her mother asked as she watched with a mixture of worry and reproach while Ŭn-su applied makeup.

"I'm going to the bank. I have to see Sŭng-il's father."

Ŭn-su got off the bus at City Hall, checked the digital display atop the building, and reset her watch at ten o'clock before starting down the underground walkway that led toward the Great South Gate. There was no need to rush since she hadn't made an appointment with Se-jung, and walking would give her time to think things out. In any case, he would be at the bank all day. Though she was determined to see Se-jung, in reality she hadn't planned what to say or what manner of solution she might offer when she met up with him. Arriving in front of the bank, she wondered briefly whether to go downstairs to the tearoom where they had met the previous time, but instead she proceeded inside. She was afraid of his reaction if she were to telephone him. Actually, she had called home several times when Se-jung ought to have been there. But when she heard the faint purring of the all-too-familiar telephone that sat on the table beside the television in the room where they had spent so much time, she felt as if she were calling a lover whose feelings toward her had changed. Overcome with fear and tension, she would simply hang up—sometimes after hearing Se-jung answer.

It was midmorning, and the bank wasn't that busy. Se-jung had been transferred to this branch two years before. In that time Ŭn-su had never visited him here and had no idea where to find him. She took a seat in the waiting area and pretended to read a magazine as she looked around. She realized that her fear and timidity probably made her look all the more shabby and unseemly, but she couldn't keep from shrinking back and cowering. She had to scan the bank several times before she was able to spot Se-jung at his desk. He blended in well with all the other men in their short-sleeve shirts and neatly knotted ties. A teller had just brought him a cup of coffee from a vending machine and was setting it down in front of him. Remaining bent over his work, he thanked the young woman.

Se-jung at work looked different to her—but not because of their lack of contact all this time. "Chi Se-jung, Associate"—well matched with the mother-of-pearl nameplate on his desk was this sincere and competent worker, both friendly and businesslike. His face was a bit pale, but perhaps this was not so much the manifestation of a worried mind or an illness as it was the common fate of those who worked indoors and rarely saw the sun. There was nothing about him to suggest he had driven his wife from their home, no apparent difference between him and those working men whose wives bestowed meticulous attention upon them, whose children waved affectionate goodbyes. Though he answered the telephone briskly and didn't speak at length, he exhibited a delightful laugh or tossed off a joke, then bent over his work again, all the time never noticing his shabby, hunched-over wife. After observing him for an hour, Ŭn-su found herself choked with tears of profound betrayal—though this feeling was not directed at anyone in particular—and she unobtrusively rose.

"How are things with you? Me, same as always. Kind of busy these days."

She could hear Se-jung on the telephone as she left. She caught a taxi in front of the bank, asked the driver to take her in the direction of their house, buried herself in the seatback. She felt like a gambler who had suddenly lost a closely guarded card. In any case, today she would somehow have to arrive at a decision.

"Can't keep drifting along like this," Ŭn-su mumbled as the wind blew in through the open window and swept her scattered hair across her forehead.

As the taxi left the downtown area, Ŭn-su realized Sŭng-il was probably at kindergarten, and she asked the taxi driver to go there instead.

Recess was just ending as Ŭn-su stepped through the iron arch of the gate of Hyewŏn Church, the bell jingling and the children thronging inside the kindergarten. In no time the playground, which had resembled a flower garden because of the children's yellow jumper gowns, was practically empty. Only two children remained, one scooping sand in the sandbox, head bowed, and the other at the top of the slide trying to work up the courage to come down. A teacher appeared and lifted the boy down from the slide, then helped up the boy in the sandbox and dusted him off. One of the boys turned briefly toward Ŭn-su, and immediately her eyes blurred over. It was Sŭng-il.

She frantically reached out toward him, silently called out his name. But Sŭng-il didn't see her before he was led inside by the teacher. The door closed behind them, and presently Ŭn-su heard the screech of the children singing more or less in unison, accompanied by a piano.

Ŭn-su drew close to the boy's classroom and peered through the window. The children, still singing, were milling about getting resettled in their places. There must have been fifty or sixty of them, and they filled the plank-floored room. Some of the children were standing in the corner, sucking on a finger, pouting. Eyes wide, Ŭn-su desperately scoured the room for her son but couldn't locate him among the mass of bodies.

"Are you looking for someone?"

A young woman had stuck her head out the door of the long, straight building.

Ŭn-su stepped back from the window.

"N—no. My son's inside."

With a flustered smile, she sat down on a bench. Tall poplars grew along the church wall, but not a speck of their shade reached the playground, where the sunlight poured down. With each breath of wind the branches of the poplars whispered and swayed, the glossy, verdant leaves fluttering and glistening.

"The wind's calling."

"Why does the wind call?"

"It's all the lonely people calling and reaching out to each other."

As Ŭn-su recalled these words from her last day with Sŭng-il, she gazed up with tear-filled eyes at the crowns of the poplars, where the wind briefly touched down before continuing on its journey.

The final bell rang, and the children surged outside to board two waiting buses. As if she were taking a head count, Ŭn-su searched the line of children one by one until she discovered Sŭng-il near the end. She approached and without a word took the boy's hand.

Sŭng-il took a couple of steps before looking up unawares. His eyes immediately grew large. He drew back, as if from a stranger, and his mouth turned down, as if he was about to burst into tears.

As Ŭn-su's eyes met her son's she felt a great lump in her throat.

"Sŭng-il," she called, almost whispering. "It's Mommy—Mommy's here."

The boy released his hand from Ŭn-su's and clutched her skirt so tightly that Ŭn-su thought for a moment it might rip. The boy didn't call out to her, merely fixed her with unblinking eyes. *He can't believe it's me.*

The children aboard the buses stuck their heads out the windows and waved toward the teachers, singing, "Goodbye teachers, goodbye friends, tomorrow we meet again!"

Uneasy and hesitant, Sŭng-il looked in turn at the buses, his mom, and the teachers.

The driver of the lead bus stuck his head out the window. "Is that everybody?" he asked the waving teachers. He started the engine.

Apart from the three teachers there remained only Ŭn-su and Sŭng-il. One of the teachers approached Ŭn-su.

"Have you come for Sŭng-il?" she asked respectfully. "Are you his mother?"

The teacher's smile radiated warmth and kindness, but beneath it Ŭn-su sensed a tension, a note of precaution and inquiry. If you accepted the responsibility of caring for young children, you needed to be able to notice strangers. It was to be expected that the teacher didn't remember Ŭn-su, who had appeared at the school only for the entrance ceremony and the first month's parent-teacher meeting.

"Yes, I am. I was on my way somewhere and happened to be in the vicinity. . . ."

"I see."

The teacher nodded toward the driver and closed the door to the bus.

"Goodbye teacher!" the children shouted all together as the buses set into motion.

"Sŭng-il's a wonderful boy," the teacher said, patting him on the head. "He's in the youngest group, but you wouldn't believe how grown up he acts. When we did home visits last month, his grandmother was the only one we saw. She said you'd gone down to the countryside for a few days."

"Uh, yes, that's right," Ŭn-su said and managed to produce a vague smile.

Head bowed, maintaining his hold on her skirt, Sŭng-il dragged his sneaker back and forth across his shadow.

"Well, then, goodbye." The teacher nodded, then returned to the kindergarten.

Ŭn-su led Sŭng-il off by the hand.

"Would you like to ride on my back?"

Sŭng-il looked back at the kindergarten and shook his head.

"It's all right; Mommy just wants to give you a piggyback ride. Nobody's going to laugh at you."

Every few steps Ŭn-su offered Sŭng-il her back—she didn't want him to see the tears streaming unchecked from her eyes.

Finally, when they were far enough from the kindergarten that only the spire of Hyewŏn Church poked up above the roofs of the neighborhood houses, Sŭng-il climbed onto Ŭn-su. He clung fast to her neck and buried his face in her back.

"Mommy, where did you go?"

For the first time his voice was full of displeasure.

"Mommy, are you back for real? Grandmother said you went far away, much farrer than Karhyŏn-dong Grandmother's house."

As the bright voice rang in her ears and the breath fell warm on her neck, smelling like sour milk, Ŭn-su stumbled and barely avoided falling. Not that the boy's weight was difficult to manage; rather he kept calling out "Mommy!" and turning Ŭn-su's head around so he could look at her.

"You didn't cry when Mommy was gone? And you didn't catch a cold?"

"No. In the morning I lift weights with Daddy. I'm real strong now."

"Weights?"

"Daddy bought some weights. His are real big and heavy. Mine are little ones. And we got a puppy. A cute little puppy. His name is Furry. He doesn't have his own house. He sleeps in a box on the veranda. But he cries all night. That's 'cause he's a baby. Grandma really yells at him. I sneak out and get him and put him under my quilt and he doesn't cry. Mommy, he cries 'cause he wants to be in my bed with me—Grandma doesn't know that."

Arriving at a main street, Ŭn-su let her feet continue to lead her. She wondered where to go. As a matter of course she should take Sŭng-il home. But the thought of facing her mother-in-law scared her. The last time she had gone home, she had met, protruding from the open gate, the older woman's icy countenance. Her mother-in-law made no attempt to conceal her pride, her sense of superiority, at having devoted her life to managing her home and raising her children, and she had spoken coolly to Ŭn-su, had disdainfully taken stock of her appearance. "Look at you—a flea has more sense of shame than that. I have to talk with the boy's dad before I can let you in. Don't be upset—you brought this on yourself." But what fazed Ŭn-su more than anything else now was the prospect of taking Sŭng-il home and having to give him up again.

It was a hot day, and Ŭn-su's back beneath the boy grew clammy. He had to get down, she told him. He did, and now her back felt empty, cool.

Sŭng-il looked up at Ŭn-su, noticing they weren't following the route of the church bus.

"Mommy, where are we going?"

"Aren't you hungry? How about something yummy?"

Sŭng-il shook his head.

"I had a snack at kindergarten."

"You did? Well, why don't we just go somewhere and have some fun together?"

"Mommy, you're not going away somewhere this time—promise?"

The boy clutched her hand and drew close to her.

"Mommy's going to be right here."

Ŭn-su gave him a strong hug. The boy smiled, seemingly reassured, and buried his face in the folds of her skirt.

Ŭn-su hailed a taxi. She needed to go to a bank. Then she would think about what to do next. After cashing one of the four checks from Se-jung, she took Sŭng-il to a Chinese restaurant nearby. She had to press him to say what he wanted to eat, and finally he responded— noodles in black-bean sauce.

"That's all? Don't you want anything else?"

Not knowing the reason for his mother's anxious insistence on feeding him, Sŭng-il petulantly shook his head at the repeated question. Ŭn-su wiped the boy's mouth, studying him as he ate.

"Did you call Grandma? She's waiting. She waits for me every day at the bus stop."

"It's all right. You're with Mommy; Grandma doesn't have to worry."

Sŭng-il blinked in the sunlight streaming through the window. The down on his cheeks had taken on a golden radiance. Ŭn-su was about to draw the curtain but paused to observe the boy. The dusty, luster-less hair covering his ears and forehead—when had it last been sham pooed? The dim, gaping eyes. The small knees, scabbed all over, show-ing below his shorts. Every night her heart had burned with despair as she yearned to hold him in her arms and put him to sleep, to examine his features for as long as she wanted. Could any desire be more ardent than this? Her despair had built to desperation, and now her only wish was to shield the boy from the eyes of others and never to release him unconditionally from her breast. Hadn't she prayed, believed, when she gave birth to Sŭng-il, that this tiny living thing would be her per-fect anchor? But now, as the small boy across from her looped noodles about his chopsticks, oblivious to her thoughts, Ŭn-su's face contorted in pain. He represented all the things she had lost, all the things she couldn't do, and out of sight beneath the table she wrung her hands.

And now she was all the more anxious as she imagined her mother-in-law fidgeting and pacing, wondering about Sŭng-il, all the more anxious as she felt the bulk of the thousand-_wŏn_ notes in her purse.

As soon as the boy had finished, Ŭn-su left with him for Seoul Station.

"Sŭng-il, would you like to go for a train ride with Mommy? You've never been on a train, have you?"

The boy jumped up and down in delight. He had never seen a train except in a children's book.

The waiting room was crowded with passengers departing and arriving seemingly at random. Ŭn-su scanned the timetable, considered the stops on each line and the departure times from Seoul, calculated distances and possible return times, and finally her eyes came to rest on a familiar place name—M City, the port where she had grown up. She hadn't seen it once in the twenty-plus years since she'd moved away. That she had never turned her steps toward that city among all the places she'd wandered, a place only one and a half hours distant by train—was there a fear at work here, a fear buried deep in her consciousness? Or had she been thwarted by the prospect of the bittersweet sorrow that comes with returning to a place from one's past?

Thirty minutes later, tickets punched, they boarded a coach. In no time the train was under way.

"Mommy, the train's going backwards!" Sŭng-il exclaimed as he stood on their seat, which faced the rear of the compartment.

As she removed the boy's shoes, Ŭn-su felt she was leaving for the distant past, that she was part of a film being shown in reverse.

In Insu-dong, at the foot of the other side of the hill from the docks, was a street lined with rundown Japanese-style frame houses. To this day, the street existed in Ŭn-su's mind as an abstract noun signifying her childhood.

A cutting wind, cold and harsh, always blew in from the far end of the harbor. Every morning on their way to school the children from the neighborhood near the docks passed the park with its stone steps, hundreds of them, climbing toward the heavens. If you stopped to rest along the way and looked back, the bombed-out ruins of the urban district, awakening like a lazy harlot from the deep sleep of dawn, and the foreign vessels with their multicolored flags moored along the piers would enter your vision.

At night the docks were always festive, flourishing with foreigners and the resplendent mass of lights from the ships.

On rainy days the children would avoid the shortcut through the park and go to school through the thronged market area. For when the wind hit the high-tension wires running through the towers standing in the park, it produced an eerie cry that chilled them, clutching at any loose strand of hair and raising goose bumps. It was a ghost crying, the children said.

But to Ŭn-su all of this had become a dim, secluded phase of her existence.

As she walked the unfamiliar streets with Sŭng-il, no trace of the past came to mind.

As in most of the other cities outlying Seoul, the children finished their classes and walked home from school, just like children from her past, on streets that were almost frightening in their bleak expanse.

They caught a taxi and sped toward Insu-dong. Ŭn-su had no idea which direction they were going. Deposited outside the taxi, she examined the surroundings. The neighborhood of small, shabby, two-story Japanese-style houses planted so firmly in her memory was no-where to be seen. They had crossed the hill rising up from the docks, but here there was only a broad, paved street with a drugstore, billiard hall, supermarket, and precinct station. Feeling like a blind woman with Sŭng-il her guide, Ŭn-su lapsed into a vague sensation of un-reality as she felt her way around street corners she didn't recognize, Sŭng-il firmly in hand, seeking the house of her memories. It was as if she were walking hand in hand with herself when she was a little girl.

A vertical sign was painted white with black letters: "Doctor Ch'oe—Dental Clinic." The ground floor of the small, two-story wooden house had been used by her father for his clinic; the family liv-ing quarters occupied the second floor. As she lay in her tatami room upstairs doing her homework, young Ŭn-su might hear the rattle of instruments and her father clearing his throat. She had always felt un-easy around her taciturn father.

"Mommy, where are we going?" Sŭng-il kept asking, looking up at

Ŭn-su. He was tired and bored, this area they were passing through offering nothing for a young boy to marvel at.

"This is where Mommy lived when she was little like you."

"Mommy, were you really five years old?"

Indeed, was she five that time she perched halfway down the steep flight of stairs from the upper floor, afraid, so afraid, shouting, weeping, unable to go down? According to her mother, it had happened not long after Ŭn-su moved in with them.

The steps leading up through the park were still there but seemed laughably small now. Taking those steps as a point of reference, she guessed that the laundry she saw now occupied the space where the dental clinic used to be.

Inside the laundry a youth in an undershirt was ironing clothes. Steam rose from the iron. Leather jackets reeking of benzene hung outside. Ŭn-su peered in through the open door, and the next instant the strong odor of the cleaning fluid had her visualizing the dental clinic, always filled with the smell of cresol. But then she shook her head. The rundown building that housed the clinic was no longer of this earth. This was as clear as the fact that she was no longer the little girl of that time. Was there anything to be gained by groping for a past that had vanished, by searching for a tiny trace of she knew not what?

Ŭn-su walked slowly away from the laundry. She set foot on the stone steps she had gone up and down all those mornings and afternoons in the past and climbed up through the park. It was the city's only park and also its highest point.

It was early summer, and the sunshine remained hot long into the afternoon. The crest of the park was an open area covered with sand and scattered with benches. Like so many porcelain chips, the white sand glinted and danced in the sun's strong rays.

As she watched the bleached sand, disheartened, Ŭn-su was swept with a feeling, odd in its suddenness, that she had come to a place she knew, that everything about her was not after all unfamiliar. Here, it seemed, was the place she always went in her dreams, yet the place she could never remember upon awakening, a place that was faintly familiar.

How she wished she could explain this mood into which she sank at odd times when she was beneath the blazing sun, this chilling sensation, this fear. What was this thing that would crack the hard shell of oblivion and rise faintly to the surface, like the prow of a ship that has sunk to the bottom of the sea and slowly rusted away, only to be revealed long after by the ministrations of deep-sea divers?

But when she desperately reached out, it would slip, formless, between her fingers and vanish. She could advance no further in her memory than the sunny yard and the pair of black rubber shoes. Someone must be there, in the front of the yard. *But where am I?*

"Mommy—look how big the ocean is! It doesn't end! There's a big, fat land floating on it, Mommy!"

Sŭng-il clutched her arm and pointed toward the sea, clearly visible below. It was the first time he had seen the ocean, the first time he had seen an island.

"The world's made up of water and land. If you go on a boat far, far away, you'll reach another land."

The sunshine was brighter now, but the sea, turbid and indigo, was impassive.

The day she had learned from her cousin that she wasn't her mother's natural daughter, Ŭn-su had sat on the breakwater near the docks, watching the ships lying at anchor and thinking she ought to run away. Anyplace would be good, as long as it wasn't here. She didn't realize at that stage of her life that since the world was round, if she kept traveling, she would eventually end up at the very place she had left.

That stage of her life was like a mirage. Only a few vague traces of it remained in her memory.

As Sŭng-il sat gazing at the sea, he sucked through a straw on a bottle of citrus soda. Then with vacant, sleepy eyes he leaned against Ŭn-su.

Insects appeared from the grass, chirping insistently to hasten the onset of dusk.

Night fell and Ŭn-su remained with Sŭng-il in M City, even while telling herself they should return to Seoul. The faces of Se-jung and her mother-in-law waiting anxiously for Sŭng-il flashed through her mind, but she shook her head determinedly, telling herself she was only a mother taking her son somewhere—it wasn't as if she was kidnapping him. Her mother-in-law would have telephoned the kindergarten when Sŭng-il failed to appear, and the amiable teacher would surely have reported that he'd left with his mother.

It was not that Ŭn-su had expected all along to spend several days scouring the area and to find at least one person she knew. She realized her roaming about was as fruitless as grasping at the swirling wind or searching for a needle at the bottom of the sea, but she couldn't simply leave. For a shadowy presentiment had begun to spread like haze through her mind.

This presentiment, as she thought of it, was surely the faint, stealthy feeling of familiarity she had experienced in this street that had changed into something completely unfamiliar, a street in which she couldn't detect the faintest connection with the images of this city left in her memory. It was like a thin, faint shadow that might disappear if she let down her guard for the space of a breath. But when it came to presentiments, conjectures, that sort of thing, weren't they most of the time a dressed-up feeling of betrayal manufactured by her own illusions?

With nightfall the boy whined to go back home. For in addition to the dark, unfamiliar streets he had felt his mother's vague unease as she spent this reunion of theirs walking, wandering, carrying him piggyback through an area that lacked a zoo or any other entertainment for children.

Ŭn-su for her part wanted to detain passersby and ask them questions. She wanted to stop these people who somehow seemed familiar but whom, it was clear, she had never seen before; she wanted to remove the masks of composure they wore and give voice to her real feelings: "Do you remember the children who lived near the docks? Do you remember a little girl? Do you remember a day of blazing sunshine in summer, or maybe fall? About thirty years ago—they tell me it was during the civil war. Are you familiar, by any chance, with a yard surrounded by a fence painted with coal tar? Something happened in that yard. Could you tell me where that house is? Could you tell me what it is that keeps pushing me, that keeps grabbing me by the neck and shaking me? I'm frightened by this yearning I have inside me that blows me about like the wind and then sets me adrift. I've paid a great price—I've lost everything except my shell. All I see ahead of me is a dark, solitary, hopeless future—a confinement. All I see is a sour, ugly old woman spiteful and anxious about the things she's lost, the things she can't recover. What could it possibly be, this thing that prevents me from staying put, that tears me away? Eyes I can't see are examining me—whose eyes are they? A soul I can't see has set me drifting—whose soul is it? The wind constantly flies through my hair, murmurs at my ear, sweeps away the vestiges of my life, makes them into nothingness. And now I'm like a phantom—I don't even have a shadow. I look back and see no trace of myself. All I do is wander, rootless, imprisoned in the wind's vortex. The eyes of the wind are hidden fast, and I want to know where."

Ŭn-su returned to Seoul late the following afternoon, after spending the night in M City at an inn near the docks. As she made her way through the congested plaza of Seoul Station, she felt as if she hadn't left there the previous day. She briefly wavered in her decision to take Sŭng-il home, exhausted as he was by the overnight outing. But before long her indecision had vanished, and she was in a taxi headed for Karhyŏn-dong.

The boy had awakened several times the previous night in their unfamiliar room, but upon seeing his mother watching him, he had fallen asleep again, relieved. Her purpose in taking him home with her was to get him a nice haircut and buy him a new outfit after giving him a bath to get rid of the dust and sweat.

Sŭng-il looked out the taxi window into the thickening dusk and cocked his head dubiously.

"Mommy, isn't this the way to Karhyŏn-dong Grandma's house?"

Amazingly enough, the boy remembered the way, though he visited his grandmother only once a month at best.

"Yes, it is—Grandmother wants to see Sŭng-il, so we should say hello, shouldn't we?"

Hastening to forestall in this way the boy's next question—why weren't they going home?—Ŭn-su at the same time feared that Sŭng-il would instinctively sense the abnormal circumstances reflected in her Karhyǒn-dong room, furnished only with a worn-out clothes cabinet and a few chests of sundries piled atop one another. To anyone's eyes the starkness of the empty room was not welcoming; it was a room unwarmed by a shared life. How would her insecure situation be reflected in her young child's eyes? How would he perceive it?

The taxi stopped in front of the Karhyǒn-dong house, and Ŭn-su's mother flew outside in a fluster, dishcloth in hand.

"Crazy thing! Why can't you tell someone when you're going somewhere?! Do you realize the entire family is up in arms?! Hurry up and get inside—Mr. Chi's here."

In spite of herself Ŭn-su pulled up short in front of the gate. Se-jung was here?

Sŭng-il was holding onto Ŭn-su's skirt and staring at his grandmother. The older woman whisked him into her arms and led them inside, blaring, "Look—she's back! What did I tell you? Didn't I say she'd be back soon with the boy?"

Her mother's abruptly loud voice and loquaciousness all too clearly told Ŭn-su how resentful and anxious she must have felt waiting for them, how embarrassed she must feel in Se-jung's presence.

Se-jung, sitting on the plank floor of the veranda, which was unlit in spite of the dark, got to his feet. Ŭn-su couldn't make out his expression, but the moment she saw his outline, she felt her stomach clench.

"Are you still out here?" said her mother. "Didn't I say you could go in and lie down—you must be exhausted. And the least we can do is turn on the light. . . ." And she hastened to do so before leaving for the kitchen, happy to have found something to distract her from the tension between the couple.

Se-jung shot Ŭn-su a cold look that was at once contemptuous and scornful.

"What the hell do you think you're doing running off with the boy? And you have the gall to show up like this?"

Ŭn-su squared her shoulders and looked straight at Se-jung. "Running off? How can you talk like that?" She realized as she said this that not only was she trying to hold her ground and put Se-jung on the defensive—after all, it wasn't as if Sŭng-il belonged to him alone—she was also compensating for her disappointment in herself, the scorn she had heaped on herself for being so shabby and timid ever since she had seen Se-jung at the bank the previous morning.

"Are you trying to play tug-of-war with the boy or what? It's disgusting, low-class."

"Sŭng-il isn't yours, and he isn't mine—he's himself, and that's all there is to it."

Ŭn-su released the hand of the boy, still holding fast to the hem of her skirt as he watched with a fearful expression these signs of alarm coming from his parents. Leaving him on the veranda, she went not into her own room but into her mother's room. She didn't want her boy or her husband to see the stark, uninviting room she'd been living in, with its metal clothes cabinet and the stacked chests—the sight of which would have revealed the life she had been living in Karhyŏn-dong along with her inner desolation.

She heard her mother bustling about in the kitchen preparing dinner, smelled the pungent odor of the bubbling stew. Amid her preparations her mother would look out to the veranda and speak to Se-jung: "What are you doing just standing there like that? The house isn't going to fall down on you. Sŭng-il, now you go inside with your dad. It's been so long since all of you were here, the house is actually starting to feel lived-in. Yes, indeed, there's something to those old sayings. People have a dozen crises in the course of a lifetime—right? A lot of rough times, a lot of ups and downs. Why not make a break with the past—it's water over the dam."

Knowing for a certainty that Se-jung must have been frantic as he rushed to Karhyŏn-dong to look for Sŭng-il and that a venomous hatred lay coiled in his heart, Ŭn-su's mother was nevertheless acting distracted and boisterous, talking like a chatterbox, as if she were welcoming a pair of newlyweds. She had never behaved like this before. Se-jung, standing on the veranda, remained tight-lipped.

Ŭn-su's mother carried the dinner table out to the veranda, calling to Ŭn-su, "Could you come help me with the table?" But by then Se-jung had stepped down into the yard.

Ŭn-su's mother turned pale.

"Now hold your horses; I just brought out dinner. I'll call your mother, so you can eat here and take your time getting home."

Though she couldn't bring herself to take Se-jung by the sleeve, she tried to detain him by repeating these words over and over.

"We're leaving," Se-jung replied. "Sŭng-il, get your shoes on."

Sŭng-il inched his way down from the veranda to the yard, looked back tearfully at Ŭn-su as she rose to her feet from the threshold of her mother's room. Intimidated by his father's frigid attitude, the boy moved like a windup doll.

"What a heartless man. You frighten me. Can't you help an old woman save face?"

Oblivious to the older woman's complaints, Se-jung bent down and worked at the flattened heels of Sŭng-il's sneakers, which the boy had been wearing as if they were sandals.

Ŭn-su stood stock still, riveted by the scene unfolding before her. Her eyes burned, but she glared with all her strength, feeling that all of this would disappear like a mirage if she but blinked, would be reduced to ashes at the slightest impact.

Se-jung's drooping outline and the boy's small form slipped out the front gate.

A moment later there was a faint, choking cry—"Mommy!"—and then stifled sobs receding into the distance.

Ŭn-su's mother remained perched on the edge of the veranda staring dully at the empty space framed by the open gate, which was even darker than the darkness about it.

"The soup's getting cold," she muttered.

The dinner table with its four sets of spoons and chopsticks loomed in the middle of the veranda. The steam from the meal had long since dissipated, and the hastily prepared food had grown cold and seemed to have changed color, looked almost unsanitary. A moth flitted about the fluorescent ceiling light, but neither daughter nor mother were of any mind to close the front gate or shoo the moth away.

Ŭn-su picked up the bowls of soup.

"I'll warm it."

"Bring the liquor kettle too—it's in the kitchen," her mother said without looking at her.

The small kettle was full of a clear beverage tinted the color of the inside of a pumpkin. Undoubtedly her mother had brought this out for Se-jung, visiting for the first time in a long while.

Though Ŭn-su presumed her mother had virtually no occasion to receive visitors or special guests, she was aware of her mother's habit of preparing a fruit liquor every year and keeping it buried in a crock in the corner of the back yard. Her mother had always been very proud of the praise drawn from her son-in-law by the aroma and taste of this clear, filtered beverage, to which he was treated during his incidental visits.

"Mother, please eat."

Ŭn-su sat down at the head of the table, and her mother poured her a drink in a small porcelain cup.

"I made this last year, so it ought to have some taste by now."

Her mother then filled her own cup and gulped down the contents—just as she had done the first time Se-jung had visited. Had it already been six years? And now those six years had stolen past their backs, leaving the two of them here in the same place, unchanged except for having aged considerably more than six years.

"You drink too. There are times when we need to drink, just like insomniacs need sleeping pills. Did you latch the gate? No need to leave it open—we're not expecting anyone else."

The aromatic liquor burned bitter on Ŭn-su's dry lips. The drink produced a warm, soothing glow that eased the exhaustion she felt in her body and soul.

After several drinks in quick succession her mother grew red around the eyes. Neither of them had touched her spoon and chopsticks.

"Why are you drinking like that? I wish you'd eat some dinner instead."

"Don't worry. My crazy, wandering daughter, sitting across from me, telling me to eat! So where did you go? And what are your plans now?"

Her mother forced a bitter smile that made Ŭn-su sit up and take notice.

"I'm not sure yet. But I don't think I can live this way anymore. The more important thing is, there's something I need to know. And I want you to tell me. I went to M City. Of course it's been more than twenty years, and the place has changed incredibly—nothing I could remember was there. But there *was* something. It was like a faint shadow following at my heels. I want to know what it is. And who I am. Where did I come from? I can look all I want, but without some help it's no use."

"Is that the reason? I didn't know you'd been tortured so much. Well, you must have done something in your previous life to deserve this."

Her mother put down her drink and with a distant look in her bloodshot eyes she gazed at Ŭn-su.

Two little girls with short hair that's cut straight across the back sit in the yard, heads touching, peering intently at the ground. They're trying to catch ants. If you catch a carpenter ant and lick the hole in its underside you taste something that's sweet and also a bit sour. The girls' stomachs are constantly growling, for they've had to make do with a handful of roasted beans for lunch.

"In wartime we have to get along on this," their mommy explains to them time and again as she takes out one of the basins she has hidden beneath the kitchen floor and produces a handful of wheat flour or rice with which to boil some wheat-dumpling soup or cook some watery rice gruel. The girls listen with ravenous expressions.

It's an afternoon in early autumn, and the sun beats down white-hot. The neighborhood is deathly still. No sign of those who locked their gates and fled the war. Sometimes the girls go next door and peer through the gate nailed shut with two crisscrossing planks. Growing in the yard are weeds as tall as they are, and the tile roof is lush with green grass. It looks so desolate and mysterious—does a ghost live there?

Every night from the downtown area the thump of bullets buffets the sky. Their mommy has the front gate barred, and she keeps the children hidden inside day and night. Father hides in the loft, coming down to join the family only at night. Mommy often whispers to Father. "The robbers are everywhere. They break down the gates of the people who have left and take food, clothing, anything they can get money for. People scare me. They're getting more and more like animals."

But for the girls, all that matters is their empty stomachs. Their playmates are gone, everyone is gone, but they don't lack for things to do. Because for a long time, ever since they were born, they've played with each other, and only with each other, and they're used to this. For the two girls are twins. Identical twins. No one but their parents can distinguish them. But not always. "How can you two look so identical? You're the mirror image of each other. If you want to see your face, just look at your sister."

Mommy always dresses them in clothes of different colors. She wants two equally fine husbands for them—she'll marry them off on the same day, at the same time. One girl removes the black rubber shoes they both wear and puts the ants they've caught inside. Suddenly there are footsteps, many footsteps, outside the wall. The gate rattles and bangs. Its planks give way easily, and men lunge into the yard.

Startled by these intruders during the midday stillness, the girl who's removed her shoes scampers onto the veranda calling for Mommy. Instinct and fear drive the other girl into the outhouse in the corner of the yard. She locks the door. Between the loosely fitted planks of the outhouse the L-shaped living quarters are clearly visible.

The men bound onto the veranda, shoes and all. Each is armed with a pickaxe, a crowbar, or some such thing. There, at one of the doors— is that Mommy's face? A scream. I should go to Mommy, the little girl thinks. But an even stronger fear has seized the hand that holds the outhouse latch and won't let go. The men come out through the door and head for the kitchen. Mommy crawls out behind them, blood gushing from her head, and grabs one of the men by the pant leg. He nonchalantly chops at her with the pickaxe.

A short time later the men disappear, toting a sack of rice and a fat bundle of something or other. It all seems like a lie—did it really happen? The little girl emerges from the outhouse. All is still. The dancing, white-hot sun filling the yard, the pair of black rubber shoes looming in the deathly still noonday—there is nothing else. Where is everybody? Come on out! Standing in the yard, the little girl softly calls her sister's name.

The woman has just finished what you might call brunch. She hears a faint sobbing outside her gate. Are those sobs real—whoever it is must be exhausted—or is she hearing things? But then at intervals it sounds like someone's knocking on the gate. When the war broke out, her husband was drafted as a medical officer, and the woman keeps waiting for him, as if he will suddenly materialize out of the blue. Instead of fleeing with all the other refugees, she keeps the house all by herself.

The woman wavers, then looks out between the planks nailed across the second-story window.

A little girl squats at the gate, weeping. Even the baby ants dare not show themselves on the street. With street fighting erupting without warning several times a day, those people left behind hide inside, concealing their very existence. Going outside is unthinkable.

The woman sweeps up the girl, takes her inside, and bolts the gate. Whose girl is she, and what could have brought her weeping to the woman's gate? All she will say, speaking between her sobs, is that she's hungry. The woman feeds her, washes the dusty, tear-streaked face, combs her hair, and finally she realizes the face is not unfamiliar. A friend of her husband has twin daughters, and this is one of them. The woman scolds herself for her faulty memory, but then again it's not surprising.

For it's been about a year since she last saw the girl, and during that time they've grown, changed almost by the day. In 1947, two years after the nation was liberated from Japan, a classmate friend of her husband showed up at her door, along with his wife. The young couple had migrated south from the northern part of the country, leaving their parents behind. The wife, a woman with large eyes and a beautiful voice, has graduated from a training program for nursery school teachers. At the time her stomach was bulging. After a month's stay at the woman's house they took a rented house in the outskirts of the city.

Not long after, the wife came to term and gave birth to twins. Meanwhile, the husband had found a job as a middle school teacher. Though the husband had said he was a friend of the woman's husband, it seemed to the woman that the relationship between the two men was not that close, for the couple's visits grew sporadic. The wife would come calling with the twins a couple of times a month, but then the visits abruptly stopped altogether. Was that just the way they were? the woman wondered. Then again, it seemed they were busy establishing a foothold in this new environment. The woman tried to erase her misgivings. And then the war broke out.

"Where's your mommy? And what about Daddy? Did something happen at home?" The questions are urgent, but the response to each is the same—a blank look, a shake of the head. She seems to remember nothing. The last time she was here, her mother guided her. And now, a year later, this five-year-old-girl has found her way here through bombed-out streets where no one would venture forth, walking from one end of the city to the other. How is it possible?

The woman applies ointment to the knees with their layers of clotted blood—the falls she must have taken!—and to the tiny, blistered feet. "Now don't you worry. Tomorrow I'll go home with you." But not until she receives word that the street fighting has stopped and that the enemy has completed a total withdrawal does she step outside.

Back at her home, all the girl does is stare vacantly at a pair of dusty black rubber shoes lying in the sunny yard. She absolutely refuses to go inside the gate.

Leaving the girl, the woman ventures inside. At the door to the kitchen is sprawled a woman; upside down on the stairs to the loft lies a man; lying prone on the veranda is a girl—the three bodies already decomposed beyond recognition.

"Who could have done such a horrible thing? What could possibly have happened to the family, and little you somehow surviving and finding your way all that distance to our house—did somebody bring you? I never found the answers. You didn't remember a thing, and afterwards I never explained to you what I saw. I could only guess someone had broken in to steal food. It wasn't all that unusual, they tell me. It was wartime, and many of the people who stayed behind starved to death. The ones who managed to stay alive all turned yellow and puffy. I took you in, and while I was raising you I was thankful you'd forgotten everything about your family—your parents, the twin sister who was your constant companion, as well as your life in that house. And it wasn't just because I was greedy to make you a child all my own. You see, I wondered if you could ever hope to live out your life in peace after that awful experience."

Ŭn-su's mother slumped back against the wall and closed her eyes.

The night was far along. The intermittent footsteps passing by outside had long since ceased. Swarms of insects flitted about the fluorescent light, fleeing the deepening darkness and the chill in favor of brightness. With nightfall the wind had gradually come up, and now it whispered through the branches of the several trees in the yard.

"Is somebody out there? We didn't latch the gate, did we?"

Her mother was motionless, eyes closed.

Ŭn-su clearly remembered the gate being locked, but she donned sandals and stepped down to the yard. Someone was there, she sensed. But the bolt had indeed been drawn. She gently released it and looked out into the alley buried in gloom.

Round the corner of this pitch-black alley, and there! Bright daylight, blazing sunshine, and a little girl walking this way from the far end of a familiar street. From what far place has she come? Where did she leave her shoes? On she plods, one bare, sunburned foot in front of the other.

A street broken up, unrecognizable, an empty, dead, bombed-out street devoid of human life. Down this street the girl walks, an innocent expression on her face. From time to time she looks back. Is someone pulling at her? Is a voice calling out anxiously to her? But never is anyone there. She doesn't know where to go, can't remember where she's been. But nestled within that slender life is an instinct of frightening power. It moves her along, step by step, leading her where it will in search of one faint surviving strand of memory.

The sun beats down white-hot; sweat streams down her face. But why does she constantly feel chilled? All that she knows is that if she keeps walking, ever walking, there will appear the small, two-story frame house that lives at the verge of her memory. The girl comes to a vacant house. Up from the luxuriant growth of weeds in the yard flutters a white butterfly. With both hands she reaches for it. And then she is walking again.

Come to me, spirit of my childhood, spirit on the wind, spirit of the wind, ease my troubled longing and come back to me now.

The Red Room

Im Ch'ŏr-u

One

"So, what's new? Anything different . . . ? Don't hold your breath."

I'm flipping through the newspaper. The world is the same today as it ever was. You take the most commonplace occurrences and report them in commonplace, reassuringly soporific language, and there you have it—nothing different from yesterday, the day before, or the day before that. You can feel it in the front-page articles with their big headlines, in the photos wedged haphazardly among them like bits of dinner stuck between your teeth, the feeling you get from stuff that's stale and worn out. Here, tucked away in the lower-right-hand corner, a few lines about a university demonstration, there a scrunched-up paragraph about factory workers in Inch'ŏn, Masan, or some such place getting tear-gassed—and not a word of commentary about any of it.

The newspapers don't have a face you can see; the articles don't have a voice you can hear. It's all a facade. Everybody wears that facade; everybody's jockeying to be part of it. Someone was ranting last night at the bar—was it Yu? Why do you suppose he wears that very same facade himself when he says those things? Beats me. But then weren't the rest of us just sitting there behind our own dead masks, our own heavy, leaden expressions? Struck by these thoughts, I pore over the tonic ads and movie ads at the bottom of the page. Nothing new there either.

I call out from where I sit on the pot: "Honey, what's the exact time?" I raise my voice because of the water dripping from the leaky faucet. Still, I have to repeat myself more loudly before an answer arrives from beyond the bathroom door.

"Thirteen minutes—oops, twelve now—before the hour. Will you be much longer?"

"Got it."

Have to move fast. What a day for my innards to let me down! Damn bowels—why can't they cooperate? It's a miserable performance, and I realize it's because of the booze I put away late last night. I was afraid this would happen, and that's why at the bar I made a point of slacking off and not slugging down shots like the other guys. But it didn't help. At my age these things shouldn't be happening. Actually it's not just my pathetic bowels that are to blame—there's more to the story: Why can't I find someplace else to work, where I can take my time on the pot instead of my wife having to report the passage of the minute hand on the wall clock while I try to squeeze something out of my wretched intestines? A job where I can arrive at work half an hour later. The way it is now is *too much*. Up at dawn and off to school, and after school the supplementary classes, and I'm not home till nine—what kind of a life is *that*? All right, enough harping on my stupid grievances—when did I start whining like this anyway? I heave a pointless sigh.

"Honey, you're going to be late. It's six-fifteen. If you miss the bus, it's all the harder to catch a taxi."

"Don't you think I know that!"

And so, business unfinished, I flush the toilet and splash a few drops of water on my face. From here on in, everything has a fixed order: on with the dress shirt, tie, socks, and suit, watch around the wrist, maybe plop down at the meal tray for a few hurried spoonfuls of breakfast, and then up and out. The same damn routine, the same rush, day in and day out except for the occasional holiday and—damn those supplementary classes—the all-too-short winter and summer vacations.

"See, if you'd just get up twenty minutes earlier—you're always . . ."

I'm so sick of her tone of voice, have been for a long time; wish I could fast-forward it, wish she wasn't there watching her sorry, worrisome excuse for a husband. My part in the routine is to throw on my trench coat while I'm still chewing breakfast and head for the door. My wife hands me my briefcase, lunchbox inside. Our daughter bursts out crying. I'm surprised she's slept until now.

"Now, remember what you have to do today, honey."

"Remind me."

"The loan from the scholarship fund, remember?"

"Oh yeah. Okay, you better go see what she's crying about."

Before she does that, she has one more thing to add: "You're coming home early today; no more drinking like last night."

The door clunks shut, and I can't hear our daughter's crying any more. I scurry down the corridor and run down the steps to the elevator landing. I'm in luck: with a chime the elevator door opens before my eyes to reveal . . . no one! That's more like it. I hop in, thinking that this day just might turn out all right. Consider—one elevator for a hundred and fifty families in this fifteen-story building. In the morning I'm always fretting about how long I'll have to wait for it.

Is it already a year since we moved here? After we got married, we spent a couple of years in a rented room where we had to keep a low profile, ever watchful of the landlord's family in the next room. And so having a nineteen-*p'yŏng* apartment all to ourselves—even though someone else owns it—puts a glow of pure ecstasy on my wife's face. But then the day before yesterday we got a call from the landlord, who wanted to raise the rent three hundred thousand a year. My wife pulled a long face and wondered out loud if we were going to have to overextend ourselves.

"We'll figure something out. I can check out the scholarship fund at school—teachers can draw on it for up to two hundred thousand *wŏn*. And the interest is a lot lower than it is at the bank."

So I said, but in actuality I've been putting off looking into this loan. Mainly because I hate being beholden to our pain-in-the-ass of a general-affairs section chief. He's the son of the president of the foundation that runs the school, he's a former army captain, and he talks down to any and all. He's got a sly, cunning look that makes me sick. But I can't very well put it off another day—and how many options does a guy like me have anyway? My briefcase feels ridiculously heavy. One more thing to bitch about. I switch it back and forth from one hand to the other, but it doesn't help. How did I end up like this? How much longer do I have to live like this? Here I go, carrying on again, feeling sorry for myself, the same old grievances that I repeat to myself dozens of times a day, and I'm so used to it that I can check my watch, get my legs moving, and scuttle off on my way all at the same time, and that's what I do now.

Looks like we're in for some snow. The sky's glowering, clouds spread out far and low. The air has a cold tingle to it, the way early-winter mornings do. The young woman who runs the grocery store is setting out crates of fish; she blows on her hands to warm them up. I look down, avoiding eye contact. She started saying hi to me a while back, and I finally figured out it's to get business from those of us in the apartments. I don't appreciate it.

At the pharmacy I turn the corner, and there on the far corner are the two three-story town-house buildings side by side. Go around them to the right and you come out onto the main street. From there it's exactly five minutes to the bus stop. Past the pharmacy I'm practically running—I'll miss my bus if I dawdle. The way things work in these satellite neighborhoods, the buses only come by every ten minutes. So if you're running late and you miss your bus, you're not going to make it to work on time.

I take another look at my watch as I hustle around the corner where the two town-house buildings are, and that's where I almost bump into the man. The navy blue windbreaker is the first thing I see. Somehow I manage to avoid contact with him. But instead of going on his way, the man moves straight toward me. I look up. *What's he doing?*

"Just a minute, there."

He's not that tall, but he has the build of an athlete, muscular and agile-looking. I inspect the man, wondering if the curt, low-pitched "Just a minute, there" really came from him. He has keen, narrow eyes set in an expressionless face. He speaks again, his lips scarcely moving.

"Beg your pardon. O Ki-sŏp?"

"What's that? Oh, right. And you are . . . ?"

I search my memory for the man's face. Is he the father of one of my students? Someone from our building? I'm drawing a blank.

"We need to have a little talk. I'll explain along the way." And that's it. He plants his hand on my left shoulder. And then another hand grabs me tight at the armpit and shoulder blade. _Two of them._ While I was face to face with the first one, his partner must have been a few steps behind me, in the direction of the main street, cutting off any escape route and managing not to draw attention to himself. This second man has an imposing build and massive hands.

They've got me.

"What's going on? Who are you?" I shout. I'm choked up, can't breathe right. My heart begins to pound with an urgency that frightens me.

"Easy now. We're going to talk real nice to you. Don't want to make a scene in your own neighborhood, do you?"

"Hurry up and get him in the car!" The second man's arm loops around my waist like a serpent's tongue and it's like I'm being swept away—the man is unbelievably strong. We're going toward a gray car; it's parked no more than fifteen feet away. It must have been waiting there. Why didn't I see it? But people don't notice things like that. Should I scream? Who the devil are these two? Police? And why me? What did I do? A dizzying profusion of thoughts come together in my mind, unravel, and come together again as they carry me along. They open the back door. I tense and shout, "Let go! What are you doing? Dammit, who are you?!"

"Huh, damned if this guy's going to go easy."

"Look, I said we're going to talk to you real nice. If you know what's good for you, you'll shut up and go for a little ride with us. And then we'll give you all the answers your little heart desires."

The men's faces are hard—they look like they want to hurt me. Suddenly the second man has my necktie wrapped around his wrist. His eyes are wide open, fixing me with a glare that frightens me. I feel my willpower weakening, my resistance fading. My briefcase, which I've held fast till then, tumbles to the pavement. *My wife put together that lunch for me, and now they've gone and spilled the kimchi.* Funny, I think—it's spilled kimchi that makes me realize how indignant I am, how humiliated I feel.

"My briefcase—" I blurt out. By then they've shoved me into the back seat. The first man gets in the front passenger side. The second man gets in back, next to me, and yanks the door shut.

"Here—your briefcase."

I take it and hold it close.

And then we're moving. Through the window I watch the street rush past. Everything out there looks heavy and sunken, as if we're under water. And then I realize it's because the windows have a dark gray tint. I'm still not thinking straight, but in spite of the sudden confusion I will myself to steady my breathing. I have to protest, but how? I have to show them I won't just be led away meekly.

"Who do you think you are grabbing someone off the street who's on his way to work? Show me an arrest warrant."

But my voice is too soft and shaky to convey the anger I feel. *Pathetic!*

The man in front turns and looks over the seatback at me. "A warrant?" he scoffs. "Not our department, big-shot teacher. You'll find out all about warrants when we get to where we're going."

"What do you mean? There's such a thing as the rule of law, you know."

"Rule of law? If you're so keen about the rule of law, then why did you break the law? It's people like you who are the lawless ones. You're going to find that out for yourself in a little while."

"Oh yeah? So which law did I break? What am I—"

"Teacher, will you *please* quiet down?" This time it's the man beside

me who speaks, a look of naked malevolence on his face. "We
are three very tired men. And we haven't had our breakfast yet." So
saying, he fixes me with a menacing scowl. I'm scared he's going to
take a swing at me with that huge fist. But instead he produces a
vocal, cavernous yawn.

I realize it's no use protesting, and I give up trying to resist. They're
not going to listen to reason. Better for me to organize my thoughts
quickly. First of all, _where_ are they taking me? And I broke the law?
That's what the guy in front said. What did I do? I curl up, embracing
my briefcase more tightly while I search my memory for anything
suspicious I might have done. But this first quick scan yields no hints.

Did I say something I shouldn't have? Once in a while in class
I'll put a political spin on something I say—but that couldn't be the
reason, could it . . . ? Well, one of my professors was supposedly
grousing about something after a few drinks and got put in jail for
spreading groundless rumors. But he wouldn't have harmed a fly. . . .
I've never vouched for someone taking out a loan, have I? And even if
I have and the loan went bad, that wouldn't rate the wildcat-snatch-
ing the-chicken treatment. Maybe one of the parents filed a complaint
about me? Is someone trying to frame me? No, I don't think so. Or
maybe—? And then it hits me; my heart sinks, and I feel dizzy. There
he is in my mind's eye—him and his drawn face and the black overcoat that the old men wear. He's lived there in the deepest and darkest
recesses of my consciousness ever since I was old enough to know
better, a scar in my memory, his image popping out at random
moments, oppressing me.

_He_ meaning my father's older brother. I've never seen his face in
real life, not even a photo of him, but he's always there in a dank corner of my mind, standing silent, black overcoat, formless except for the
haggard, gloomy face. _Don't tell me he's turned up!_ He was supposed
to have gone north; they said he didn't leave a trace. But that was more
than thirty years ago. And now? Is he a spy? Was he sent south on
some grand mission? No, it can't be. My hands are shaking. I'm seized
with the fear—and I know it's ridiculous—that some improbable
scenario hidden till now beneath my daily routine is about to material-

ize before my eyes. No, how could it—it's a story that could never be. Maybe on television or in a movie . . .

I'm too hunched over. I stretch, trying to relax, and look outside. Now it's my knees that are shaking. I place my hands on them and press down. *I know this street.* Dark smoke issues from the smokestack of the public baths. And that drugstore—I bought breath mints there. That shop sells goldfish. There's the hairdresser's. And the realtor's office. I went there before we found our apartment; I wanted to see what was available. The second floor of a town house was on the market—was it the one that was repossessed by the bank? Anyway, I soured on it.

"What's with the yawning, Detective?" Windbreaker is talking to the man next to me. "When did you get home last night, anyway?"

"Not till after two. Shit—I don't want to think about it. Once that asshole starts drinking, there's no end to it. We went to five different places—can you believe that?"

"Boozing again. That asshole meaning . . . ?"

"Section Chief Ch'oe—Ch'oe Tal-shik. He calls and says it's time he treated me to a drink—I couldn't get out of it. I'd worked two days straight, just gotten home, but oh man, the wife is all weepy, the kids are bawling for God's sake, and I just didn't want to stick around."

So saying, the man beside me produces another gaping yawn. Sure enough, that's liquor I'm smelling on his breath.

"Ch'oe Tal-shik? I remember him—transferred to your section last year? Same seniority as you, right?"

"Nope. Same age, but I started a year after him. Sounds like he's made quite a career for himself, and now he's sitting pretty. He was damn animated last night—said he really put the screws to someone earlier in the day."

It's like they've already forgotten me. I could almost believe I'm going to work like on any other day, only I'm sharing a ride with a couple of strangers. Almost. What I'd give if that were in fact the case!

We're stopped at an intersection. The back of a bus looms large through the windshield. It's the 38, the bus I take to school. How can this be? I'm supposed to be on that bus, burrowing among the throng like I always do till I'm two-thirds of the way toward the back, then grabbing onto a rail before I can relax enough to gaze out the window, or else have the good fortune to be comfortably settled where one of our students has given up his seat for me. Instead here I am, sitting in this car for some ridiculous reason. This isn't any way to treat a person. It's outrageous, damned outrageous. I consider in turn the faces of these two men I've never seen before as they jabber away. Nothing unusual about their expressions; their tone of voice is nonchalant; they laugh like normal people laugh—and yet they might as well have come from outer space, that's how alien they feel to me.

Nothing's going to happen. It's all a misunderstanding. I'm getting a very bad feeling about this, I'm cringing into a ball, and I keep repeating these words to myself because I want to deny what's happening to me. I look out the window, trying my best to appear indifferent. Surprise: the outside world is just as I left it—pedestrians crossing the street, the empty faces of children looking absently in my direction out the windows of packed buses, drivers chomping on gum as they wait impatiently for the light to change. Nothing out there is different. Tedious and ordinary, everything moves along in blissful ignorance, just as it did yesterday and the day before. The only thing that's different is me. Everything was fine till I came out of the alley outside our apartment building, and then something changed; something is happening to me that I never could have imagined.

What am I feeling? Mostly numb, numb all over, like I've been plunged into deepest darkness. And a fathomless despair. *What's my wife doing now?* My daughter will be a year old in another three weeks. The morning meeting at school gets under way any moment now—there's my place at the big table, empty. Today's a heavy day, six hours of classes starting right from period one. Who's going to take my classes? The vice-principal's going to call me at home; he'll be pissed for sure. I realize for the first time—and I have trouble believing this myself—that I have a warm affection for all these various things; I long for them. I'm angry, and terrified, at whatever it is that's about to deprive me of these things. My knees are shaking again. The car has slowed to a crawl; it's stopping at a massive white building. At the entrance is a uniformed guard. He snaps a salute and barks out something that sounds like a war cry.

Two

We'll get a dumping of snow tonight for sure. The weather was turning bad, half the sky dark and gloomy with a thick cluster of clouds the color of bloody pus. Against this backdrop the windows in the highrise apartments began to blink on.

I'd just come out from the public baths and found myself thinking how nice it would be to have a smoke. I felt for the pack, then realized I was wearing my sweatpants, then realized I wouldn't have found cigarettes even if I were wearing street clothes. *Got to kick the habit for good.* I crossed the street to a mom-and-pop store and bought a pack of Sol. How about that—almost five days since my last cigarette.

Good heavens, how do you expect me to live with this stink? You're an embarrassment is what you are. You listen to me, dear—the last time the pastor was here, I was so embarrassed, I could have died. I asked Chŏng-sun, I don't know how many times, to hide the ashtray, and she goes and puts it smack dab under the living room table—right in front of where Pastor Kwŏn was sitting. He had to pretend it wasn't there. And here I am living with a believer, a so-called deacon, who smokes like a fiend—what are you going to do about it?

Once the little woman opens her mouth, it's yap-yap-yap, scold-scold-scold. Well, she does have a point. When we go to church, I make sure I've brushed my teeth and changed into clean clothes—but that's not about to get rid of the cigarette smell that comes from *me.* And when I'm flipping through the hymnal, I wish I could hide that yellow nicotine stain on my fingertips. Anybody can say he's going to quit smoking, and yet you might as well try to kick a drug habit. Last year, when Detective Yi was in the hospital with hepatitis, he swore he was going to quit, but as soon as they let him out, he was smoking like a chimney again, wasn't he? Well, hell.

I took a nice, deep drag as I went up the alley to our house. I'd had myself a good sweat in the sauna and felt light on my feet, but I had to admit, I'd overdone it with the booze last night. How many places did we hit, anyway? Four, five? I woke up at noon with a splitting headache and stayed in bed, feeling like shit the whole afternoon.

The guy I've been working on is hard-core. I thought he'd spill his guts right off, but then he must have had second thoughts because he clammed up and wouldn't say a damn thing. So I had to get involved, and I haven't had a good night's sleep in four days. Young guys these days, they look tough, but they're spineless, most of them. But this asshole put up a hell of a fight. That was his loss; it took him a while to see the light. Fucking idiot! *It was over before you started, but you didn't get that, did you?*

I spat noisily and tried to whistle a tune. The girl next to me last night at the Abang Palace was pretty good for a bar girl. Kind of tall and slender but solid, with just the right give in all the right places; she got me stirred up. She didn't do anything when I got inside her bra, but she put up a stink when I tried to go up her skirt. If it had been one of those other broads, I'd have given her a backhand upside the head, but with her for some reason I didn't do that. The other guys didn't seem to be in the mood, so I didn't let on that I was really up for a night out with a woman—it's been a long while—and instead just followed them around. Damn—I wasn't able to go home for four days, and so I really worked over that asshole, but it left me feeling played out, like a piece of shit. Thanks to him, though, I had a little treat for the wife last night—finally. And she was really hot for it. She must have had a pretty good appetite after starving these last few days, but wouldn't you know it, I felt empty inside; something wasn't quite right—it's been so damn long since I've gotten really worked up over a roll in the hay.

I just can't figure it out. It takes days to wear down one of these guys, and when I'm finally able to fill out my report and the only thing that's left is to hand it in, I have this weird feeling. It's like there's a hole somewhere inside my chest and the blood from my heart is leaking out through it. Maybe it's a feeling of being drained, maybe it's regret, but on the other hand there's a poisonous rage against something, a kind of disappointment and despair that keeps pushing its way through. It's

the same despair that sneaks over me after sex; it's kind of like someone's deceived me—whatever it is, I can't quite put my finger on it.

I turned down the street past the empty lots. Trucks had been delivering bricks, gravel, and stuff for days—already there was a house
going up. The bricklaying looked like a rush job, but still, those red
bricks were beginning to look like a house. The guys were knocking off
for the day—dusting off work gloves, jabbering away, coming down
the alley.

Our house is a two-story Western-style at the end of the street and
across from the lots. My wife is always harping about how she wishes
they'd get those lots filled with houses—they look so unsettled and
godforsaken. Guess I won't have to hear that anymore.

Absorbed in such thoughts, I arrived at the gate and pressed the
buzzer. I was greeted by the roar of an animal right above me.

"Goddamn mangy mutt!"

I was really heated. The people upstairs have a spaniel, and it was
barking like hell, with time out only to shake itself and get rid of more
of its dirty hair. I made as if to throw a rock at it, but that didn't accomplish much—it bared its teeth and barked even more furiously.
God help me, I'm going to rip its jaws open and throw it out in the street.
I felt like going upstairs then and there, but just then my wife opened
the gate.

"What's the matter, dear?"

"That fucking dog's the matter. Doesn't even recognize me, and I
own this house! Look at him jumping up and down; he knows I'm going to kill him. I'm going to take a saw and cut off his head!"

"You're right about the dog, dear. We should tell them to sell it, for
God's sake."

"They've got no sense. What the hell are they doing with a puppy
when they're renting out of someone's house? If they're going to have a
pet, the least they can do is tie it up and keep it from barking!"

"Oh, come on, dear, they're going to hear you," said my wife as she
gave me a little shove to get me inside.

"Who cares? I *want* them to hear. Damn renters, who do they think
they are?"

My voice was even louder by now. I went into the yard. We sure as hell had made a mistake renting to those people. They'd been here a couple of weeks—newlyweds, they said when they first visited, just the two of them, but when they moved in, they came with two extra mouths attached. Those two were college boys, and there was something sassy and uppity about the way they looked at me. I didn't care for them. But I couldn't very well tell them to leave on the spot. Instead I decided I'd wait a few months and then jack up their deposit, and then they wouldn't have any choice—they'd have to leave, with their tails between their legs.

As soon as I went through the front door, our youngest ran up to me, arms wide open.

"Daddyyyy!"

"Hey, my little girl!" I scooped her up and smacked a big wet kiss on her cheek. By nature I'm kind of dull-witted and not so sweet or attentive, but she was my blood, and that was probably why, when I was face to face with my kids, I felt like a kid myself, simple and uncomplicated, and my mood would lighten. Our older one was in her last year at the girls' high school and wouldn't be home till late at night. Up at six every day, out the door with two meals packed in her lunch box, and not back home till ten in the evening. And so I didn't have much chance to see her. I don't know how she managed, she being not so strong of body—it kind of worried me.

I lifted our little one onto my shoulders and went into the family room. There in front of the television, eyes glued to the screen and oblivious to my presence, was my boy. He had just started middle school.

"Han-gi-_ya_, you little rascal, aren't you going to say hi to your dad? If you're watching TV all day long, when are you going to study? Did you do your homework yet?"

When I scolded him like this, I tried not to do it in a mean-spirited way.

Even so, he responded with a sullen glance and said, "Aw, who cares? I got a lot of homework, but how am I supposed to go into my room?"

"What do you mean? What's wrong with your room? Your mom put some nice wallpaper up. Pictures from the pet zoo, just like you wanted—remember?"

He was angry about something and didn't show any signs of cooling off.

"I don't like my room, I don't! It stinks so bad I feel like throwing up."

He sniffled, and I thought for sure he was going to start crying. I got up and turned off the television.

"What are you talking about? What smell? You're making a big fuss over nothing. Keep that up and you'll catch hell from me."

I tried to look menacing, but inside I felt all tense.

Truth be told, there were times when I hit the children. It was all because I was wired the wrong way. The kids were at that stubborn age, and at times they could be contrary for no good reason, and when that happened, the next instant I couldn't see straight and lost all rationality, I'd be oblivious to the fact that the kids standing there before me didn't know any better, and I'd start punching the air. That's how I lost my oldest son. Well, maybe it was like my wife said—his death didn't have anything to do with me. But . . . I still think he died because of my fists. The poor kid—to think I did that to him. . . .

Our older daughter, Un-ok, and Han-gi were six years apart, and in between them was Han-su. At the hospital they said it was a blockage in his brain, but that didn't lessen the shock when he died. He was eleven years old, two years younger than Han-gi was now. The day I left the hospital, his body in my arms, it was raining like crazy. That day I cursed the world and everything in it, including myself with the boy in my arms. I realized that from then on I would never be able to love this world, the people in it, or, most important, myself. A few months before he died, I'd given the kid a terrible beating. It was no big deal, what he'd done to provoke me—actually it was kind of silly—but because of it I punched him in the face—*bam-bam-bam*. He went down like a rag doll, and even now the sight of the vivid purple blood dribbling from his nose is fixed in my mind. I won't forget that sight for a long time, maybe not till the day I die.

"What's this smell you're talking about? Where did it come from? Speak up."

I glared at him, blocking his view of the television.

"It's a poop smell. Grandmother had diarrhea in my room!" And then he made a strange little scream and burst out crying.

"What? In your room? What was she doing in there?"

I called my wife, shouting for her twice, but no answer. When I was too mad to wait any longer, I ran out onto the veranda. There she was, in the bathroom, squatting over some laundry. She jumped to her feet when she saw me.

"That's right. Han-gi went into his room just now, and there it was. She crawled in there when I wasn't looking. I don't know what we're going to do about her. I've had it. I can't live like this anymore. It's not like this is the first time it's happened—it's been years now. I'm forty years old—how much longer do I have to clean up that senile old woman's mess, for God's sake?"

Waiting to unload on me. She displayed the red rubber gloves she used for doing laundry; they made her hands look like a leper's, decomposed and deformed. She must have been washing the rags she'd used to clean up the mess.

"So what's new? That's a job for the housekeeper." I felt like a balloon with the air let out of it—there was nothing I could say in defense of my mother.

"Housekeeper? Do you realize how long it's been since the last one took off? Housekeepers have their dignity, you know. Are they supposed to clean up after senile old people who poop and pee on the floor? I told you, dear, I've had it. I can't take any more of this!" And with a shriek she ripped the evil-looking gloves from her hands and threw them on the bathroom floor.

I flew into a rage. *What a fucked-up world! How come I get all the shit luck? How did I get this way? It's because of my mother. At her age she ought to be dead, but instead she poops and pisses wherever she wants, eyes wide open but nothing registering; she's lost all sense of shame, and she's senile—she's the reason my family life is absolute hell!*

It felt like these angry thoughts were going to burst out the top of my head. I rushed to the corner room and flung open the door. It was dark inside—she never turned on the light, even after the sun was down. That's the way it is with her. Unless my wife or I turn on the light, she'll lie there all night long in pitch darkness, giggling or mumbling at odd hours, pooping or pissing, and when she poops, you can bet it won't be long before she's working on that lump of shit with her hands, like she's making a rice cake.

I looked into the unlit room and waited for the stink to hit me—the urine smell, the smell of sweat, the smell of an old woman's dry, flaking skin. This awful mix of smells made my nose feel like it was going to burst.

I groped along the wall near the door and found the light switch. The fluorescent light blinked several times before coming on. There wasn't much to the room. Most of the furnishings had been moved into storage and elsewhere, leaving only a squat chest for bedding against the wall. Slumped against that chest was an old, white-haired woman in her underwear, looking more ghost than human. Her hair had been roughly sheared—my wife's handiwork—the scissor marks making it look rat-eaten.

I stood at the door, unable to move. *For the love of God tell me this is a nightmare. How can that horrible, ghostlike thing gawking at me be my mother? It doesn't make sense. It's so damned unfair!* I wanted to scream.

Suddenly she produced a weird little screech. *She's laughing.* Her lips were working, and I could see her few remaining teeth, ugly and discolored. Her face had the dark blotches you see on very old people, and her skin was deeply wrinkled.

"Go ahead, kill me. . . . I know. . . . All of you, you're going to kill me now. . . . All right, do it, go ahead."

She was staring at me as she said this. Her voice was husky, and the words were like a creepy chant or a slow tune barely uttered by someone on her last legs. Some time ago she'd started this strange muttering. Why she was doing it, I didn't know.

"All right, I will!" I screamed. "Mother, you don't know how much I want to. If only we could all be killed off—you, me, the wife, the kids, all of us; if we could all be killed off. . . . I'd give anything, just to get this damn, fucking world off my shoulders!"

I slammed the door shut, feeling choked up inside, my chest heavy. I wanted to burst into tears like a little kid. I went back to the family room, plopped myself down on the floor, and sucked on a cigarette. It was true—I wanted to see an end to everything. Rat poison for each of us—that's all it would take. The next moment the image of my father came to mind, then disappeared just as quickly. _That's right. It's all your fault! Leaving me with my senile mother and with all the ugly and horrible memories of a sickening war. It was you that caused them all to be slaughtered—your parents, your big brother, your little brother, their wives._

If not for my father, our family wouldn't have gone to hell like this. Mother wouldn't have gotten weak in the head because of what happened during the war; she wouldn't have ended up an ugly, senile old woman, and I wouldn't have to listen to my wife harping day and night about having to clean up after her. If not for my father, I could be like other people—I could have finished college, gotten myself a decent job; I could walk tall. And maybe my poor little Han-su would still be alive. If things hadn't turned out this way, I wouldn't have punched Han-su in the face like an animal . . . and he wouldn't have died. But that's the infernal legacy my father left me. And that legacy produced in me a mortal grudge, a lust for revenge that ran in my blood. I crushed out my cigarette and collapsed onto my back.

I thought about my father. The policeman. He'd joined the colonial police force before Liberation. After Liberation he continued to work as a policeman and was posted on Nagil Island, off the south coast. My father, his parents, and his brothers all lived there; it was the ancestral home. My mother's family lived there too. When the war broke out, my father was called back to the mainland, while all of us stayed behind on the island. I was only nine at the time; my sister, Tal-suk, was five.

I thought about the first time I saw the People's Army. It was late one summer day, and I was playing in the shallows along the shore.

They came into our village, and that night Grandfather sent us all off to stay with my mother's family in Tongbaeng-ni. Mother led the way, a bundle of clothing on her head and Tal-suk on her back. The night was pitch dark. All along the way I was frightened—by the ups and downs of the road, which never seemed to end; by the gasping of the waves down below; and by the fluttering of the birds in the sky above, where there was no moon or stars.

When we arrived, my maternal grandfather proceeded to take us across the next hill to a thatched hut at the far end of the island. He had nets set in the waters nearby, where he caught anchovies. At a certain time of year the anchovies were dried by workers who stayed at the hut. After we had hidden there for two months, we were surprised to see my father show up one day, along with Maternal Grandfather. We learned that the Nagil Island police had had to evacuate to Ch'ŏngsan Island and had recently returned. At the same time, the People's Army had left Nagil Island. Tal-suk and I ran to Father, crying out in delight. Father embraced us and then with no warning he burst into tears. Mother sank to the ground and began wailing. Why were the grown-ups crying? Father took us back home. Where were Paternal Grandfather and Grandmother? Where were our uncles and aunts? We learned later that the local Reds had slaughtered them, killed them while the People's Army was still there. Father stood in the yard, silent; Mother collapsed on the ground. Tal-suk and I were terrified. We cried without knowing why. And then Father took me by the hand and hurried me away.

Let's go. You're going to see me get my revenge. You're going to see with your own eyes. Understand?

Father changed just then; he became someone utterly different. His bloodshot eyes bore into me. He kept repeating to me that he was going to get his revenge and that I would see it with my own eyes. He took me to the township office, and there in the yard he brought two men out from a locked shed. And he made me watch as he stood them against the wall and shot them dead.

Look, Tal-shik! he shouted at the top of his lungs, pointing at the bloody corpses. *You have to see this. Those sons of bitches are Reds!*

*They're the ones who murdered your grandma and grandpa. Don't
you ever forget. The Reds are your enemies! Understand? Sons of
bitches like that, you can grind their bones to dust, you can eat their
livers, and they're still your enemies for as long as you live! Understand?*

I shot to my feet, took a pair of pants and my black leather jacket
from the wardrobe, and changed into them.

My wife entered just then.

"Where are you going, dear?"

"Where do you think I'm going?" I shot back. "I'm working nights
again—I won't be back for a few days."

She didn't say anything. She probably knew I had to leave for work
that night, and I was sure without looking at her that she was pouting.
I crossed the veranda and put on my shoes.

"Remember, dear, you need to be back the day after tomorrow for
lunch."

"How come?"

"How many times do I have to tell you—the minister's coming. It's
our turn to host him this week. It's not good if you're not here. You're
supposed to be a deacon, remember?"

Oh yeah. It had slipped my mind that we were hosting the prayer
meeting this week.

"All right. I'll try to get away for a little while around one o'clock.
And if things go well, maybe I'll be done by then."

I crossed the yard.

"Daddy, don't forget to bring me something," said my daughter.

"Bye, Dad," said Han-gi.

I gave them a glance and left. The wind was pretty chilly. It had
been getting cold at night. I looked up at the sky; it was dark as ink. I
flagged down a taxi. We were in for a dumping of snow.

Three

Light reflects from the wall above the window of the cell. It's not
coming from outside, which tells me it's long past sundown. I check
my watch—but what's the use? I'm still trying to figure out how I
ended up here. It's been thirteen hours since those men took me

away. Thirteen hours. I was robbed of those hours, and it still feels ridiculous. But then maybe this is only the beginning—and if so, how much longer will it take for things to run their course?

The concrete floor is hard and cold, and my bottom's numb from sitting on it all these hours. I rise to a squat and stretch. There are two steam pipes, but I can't imagine them heating the entire cell. I wish I had my briefcase to sit on, but they took it away after they questioned me in the small room.

One of the other guys is clutching the bars and shouting. He's slurring his words. "Hey. Call the guy that owns the bar. He'll tell you what happened." He belches. His dress shirt is hanging out and his tie is loose. He looks like he's been beaten up, his cheeks swollen and his nostrils caked with dried blood. He must have gotten into a fight at the bar. He shouts something more, but the two policemen at the desk near the door—riot policemen—are talking to each other and they ignore him.

There are five of us in the cell—me, the drunken man, and three young men who look to be about twenty. Heads together, those three are talking among themselves.

"Fucking bastard—he gets away, and here we are."

"Still, maybe we shouldn't have ratted him out. I mean, he wasn't really part of it, right?"

"What are you talking about? Whose fault is it we got caught?"

"Shut the fuck up. What's the use of bitching now? The party's over, dammit!"

They continue muttering. It sounds like they got caught stealing something.

So here I am, asking myself why in hell those men dragged me here and then disappeared. I realize I'm chewing on my fingernails as I try to figure out what they have in store for me. As soon as we arrived, they put me in the small room, which I guess they use for interrogation. It has a single lonely wooden desk, and I had to sit there, fretting and waiting. Nobody was in any hurry to show up, and all I could do was sit there, my mouth getting dry. I had to go to the bathroom a few times—it's at the far end of the hallway outside—always accompanied by a riot policeman.

Finally a man showed up. Average height, wearing a gray jacket; I put him in his late thirties. His large pug nose made him look not too bright, but there was a peculiar gleam lurking in his eyes, and it gave me a bad feeling. He sat down across from me at the table. He started by asking personal information, which he jotted down as I responded—my name, age, address, occupation, citizen registration number, et cetera, et cetera. I kept thinking it wasn't me I was talking about but a complete stranger. More to the point, I kept wishing that the person I was talking about had no relation to me whatsoever. I guess I was praying that it was all a big misunderstanding, that they had brought the wrong person to this creepy, godforsaken place.

The man finished writing and looked over the information I'd given him.

"Tell me, will you?" I asked the man. "*Why* am I here? What did I . . . ?"

The jaundiced face with the pug nose slowly lifted, and the man shot me a look. In spite of myself my voice trembled; I felt wretched. All I could do was mutter lamely; I couldn't even finish a proper sentence. Those eyes with their peculiar gleam were full of disdain and arrogance; it was as if my questions were laughable.

"Why are you here? Is that what you said?"

But the man's attitude cowed me so that I couldn't respond.

"You're asking what you did? Huh?"

"That's right. What in heaven's name . . ."

And again my mumbling trailed off.

"Look, who do you think you're trying to fool? *You're* asking *me* what you did wrong? You've got to be kidding." There was no longer the slightest pretense of civility in his speech. "If *you* don't know, then who does? Stop playing dumb. You can save your fun and games for somewhere else." And then he cleared his throat, spat on the floor, and rubbed what he had spat with the sole of his shoe.

I was getting more and more thirsty. My chest felt tight, and I was having trouble breathing. Was this a dream? What in God's name had I done wrong? I was beginning to have doubts about myself—was there something I wasn't remembering, a monstrous crime I had committed and then managed to block from my mind? All sorts of wild thoughts popped up, then disappeared just as quickly—it was unreal. And in between these crazy thoughts my uncle's face came in and out of view.

"Yi Sang-jun got caught. Yi Sang-jun. How does that grab you?"

I sat there with my mouth hanging open. "Yi . . . Sang . . . Jun?" I searched my mind. *Yi Sang-jun*—who *was* that? Still I felt as if I were deluded. And then suddenly something in that thick fog that was everywhere around me tripped me and I fell. *Oh. . . . That was his name, right.* The realization was like a slap across the face. *Yeah, that's the guy.* I couldn't believe that I'd somehow put him out of my mind. *That's right; he told me the police were after him. So, he got caught—finally. But what does that have to do with me? All I did was put him up at our place for a week or so; it wasn't even ten days. . . . Is that what's going on here? Are they saying I hid this guy?*

Finally, a bit of relief. And more than that, with the thought that perhaps this dreadful cloud of suspicion had lifted, the shackles that had chained me out of the fear I felt seemed to dissipate.

The man handed me several sheets of paper.

"All right, you're going to write a statement for us. You're not going to hold anything back. You're going to give us the facts, right down to the last detail. The more detail the better. Got it?"

I had never in my life written a statement for the police, but I did as I was told and began to write. Most of it had to do with how I had met Yi Sang-jun and the time he had stayed with us. I jotted it all down as it came to mind. But when I had finished, two hours later, all the man did was give my statement a quick once-over, and then he put me back in the cell.

As he was about to disappear into the corridor, I called out to him, "Wait a minute—what's going to happen now? When do I get to go home?"

The man turned to me with his by now familiar sneer.

"You can cool your heels. This investigation has only just begun."

"Well, you can at least let me call home," I pleaded, gripping the bars of the cell. "How's my family going to know . . ."

Instead of answering me, the man called out to the riot policeman posted at the door to the hallway, "Hey—no phone calls for that one—he's a security risk."

"Yes, sir."

The riot policeman's boyish face glanced at me, and the man disappeared.

So there I was. My mouth felt like sand. Such a bitter taste at the tip of my tongue—as if I had a lump of salt in my mouth. All I had had for food was a pastry and a carton of milk. At lunchtime the man said he would have soup and rice brought, but I asked for a pastry and milk instead. And even that didn't go down very easily. And I didn't touch dinner. I could have paid to have something delivered, but I had no appetite—I couldn't have swallowed a grain of rice.

I wonder what my wife is doing right now at home. I can see her drawn face, can hear her asking me to be home early. She won't have a clue as to my whereabouts unless the vice-principal called to report that I didn't show up at school; she'll assume I'm out drinking again; she'll produce the occasional frown, she'll check the clock. I wonder if our little girl is asleep by now. Lately she's taken to spreading her little hands wide and waving at me when I come home, as if she finally knows who I am. She's much more active than your typical little tyke, always crawling about somewhere, never in one place for more than an instant, and anything that comes to hand will soon be in her mouth.

Day in and day out my wife is home alone with her. My wife's health has always been suspect, and having to spend the whole day taking care of the girl and cleaning up after her is a drain on her energy—I can see it in her face. I keep imagining her now, her drawn face looking up anxiously at the clock. The girl will be crying. She isn't even a year old, and she'll have burst into tears and will be pestering her mother. I can almost hear her crying, her lack of volume more than made up for by the keenness of her wails—it breaks my heart. How is this possible? The least they could do is let my family know where I am. How can they lock a man up like this, with no warrant. . . ? I'm beside myself.

I slump back against the wall and squat, head buried between my knees. Without warning a surge of exhaustion sweeps over me. My wife is waiting for me. Will I be able to return home before midnight ...? They have to at least let me call. I'm so sleepy, I feel like I'm sinking slowly and deeply into quicksand, and to keep awake I fight to hold onto the shreds of my fleeting thoughts.

I'm losing track of the time. I hear my name.

"Which one of you is O Ki-sŏp?"

My head jerks up. I must have dropped off. A riot policeman is there on the other side of the bars.

"That's me," I say, jumping to my feet and approaching him. He opens the cell and lets me out.

"Follow me," he barks, and he walks off toward the door to the corridor.

"Where are we going? You're letting me go now?" I ask as I scurry along behind him. No answer. The thought that I might finally be able to go home is gnawing at me. "Of course—how can they keep me here any longer over something so trivial?" I'm so sure of it, I'm mumbling out loud. But when I get out to the corridor, I realize I was too quick to jump to that conclusion. Two men are standing there—the same two men who brought me here this morning. My knees buckle, and in a single instant I feel all the strength drain out of me.

Handcuffs snap shut around my wrists. With a practiced maneuver each man takes me by the armpit, and they hustle me down the corridor. The corridor is bare save for several long fluorescent bulbs in the ceiling. We go out a door at the end. Waiting just outside is the gray sedan.

"Get in," says one of the men as he pushes me into the back seat. "Do yourself a favor and don't even think about putting up a fight." He gets in beside me, and the other man gets in the passenger seat in front. As the car starts up, I feel a hand on the back of my neck. "Head down," the man beside me hisses. Before I know it, I'm bent over, the man pressing down on me so hard that my forehead is practically touching my knees. And then he grabs the back of my trench coat and flings it up over my head so I can't see anything. I feel like I'm inside a sack. Can't see a thing. Here I am, cut off from the world—and so easily done I can't believe it. It's so easy to simply snuff out a person's life, and even though we live in a world of such barbarity and violence that it makes your blood run cold, people simply go about their lives oblivious to it all. No use keeping my eyes open, and so I shut them.

My heart is pounding. Where are they taking me? To a place where I'll be silently killed? It's not too late to try to escape. If I elbow this guy in the side and punch out the window and scream for help, people will come running. But these men would get me back. They'd show the people their IDs, call me a violent criminal, charge me with resisting arrest and trying to escape. The people would see the IDs and take them as the law. They always do; people don't want to get involved. *How dangerous and irresponsible is that?* I ask myself indignantly. And then I realize, too late, that this is exactly the way I myself have always been. I've never paid much attention to the countless incidents I read about in the papers and hear on the news or to the reports about the people involved in those events. Why should I—they were strangers to me. I would tell myself that none of it had anything to do with me and go about my life, uninterested and unconcerned. And now here *I* am, drawn into one of those incidents I've always brushed off as trivial. An incident others would downplay, thinking it happened all the time, something not worth a cocked ear or a glance in my direction. How can this be happening. . . ?

These thoughts set my knees atremble. *Is this really me, knees shaking like this?* And all the while the car continues on its way. We must be passing close by the city center—I can hear traffic noise all about me, as well as the sounds of busy streets. The car stops at intervals, then moves forward again—traffic lights, must be.

"Are you on tonight?" It sounded like the man in front.

"Yeah. Days like today make me want to puke. I had to go to the hospital this afternoon."

"What for?"

"Damn wife made me take her. She has the flu. Nice life some people got. Shit!"

"For the flu?"

"That's what I said. You should have heard her—'Honey, I think I'm dying!' You would have thought she was going into labor or something—I was about to ask myself what we were going to do with another baby."

The other man chuckles. "She wasn't faking, pal. The flu's real bad now. Section Chief Pak called in sick two days running, you know. It can kill—the public health people put out a warning."

"Yeah, I think I heard the same thing. Virulent, that's what they're calling it."

"You got to be careful—one person gets it, and the whole family comes down sick."

"That's what's got me worried—our little one's none too strong to begin with."

"The one in kindergarten?"

"He started grade school this year. Every day he gets a nosebleed."

"That's a bad sign. Kids like that, they stay sickly when they're older—it's hard to grow out of. Our older one was like that."

"Oh yeah? Last time I saw him, he looked pretty good."

"He better be, considering all the money we've sunk into ginseng and antler horn for him."

"Huh—guess we ought to put our boy on that stuff too."

The men chatter away, as natural as you please. I almost convince myself that I'm listening to a couple of strangers sitting next to me on the bus or in a bar. But then I feel the huge distance between them and me, and constricted by fear and oppressed by a vague feeling of despair, I begin to squirm.

We've gone maybe thirty minutes when the car suddenly starts shaking. It feels like we're on a dirt road, God only knows where. I think about the dirt road we drove down last year when our school had its fall picnic, the clouds of dust and the wretched condition of the road surface. The sides of the road were lined with cosmos caked with dust so fine it looked like flour. We were going uphill and we came around a bend, and there in front of us was a huge drop-off and at the bottom the blue surface of a reservoir. I was hit with a wave of dizziness, sure

we were going over the edge. Maybe we're approaching a drop-off like
that right now. Maybe we'll stop at the edge, and they'll haul me out of
the car and stand me there and then come up behind me and . . . I see
in my mind's eye, vivid as a scene from a movie, my own self hurtling
down from a mile-high cliff. I silently scream. I feel a cold sweat in the
small of my back.

One last violent bout of shaking, and the car comes to a stop.

"All right. Get out."

They pull me out, and then, like before, they flank me, a hand on
each arm, a hand in each armpit. And then a little surprise—a cush-
iony sensation beneath my feet. It feels like grass, and I wonder where
I am—at the foot of a hill or in the woods, in the outskirts of the city?
The air is somehow different. They march me off, trench coat still over
my head, and I feel my way along. The grass gives way to something
crunchy like gravel, and before long I feel the men stop. A doorbell
rings once, twice, three times, and then there's the clunk of something
opening. It sounds like a massive iron gate, worked by a motor. I'm
ushered inside, I hear another clunk behind me, and then I'm marched
another half dozen steps.

"You're going up some steps—seven of 'em."

I count them off to myself. Twice my foot catches on the step, and
twice the men's arms keep me upright. We cross another stretch that
must be grass, and then it turns to concrete, and then there's a metallic
creak that sounds like another door opening. I feel warm air—I'm inside. Inside a home, I'm pretty sure. The sound of a radio—or maybe
it's a television. The trench coat is still over my head. One of the men is
still pressing my head down.

"Where do you want him?"

"One-oh-one, please. The boss is waiting for him."

I haven't heard that particular voice.

"The boss? Oh, right, Section Chief Ch'oe Tal-shik."

Off they lead me again. And then an outburst of laughter—
women's voices. "What do you think, Doctor Kim? A very interesting
question from one of our housewives: physiologically, is it true that

the tear glands of women are much better developed than those of men?" "That must be a new theory." This male voice is followed by another burst of laughter. I finally figure it out: it's the television.

"You're going down some steps."

This time the man doesn't tell me how many. Again I count silently. At nine they turn me left. Down another nine steps. Now we're in a basement. *Thunk.* A metal door opening. A few words exchanged—another guard there—and the men walk me another few steps. I hear yet another door opening—it sounds a bit smaller than the others—and I'm prodded inside. The hands at my armpits finally let go.

"Stand up straight!"

With an effort I do so. The trench coat is whisked back from my head.

What in God's name . . . ? This is a nightmare. An awful night-mare—it has to be. I can't believe what I'm seeing. I stiffen all over and can only gape at my surroundings. *A bloody hell*—that's my very first impression. I just can't accept the scene I see before me. A red room. The four walls and the ceiling too have been painted a brilliant blood red. That painting by Munch—the skeletal, screaming figure with the hands clapped over his ears, a twisted, contorted figure in a mon-strously twisted background, as if the colors of the canvas have been melted down in one fast moment over flame. Whenever I see a repro-duction of that painting, a scream reverberates against my eardrums, the scream of a man in the agony of death.

That man in the painting, has he been in this room, blood dripping all over him, painting these four walls and the ceiling with his blood? Nightmarish imaginings from my childhood rise one after another—a monster house where people are boiled alive in a cauldron; a bloody hell; a vampire's lair. This room is the creation of a maniac. Who in his right mind could have conjured up something so disgusting? Am I seeing things? Maybe this is a simple and ordinary room that my mind has somehow transformed into something hideous. I want to tear out my hair. I can't stand to be in this room with its awful colors. *This is madness—a lunatic is playing with me.* I'm sure I'm going to vomit, and I begin to stagger back toward the door.

A voice comes out of the bloody marsh. "Where do you think you're going?" A cold, hard, metallic voice.

I come to a stop. I thought I was all alone. Where is it? Where's that voice coming from? I look about, my eyes sleepy, as if I'm hallucinating. There, a desk, and behind it a man sitting silently. Against the red walls and his black leather jacket the man's face is white as a plaster mask. Why didn't I spot him until now? The man's elbows rest against the edge of his desk; his hands are together, fingers laced. I shudder in response to the chill, alien sensation emanating from this man.

"Get down—there!"

The chill voice echoes in the red room.

I look about hesitantly. At first glance it looks like a hotel room—in the corner a bed and against the opposite wall a bathtub and a sit-down toilet. Between the bed and toilet a smallish wooden screen. In front of the desk three chairs; on the ceiling two fluorescent lights. And that seems to be all there is for furnishings.

I falter toward the bed.

"Not there."

I look back at him, unsure what to do.

"There, on the floor, kneel down. Do you hear what I'm telling you?"

I'm perplexed, humiliated, my body won't move. With a great effort I manage to shoot the man a look.

"Now!"

The man remains motionless, his face a dead mask.

Lips trembling, I muster my courage and speak.

"No, I won't. Why—"

Involuntarily I swallow, my throat is so dry.

"You son of a bitch, do you know where you are?" the man growls. "Hey, come here!" he barks toward the door.

At his command the door clunks open and four men troop in. They're well built, with strong, solid physiques that make them look like cast-iron robots. One of them has a club that's almost as big as a baseball bat.

"Sounds like you need a taste of this to wise you up. Take off your clothes!" one of them orders me.

My hands tremble. I remove my coat, then my suit jacket. I have a hard time with the buttons, my hands are shaking so badly. I loosen my tie and remove my shirt, and there I am in my long underwear. They order me to remove that as well. And finally I'm naked except for my briefs.

"Kneel!"

I glare at them. I feel a mixture of shame, rage, and a sorrow I can't explain. Tears well up. My knees are shaking.

"Look at this asshole!"

And then I'm being kicked from all sides, and the next thing I know, I'm sprawled out like a frog on the concrete floor. The blows rain down on me, first their feet, then their fists, and then the club. The club starts at the small of my back and moves to my thighs, my hips, my bottom, and with every blow my breath catches—I can't utter a word. All I can do is grunt and absorb the weight of the blows pouring down on me. And the weird, bestial shrieks and curses that gush from their mouths! As the shattering pain spreads through me, I cling to the illusion that this is still a nightmare. The small of my back, hips, chest, neck, arms, head, knees, thighs, back, shoulders, calves—my flesh in its entirety, and every last joint, is being destroyed. *I can't breathe. My chest, it's breaking open.*

"Stop, for the love of God, stop, stop."

Four

What a joke! How long does he figure he can hold out, a guy like that? I sat back with a grin as I watched his face turn the color of dirt. It kills me how these guys let themselves get stripped naked and squirm around in pain—don't they know how disgusting, how pathetic they look? It's ridiculous. *Asshole!* What's in it for him, holding out—he's just a skinny fuck to begin with. *Shit.* These guys are all the same— most of them, once we get them here, the jig is up and they lose their nerve, but a few of them stand right up, don't want to bend. They tell us to show them a warrant; they tell us we'll be sorry; they tell us to get ready because they'll see us in court, whatever—they act like they have some guts, but come on, don't make me laugh. They can say what they want, but all it takes is five minutes for them to wake up to the cold, hard fact that they're worthless pieces of shit.

I looked down at the sheet of paper and gave his personal history a once-over. _O Ki-sŏp. Hmm, high school teacher. Well, well, well, he's from Yaksan Island. That's a good one. Mihwang Village on Yaksan Island—now where's that? Ch'ilsan Village, I've been there, and to Myŏngsa Village, but Mihwang Village—got me._ Anyhow, that got me interested. I'm pretty familiar with Yaksan Island. It's the next island over from Nagil Island, where I'm from. You take the ferry from Haejin, and it's the island right before Nagil. Yak Mountain takes up most of the island, and it's the highest mountain in those islands—even though the island itself is smaller than Nagil. The mountain has deep valleys and thick woods, and back then we'd cross over in boats to get firewood—I remember doing that a couple of times. Those dense stands of camellias were quite a sight.

"Stop, please. For the love of God, stop."

About time. Our friend here seemed to be the kind that doesn't make too much of a fuss. Oh, the whisk of fists flying through the air and the dull thud when they land, but the only sound he makes when they're stomping on him and making a mess of him is a little moan—he doesn't open his mouth wide and scream, and he's not faking it either. I know from experience that this is the type that's easy to deal with. These guys with the guts look like they've got a lot of staying power, but once I let the air out of their balloon, they spill everything out, as easy as a silkworm spinning silk. And then there are the ones who play it real careful and act like they're going to kick the bucket at any moment, and among that type there are quite a few who pretend they'll do anything you say but deep down inside they're calculating every angle. You can give up trying to outfox sly bastards like that; they're enough to give you a migraine.

So, here we are, a guy who's been to college, a blackboard jockey, brain must be in good working order. Let's see how much he can handle—so far, I have to admit, he's not bad. Usually when they get worked over like that, you can count on some results. But even though he's sprawled out there like a frog and you'd think he's about to croak the way he's squirming around, he's not begging for his life.

"Please, will you stop . . . ? For the love of God, why . . . ? Why are you doing this to me . . . ? Oh God . . ."

Listen to you—"Why?" you ask. You still don't get it, do you?

"This guy doesn't seem to understand where he's at. Keep working him over until he begs for his life."

Business as usual. The boys got back to work with a vengeance. They're perfect for this line of work.

More grunts and groans. "Make them stop. . . . Stop, stop. . . . Help me; don't let them kill me, please. . . ."

There we go—begging for his life, finally. Time for the reluctant cease-and-desist order: "All right, gentlemen, that's all for now. You can go up and have yourselves a game of *paduk*."

I rose slowly. My helpers straightened their clothing and let themselves out. Now it was just me and him here in the Red Room.

"Listen, Mr. O, there are reasons things work the way they do in this world, and sometimes it's best simply to abide by those reasons. By now you ought to know where you are. . . . And so it's up to you to choose the wise course of action."

I found my cigarettes and held out the pack toward him. The guy just gave it a blank look, didn't make as if to take one. His hair was all messed up, and his eyes had the dull glaze of the eyes of a rotting fish. I took a cigarette from the pack, put it in his mouth, and lit it for him. Then I did the same for myself. He took a couple of drags.

"So, Mr. O, you're all done telling me you don't know why you're here—right?"

As I asked him this, I stuck my free hand in my pocket. The way he was kneeling on the floor, his face was right near my knees.

"Something about a crime . . ."

I could make out his lips quivering. He had a terrified look on his face. I'd have to get straight to the point with this one.

"Yeah, I know everything. You're a socialist. Aren't you?"

"What? What are you talking about? I don't even know what social-ism is."

Just what I figured—he's going to flat-out deny it. Arrogant idiot. Still, he's got his eyes on me, and he's obviously scared.

"Well, I guess you're not quite as bright as you look. Okay, I've got an idea—we don't beat you up anymore, and you confess—how about it?"

"If I had something to confess, I'd tell you. Really."

"So this is how it's going to be?"

"Believe me, please. I'm telling the truth. I don't know anything. I have no idea what's going on here."

And then the guy grabbed me around the knees.

"So, you don't know anything."

I took off one of my sneakers and smacked the guy across the face twice, hard. I've learned from experience that that's the best medicine for cutting these arrogant bastards down to size. The guy squealed, covered up his face, and fell to the side.

"Get up, you son of a bitch! Now!"

The guy was holding his cheeks, and I thought he was glaring at me. I felt the blood rush to my head, and I started kicking and stomp-ing and punching him. What a spectacle—moaning and groaning and flopping around, front, back, and side, and squirming like a worm. _"Believe me"? Huh, that's a good one. You all sound the same. You're all a bunch of calculating assholes. "Believe me"? Believe who? Calculating bastards. You think that act is going to work with me?_

Tal-shik, look. Look with your own eyes. Those Reds are your en-emies—the ones who killed your grandfather and grandmother. They're your enemies for all time. My father had taken me to the town office and was pulling me to where two bloody corpses were laid out in the yard. _No, Dad, I'm scared._ I tried to get away, but he held me tight and marched me toward the bodies. _Look, I want you to look. The Reds are your enemies, every last one of them. Your enemies for all time—we have to kill them all off, so they don't leave any children behind. You understand, Tal-shik?_ He lifted my chin and made me look at those bodies. They scared me. *Look at them, Son. What's there to be afraid of? You can't see your enemies if your eyes are shut. How are you going to kill off the Reds if you're so scared? Look at them—now!* I barely managed to open my eyes. One of the men was someone I knew very well. He was a helping hand at the Hans', on the other side of the hill, and Father and I used to visit there. We called him Uncle Yong-sul. Once he picked some edible grasses for me along one of the paths through the paddies, and once he made a little flute for me from a barley stalk. Bright red blood was pumping out of Uncle Yong-sul's broad chest. The chest and the neck of the man beside him were clotted with blood. That red color was so beautiful it made me dizzy. I had never seen such a vivid red before.

So here this one was, sprawled out naked on the floor, looking like he wasn't quite all there. Bruises and swelling on his thighs and back. Pitiful the way his shoulder blades stuck out all bare like that. *What did I tell you, asshole? Just 'fess up real nice, and everything will go easy for you. Come out with that other crap, and this is what you get.* I looked around the four walls and the ceiling, all dressed in blood red, and snorted.

"Okay, get up. You can sit on that bed over there," I said in a nice, relaxed tone.

But either the guy didn't have the energy, or else he didn't understand, because he didn't move. I took him by the elbow, figuring I'd help him up, but the moment I touched him he flinched and began shuddering all over. To be honest, I couldn't help feeling a bit of pity toward a guy when something like this happened, but I'd sloughed off my greenhorn timidity a long time ago. Cheap sentiment like that is for the new ones, the ones who miss mommy's tit. This is a war— make no mistake about it. It's violent, it's bloody, and you either cheat or get cheated. There's no place for the soft of heart. Kill or be killed, swallow up or be swallowed, that's all there is. And if I don't want to get killed or swallowed, I have to cheat the other guy first. If I let my guard down, I'm the one who gets cheated, and if that happens, the interrogation and the investigation don't work, and I'm the guy that gets jerked around, playing the other guy's game. The first thing you have to know about these guys is that their gray matter works differently from your ordinary petty crooks. Most of them have been to college and have some book-learning, and they know how to yap, so they've got some crap filed away in the gray matter, which means they need extra persuading. If you pay the least bit of attention to their word games or their excuses—and they come up with some doozies—you can bet they'll play you for all you're worth. They'll latch on to everything you say, they'll give you all sorts of reasons, and they'll find a way to get your dander up. You wouldn't believe how many of these assholes there are, always trying to put down a guy like me, who's never been near a college in his life.

You can't trust anyone. Not a soul. Humans are basically a cunning and dirty breed. Hiding behind a mask, always looking for an advantage over the next person —that's the race of animals we call human. And you absolutely have to be ready for those bastards that have the Red ideology in their heads. You could call that my credo for life. Actually those were my father's words. He was the police chief in that town, and he was forever repeating those words. Long before, he had told me something similar. Long before, in the yard of the town office, on that day when he shot those two men from our town.

Look, Tal-shik! Those are your enemies. The ones who killed your grandfather and grandmother, your big uncle and aunt, your little uncle and aunt. The Reds are your enemies, every last one of them. Remember that. We can't allow a single one of them to live in this world. They're the devil. The Satan mentioned in the Bible, that's exactly who they are. But there's no way of telling who the devil is. You don't know just by looking. And that's why you can't trust anyone. Do you understand me, Tal-shik?

My father was a fervent Christian, and his face was flushed like he'd been drinking as he shouted these words, looking back and forth between me and the awful bodies of the two Reds. And then he spread wide his bloody hands before me. Hands stained with the blood of the enemy.

I was scared, but I didn't cry. I couldn't cry. I knew that when I was grown up, I shouldn't cry, but even back then I think I was faintly aware that I just couldn't allow myself to cry. I looked down at those two foul, blood-covered bodies sprawled at our feet, two men who no longer breathed. My father reached out and silently took my hand in his. The damp, sticky feel of the blood on my palm and the back of my small hand, still lukewarm, the fishy smell—they are still clear in my mind. At that moment it was as if everything in my world had turned bright red. The sky, the earth, the trees, the flowers, the town office, the school—it was all turning the vivid red color of blood, right before my eyes.

I reached for the pen and notepad on my desk.

"When did you first meet Yi Sang-jun?"

"In the fall—last fall."

"When last fall?"

"It was . . . let me see . . . the middle of October . . . I think."

"October thirteenth. A Saturday. Right?"

"Uh, yes, I think that's right."

"Where did you meet him?" Here the guy hesitated. I could almost see the wheels starting to spin in his little brain. "Might as well tell the truth. We've already got Yi Sang-jun. He's right across the hall. Want to know more? We rolled out the red carpet for Sŏ Chŏng-min too. They told their story several days ago—you're the only one left. So keep in mind that you can try to bullshit me all you want, but I'll see right through it."

That got the guy's eyes open—and then they kind of closed down again. He looked surprised. Which was only natural.

"Okay, let's try again—*where* did you meet him?"

"Let's see, it was Saturday afternoon. . . . It was a tearoom, uh, the Songjuk Tearoom—I'd arranged to meet Sŏ Chŏng-min there. . . . So I went there, and Sŏ Chŏng-min said there was someone he wanted me to meet, but he didn't want to talk about it there and so he asked me to go somewhere else. . . . And . . . that's it. That's all there was to it. I didn't know what was happening. And I still don't have a clear idea who Yi Sang-jun is."

"That's a lie! You're trying to pull a fast one on me. Look, you, I had you figured for better than that. Well, you're not doing yourself any favors."

"No, it's the truth. Sŏ Chŏng-min said I had to help him; he asked me for a favor."

"How did you get to know Sŏ Chŏng-min?"

"We were in the army together. We got to know each other in basic training, and then we were stationed at the same base. We spent three years in the same unit, and we got to be good friends. After we got out, we met from time to time; we'd have a drink together . . . and that's about it."

"Ever think about what kind of a person he was? Do you know what he did for a living?"

I quickly scanned the guy's statement.

"Not exactly. I remember him saying he was part of some social movement I think he said it was a Christian organization somewhere. And I had the impression he didn't have a regular job. . . . Oh yes, and he said he taught at a night school and he put together a newsletter. . . . And that's pretty much the extent of what he told me."

Nothing new here. We knew all this stuff plain as day. This guy must have thought I was like the teachers when they call the school kids in to ask them their family details. Just kept grasping for straws, reciting information that we all knew. Was he playing dumb? At first glance you would have thought he really _didn't_ know anything. . . . But you can't jump to conclusions. I'd have to keep after him, no matter how many times, till I had something rock-solid. And even if he _was_ so simple that he didn't know what was going on, it didn't really matter. Well, I never expected much anyway from this one. We only brought him in on the off chance we might get lucky with him and actually learn something. Or else, seeing as how Yi Sang-jun and Sŏ Chŏng-min were flat out denying everything, maybe we could work this guy over enough to tie up the loose ends.

"Oww, Father!"

Screams from next door. The boys were back in action.

"Oww. Somebody help me!"

Sŏ Chŏng-min. Listen to him squeal—must be a pain in the ass to deal with. There was a thumping sound, like somebody rolling around on the floor, then some dull thunks. I wondered about the guy in front of me and gave him a quick look out of the corner of my eye—he was plenty scared, it was plain to see. His eyes were darting every which way, and every time there was a scream or a shout from next door, he gave a little shudder.

"Feeling a little anxious, Mr. O?"

"Huh? What?"

He gave me a stupid look. With his scared eyes he looked like a puppy caught out in the rain. A puppy whose soaked fur is a tangled mess and sticks to its hide.

We had a puppy like that once. It had long brown fur that flopped around when it moved. I forget its name, but it was a foreign breed. The wife got it from some relatives who moved overseas. I gave it a kick in the belly the first time I saw it and shouted at her to get rid of the mutt right then and there. I never expected the kids to make such a racket—they sobbed like they were the ones getting kicked. *Dad, you're bad! Dad, I hate you! You're not my dad anymore!* In particular my son Han-su liked that puppy. At mealtime he got so obstinate about taking that son of a bitch to his room and eating together that I had to scold the shit out of him, and from that point on I sensed he was trying to keep the puppy out of my sight. . . . Well, we had that puppy more than three years. Right after Han-su died it disappeared somewhere. . . . My wife said it was a good thing: "I'm glad it worked out that way. Otherwise I'd be thinking of Han-su, the poor boy, whenever I looked at it. . . ."

"You're anxious, aren't you? How does it feel? You know where you are now, don't you? You could die here, and nobody between heaven and hell would know the difference—we don't leave a trace. You can work that little brain of yours and play all the games you want, but you won't leave here in one piece. Got it?"

The guy didn't say a word. He gave me a little look and then dropped his head and gaped at the floor. His bony shoulders were slumped over. *Dad, you're bad! I don't like you, Dad!* Little Han-su took that puppy in his arms and burst out crying. I saw that mangy puppy trembling in his arms.

"Okay, Mr. O, I'm going to give you some advice. All you need to do is go along with us real nice and tell us everything just the way it happened, and things will work out fine—you don't need to be like the guy next door, going through living hell—right? You and me, we're not ignorant laboring stiffs; we know what's good for us, so what's the use of resorting to violence like a bunch of savages? I know as much as the next guy, and, you know, if you and me had met some other place, we'd probably be dressed in suits, sitting across from each other like gentlemen, having a drink—don't you think?"

I tried to read him as I kept buttering him up like this.

"Well . . ."

"So that's why I'm saying, tell us everything, just the way it happened."

"But I'm telling the truth. I'm not trying to trick you— I mean it. I've told you everything. For heaven's sake, believe me."

The guy was getting desperate; I could see it on his face. Maybe he was telling the truth. Maybe he had just hidden this wanted guy for a few days and didn't think he was doing anything wrong, and that was it. But . . . I shot the guy a look. His bony naked body was nothing to look at, and that, combined with his face, which was fair and pale like a broad's, and his pleading expression, for some reason irritated me, left me with a bad taste. And then the bad taste turned to disgust. I couldn't figure it out. I absolutely detested anything that looked weak and powerless. Things that were weak and that broke easily—whether it was a window or the expression on the face of someone who was fawning and groveling—one look and the hate swelled up inside me like the bloated body of a decomposing corpse. I couldn't help feeling an urge to break, crush, stomp on those things.

"I'm telling the truth. Why can't you believe what a person says?"

"You asshole! You asked for it!"

I jumped up, threw off my jacket, and gave him a good solid taste of my fists.

This guy was a bleeder, and once his nose was running red, I decided to call it quits. I put my jacket back on and tidied myself up. Loosening up the arms and legs like this, I'd worked up a pretty good sweat in the small of my back.

I lit a cigarette. Took a deep drag and blew it out. _Dear, I can't understand why you don't just quit a habit that's not good for you._

*Doesn't it embarrass you in front of the people at church? The impor-
tant thing is your health. Besides, someone who's been hospitalized with
bronchitis needs to be concerned about his throat. And I can't believe
one pack a day isn't enough for you. I'm thinking about the kids, you
know. What are we going to do if something should happen to you?* Her
bitching was ringing in my ears. Once she hit forty, it got noticeably
worse. In the past I would have ripped out that damn yap of hers. *I
must be getting old, the way I give in to her and put up with it now. Shit!*

"Okay, chin up and let's get you dressed."

I tossed him his clothes. He was sitting on the floor like a rag doll,
head hung low. Guy must have felt like crap. I'll bet he was fed up with
the whole damn world; whatever love of life he might have had was so
far gone he'd never get it back. And he didn't realize what I was doing
to him, and how important it was for me to make him like that. Once
you strip away a man's last ounce of pride and honor, he's as good as
naked and he'll start 'fessing up. *You guys might have looked presentable a little while ago, but once you set foot in here, you're not worth
ass-wipe, and that's what I have to make you realize. So what if you've
been to college? While you were going around with full bellies and a nice
school bag to show off and having fun fooling around with girls, thanks
to your parents' money, I was bitter because I couldn't even dream of
going to college, and I went around with a hangdog look. You think I
was any more stupid than you? It wasn't always that way. At one time
my family could hold their heads high. If the Reds hadn't slaughtered
nine of us—my grandparents and my uncles and their families—my
father wouldn't have been eaten up with hate; he wouldn't have come
home drunk every day and beaten up Mother and myself and Tal-suk
like some mad dog; his drinking wouldn't have gotten so bad that we
got kicked out of our rental with just the shirts on our backs; and in the
end he wouldn't have sunk so low that he had to kill himself. It's the
damn truth—if things hadn't turned out that way, my mother wouldn't
have been senile and started shitting and pissing all over; I would have
graduated from college like all of you; I would have landed a decent job
by now; I'd have a respectable look to me, sitting at a desk with a respectable name plate on it; I could have walked tall, lived high off the*

hog. _There was a time when I wanted to work at a bank. In no time I'd
be president; I'd ride in my black sedan to the golf course; I'd take my
family to a classy Western restaurant for a fancy dinner, build myself a
red-brick, Western-style house on a quarter-acre lot, put in a carpet of
grass in the yard, grow orchids year round, a beautiful, classy, elegant
life—that was my dream. I didn't accomplish any of that. Why? Because of the Reds, dammit. My enemies till the day I die—they ruined
my family, made me what I am today. But I have to say, I don't envy
anyone. Why should I? Because once you guys break the law and we get
you in here, you're a buck-naked little frog; doesn't matter that you have
money, good education, a bright and shining life, a swelled head that's
so heavy it's about to break your neck. Equal treatment, justice for all,
an established order, that's what we offer here—where else can you find
something like that? Here we don't discriminate on the basis of what you
do—you can be a company president, a director, a professor, a Ph.D.,
a day laborer, a construction worker, a doctor, a minister, a prostitute,
a lady, a student, a peddler; it's all the same to us, and that's what I'm
talking about._

"Come on, get dressed. Didn't you hear me?"

Finally the guy started to move. He got up, but he was so unsteady,
it looked like he was going to fall when he bent over to put on his pants.
I checked my watch—almost one in the morning. _Already. Throat's so
dry—what I'd do for a cold beer. Getting tired—maybe I ought to take
a break._ Not a peep out of the guy next door. I sat this one down in a
chair. Time to write another statement. I shoved pen and paper at him.

"Uh, I already did this," the guy whimpered. He looked like he was
done in.

"Doesn't matter. Do it again. You might have to do it a dozen times.
Of course if you decide to be truthful and write out everything the way
it happened, then once is enough, and it's all over."

The guy didn't say anything.

"To be honest with you I'm sick and tired of this. I want to drop everything, stretch out, and go to sleep. It's the truth. Same with you, I'll
bet. For the love of God, how about cooperating? I'll be back by and by,
so be sure you write everything down."

He still didn't say anything. He sat there in a heap, head hanging down. I let myself out. Before I shut the door, I looked back for a moment, and he was sitting the same way. Sitting like an idiot, all by his lonesome, there in the Red Room he looked like a little caged animal.

Five

What's that? A horrible strange sound. I'm awake. What's wrong with my eyes? The lids are stuck together, feels like sand inside. Splitting headache. Throat's burning. Everything red. The four walls and the ceiling, all blood red. And now it's like that red's inside me and I'm turning red all over. Did I doze off? With an effort I look up, and then around the room—I'm alone. I feel light-headed. Like I'm weightless, floating on air—a weird sensation. The desk, chairs, toilet, bathtub, showerhead, the bed I'm lying on—where did they come from? They look like stage props. Maybe it's because the room is filled with red. Red is the color of madness, and the objects framed by that color look bizarre, warped, distorted. I can't help shuddering.

It has to be a nightmare. I'm dreaming. I'm scared, I can't take it, I'm shuddering. I shut my eyes tight, I want it to go away. That strange noise again, coming through the wall. Such a painful sound, it makes my skin crawl; a noise like that can't possibly come from the human body. Who could it be? I hunch down, listen carefully, try to figure out who that voice belongs to. Yi Sang-jun? Sŏ Chŏng-min? Hard to tell. According to that man, there are others here, not just those two. So the man who's screaming could be someone I don't know. More screams. Coming from the room across the hall or else next door. I put my hands over my ears. Meat filling a large display at the butcher's, lit up by the red light. Bony slabs of ribs, haunches, beef and pork, hanging from hooks—ghastly images flickering on and off in my mind's eye. Am I going to die, stuck here like this? How are they going to get rid of me? Weigh me down with concrete and throw me into the ocean or the river, nothing left of me except white bones after the fish get done with me? Dump me unconscious on railroad tracks out in the open in the middle of the night, for a train to run over me, leaving me an unrecognizable mess, shreds of flesh and fragments of bone? What a bizarre stream of thoughts, no order to them, all so bizarre. Feel like I'm laid out on my stomach, face frozen in ice, a sickening fear making my skin crawl, and I pant trying to hold it back. A dull pain in the small of my back, my knees, my hips. The insanity in their eyes when they kicked me and beat me and stomped on me; I can't rid my brain of the image. How long have I been like this, laid out prone, hands over my ears?

How did I end up like this, getting dragged here? That damn Yi Sang-jun! No, he's not to blame. It's all Sŏ Chŏng-min's fault. If it weren't for him, for that phone call from him, everything would be smooth sailing like always, back and forth from home to school. Eyes open in the morning and hit the ground running; my wife's bickering; the morning teachers' meeting that bores me to tears; the nagging of Shrike, the vice-principal; the twenty-seven hours of classes I have to teach every week; drinks with the other teachers nearby when school's out for the day; the tedious, lifeless conversation there—these particulars of my daily life, they used to seem so trivial and meaningless to me. Hard to believe I found them so difficult to put up with.

I've had a dream. A lingering desire to write affecting, gemlike poems. A dream I haven't been able to get rid of. Wilting by the end of the school day, I drag myself home, have myself a late dinner, stretch out on my side on the floor, flick the remote, my eyes get heavy, and finally I'm snoring—that's my life. And yet I can't get rid of this ludicrous dream that I'm going to be a poet. Several years now and I haven't managed to scribble a single line, and yet there are times when I go out on the balcony at night and look out over the darkened city, or when I'm inside a packed bus late at night, swaying with the press of other straphangers as ridden with fatigue as I, times when I suddenly realize that I'm letting myself die a little more with each passing day, and it sends a shiver down my spine. Every such time, I resent my lot in life; I curse it. Money, wife, child, job, the whole works, I hate them. They're the reasons I'm stuck, body and soul, in this dirty, stinking life, this rotten, meaningless life. And here I am now, teary-eyed; I miss those priceless things so much. The modest and ordinary particulars of my life, which I used to hold worthless and insignificant, have suddenly assumed such incredible meaning that I shiver because I long for them so.

"Mother!"

Again that horrible screaming. Yes, it's Sŏ Chŏng-min. Finally—I have a very strong hunch it's his voice. Well . . . So he's here too. More screaming. So urgent, so desperate, those mortal screams, each one making my hair stand on end. His bespectacled face appears in my mind. Taciturn and prudent, but the most caring person you could find. When I twisted my ankle in basic training and was hobbling around, he was always there to look after me—a memory I've never forgotten. I've held him dear, have always been proud of the fact that this man who lived for the weak and the discouraged was a close friend of mine. And that's why I felt compelled to agree to the unexpected favor he asked me that day, even though I was tempted in my fear and anxiety to have no part of it. Then again, by agreeing, I may have wanted to make up for my initial indecision and the embarrassment and self-censure it caused me. At any rate, it was that phone call from Sŏ Chŏng-min, coming to me at school on a Saturday, near the end of classes.

As soon as school was out, I went to meet him at a tearoom near where he worked. I guess that's where my trail of misfortune started.

"So, a favor," I chuckled. "You're the last person I'd expect that from."

It had been quite some time since I had last seen him.

"Well, the truth is, I had to think about whether I should really ask this sort of favor. But I felt I could trust you and talk to you. I'll say this, though—if something goes wrong, you could get into trouble real quick. So if you have any doubts, just say no and I'm fine with that. I don't want to burden you with something dangerous."

"What's it all about anyway?"

Instead of answering he led me outside. We found a secluded alley, and he began a careful account: A college classmate, junior to himself, was a dissident and was wanted by the authorities, and Chŏng-min wanted me to keep him at our house for a few days. I had mixed feel-

ings, but ultimately I said yes. To be honest, I decided it shouldn't be
that dangerous. This man was one of the organizers of a demonstration that had taken place a few months before; it wasn't as if it were a
capital offense to hide him.

Two nights later, as agreed, Chŏng-min arrived at our home with Yi
Sang-jun.

My wife immediately voiced her disapproval.

"What's the meaning of this, dear?"

"You know, there are people out there fighting for their lives, and
all you can do is complain because of a little inconvenience? I expected
more than that from a woman who's been to college."

I was so full of myself toward my wife then. And so Yi Sang-jun
hid out in our home for a couple of weeks. I let him stay in my study,
where I usually slept, and kept to the family room with my wife and
our daughter. Yi Sang-jun was two years younger than me, didn't
talk much, and seemed to be an even-tempered sort. We rarely saw
each other during that time. For one thing he went out during the
day, didn't come back till late at night, and then was in bed before you
knew it, and for our part we were as careful as could be not to bother
him. I played *paduk* with him a couple of times, and the night before
he moved on to the next place, we marked the occasion with a beer,
but apart from that there were hardly any occasions where I can even
remember what he and I talked about. And that was it, I'm sure of it.
And that's why it was possible for me to forget all about it once he and
Chŏng-min left our home in the middle of the night, and I couldn't for
the life of me have imagined that those two weeks would one day lead
to the indignities I was suffering now.

I open my eyes and sit up. I have to pee, and I can't wait any longer. The back of my head hurts like hell and I'm dizzy. I try to stand,
but my knees buckle. I've broken out all over in a cold sweat. I stagger to the toilet and do my business. It's all my legs can do to support
my weight during that short time. I plop myself back on the bed and
inspect myself—arms, legs, everywhere is black and blue. I still can't
believe this is happening to me. Those men beat me like a dog, beat
me all over, beating first and asking questions later. What in heaven's

name makes men act that way? There was a strange gleam in their eyes, a gleam of joy and pleasure, something I've never seen before. That one human could treat another with such utter hatred and violence is beyond my belief. What made them like that? An organization? The blind, savage frenzy that we call loyalty?

The door clunked open. That man. I hunch up, suddenly cold.

"Let's see what we've got here. Everything written down?"

He's muttering to himself as he plops down in the chair. He picks up the sheet of paper and reads. My heart begins to race. I've written down practically everything that happened. But I have a feeling it's not what he's looking for. He seems to be giving it a quick once-over, doesn't look too interested in what he's reading.

"Look, Mister O."

He thumps the sheet of paper onto the desk and observes me, making me wait for the next words to fall from his lips. And now he's on his feet again, and against the red background of the walls his bulk suddenly looms impossibly large, filling my field of vision. His leather jacket is black as charcoal.

"Mr. O. No use trying to lie your way out of this. Your organization is broken up, finished."

The man shoots me a cold look, his expression unwavering.

Organization? I gape at him. A chill hits me, and I feel like curling up in a ball.

"Sŏ Chŏng-min came clean just now. And it's only a matter of time till Yi Sang-jun spills his guts too. So now it's your turn. What we've got here is enough to arrest you. So talk. What were you and Yi Sang-jun cooking up?"

"We weren't cooking up anything—we hardly had a chance to talk. Once in a while he'd ask me for a newspaper, and we'd talk about this and that, but . . . beyond that I don't know anything—I mean it."

"Bullshit! It's all a smokescreen. Yi Sang-jun is a damn socialist. Said so himself. Said he'd rounded up a bunch of malcontents; they were going to overthrow the system, they were planning a violent revolution, they were cooking something up. And he was using your place as a den. Isn't that right?"

"No, it's not. It's like I said—I don't know a thing about all that—honestly."

"I'm telling you, it's no use. How about we put you up against Sŏ Chŏng-min, face to face?"

"All right. That would be better. Now?"

"Look. Just cut the crap and listen up. There were some guys who sneaked into your apartment to see Yi Sang-jun. Who were they? I want names."

"I don't know any names. Sŏ Chŏng-min dropped by a few times at night, but he was the only one."

"Let me refresh your memory—Pang Han-sŏng . . . Ch'ae Hyŏng-t'aek . . . ring a bell?"

"No, never heard of them."

I look at the man's dead-mask face, shaking my head as vigorously as I could. It's true—I've never heard those names before. This man is fabricating a fantastic plot, and he wants to implicate me with a couple of guys who don't even exist. And he needs evidence from me so there won't be any loose ends. And if that's the case. . . . Suddenly all my nerves are on end. If that's the case, doesn't it mean the fate of the others is hanging on what I say? That I'm solely responsible for what happens to Sŏ Chŏng-min and Yi Sang-jun and Pang and Ch'ae?

"I don't know who they are—believe me. I've never met two men by those names. And I still don't know much about Yi Sang-jun. I wrote down everything I know on that paper. Can't you see, sir?"

I feel like getting down on my knees and begging. I'm a spineless, cowering wretch.

"Talk, you arrogant asshole! The name of your organization, how many of you there are, and what you were scheming—talk!"

"There's no organization and no plot. For God's sake will you *please* believe me? If you won't believe what another person says, then what *will* you believe? Show me those two people. Then everything will be cleared up."

"No way. I guess we need to work you over some more."

The man's face is twisted and mean. He goes for the door, it clunks

open, and he calls out. Men swarm in, the same men as before. A
shock hits me, and I can barely keep myself from plopping down on
the floor.

"Strip him!"

The men jump me, grabbing me by the arms and the hair.

"Let go—I'll do it myself!"

I'm not sure where that came from. I can't explain it, but I feel calm.
They let go of me, and I don't put up a fight—I start to undress. First
my shirt, then my pants, then my long underwear. I still have the dry
mouth, but this time my fingers aren't trembling. And then I'm standing in front of them with just my underpants on. Practically naked, but
if I'm cold, the sensation hasn't registered yet. I realize I'm slumped
over, and I try to stand straight and stick out my chest. *Got to stand
tall. Maybe I look wretched and pathetic, but I'm going to stand tall in
front of you. Got to stand tall.* I repeat this to myself, try to muster up
my courage, for what it's worth.

The man is in front of me, unblinking. He speaks coldly: "Underpants too."

I glare at him. For the first time I feel a fierce rage rearing its head
from somewhere inside me. The head of a viper whose tail has been
stepped on. Standing up straight and not backing down, I surprise
even myself. And so my underpants drop to the floor. *So there—that's
what you want.* My body deprived of that last piece of cloth, I realize
that my last ounce of pride as a human being has been plundered. At
that instant the fierce rage that has welled up inside me is consumed
and gone. I've lost the will to square my shoulders, am nothing more
than an animal.

They're standing in a circle around me, looking at my naked body;
they appear to be enjoying themselves.

"Guy's nothing but skin and bones, looks like he's never had meat
in his life. You too poor to buy meat? Look at his pecker—it's pathetic."

The man in the leather jacket chuckles as he says this; he has a cruel
smile. The others likewise wear sly, toothy grins. But hidden within
those upsetting smiles is a kind of tedium and boredom. And hidden

behind that boredom is a vicious craving for destruction, an unbearable desire to break, smash, and trample.

I wish I knew how to pray. But if there's such a thing as a God or gods, where in the name of creation am I supposed to find them? If there's a God, why does He hide himself away at the times He's needed most? I lick my lips—dry as paper; amazing. A man pulls my arms behind my back and handcuffs me. Two others take my arms and push me toward the wall.

"Okay, let's have ourselves a little shower. Makes a man nice and refreshed."

A hand grabs my hair, pulls my head back.

My head is locked in this grip, my naked body held fast with tremendous force. The showerhead. My face positioned directly toward it. And then the hiss of the water, a stream of water. . . . Stinging pain sweeps over me. The hand holding my hair tightens, pulling my head up so the water goes into my nose. Can't breathe. Can't open my eyes. The water's freezing on my face, my face is a sheet of ice, it's numb, can't feel a thing. Have to open my eyes. . . . Have to breathe. . . . I try to twist my head, but it just won't move.

"Hey, watch it, asshole, you're splashing me."

Chuckling.

"Hey, asshole." This time to me. "Quit squirming."

A shower of kicks and punches every time I try to twist free. I'm drifting. Gushing. Gushing all over me. Waterfall. I'm naked in a waterfall. Water falling from a thousand yards up, the pressure, it's amazing, falling down on me, pounding me all over. Gushing. . . . How long? No more waterfall. No more gushing—is it for real? Silence. So weird, this stillness. Feel like a rock that's sunk to the bottom of the sea. I open my eyes, and a blood-colored world pushes in on me. Feels like all the blood vessels in my eyes have burst.

"It's not working. Let him down. He's a die-hard—worse than he looks." The man in the black jacket.

I realize I'm lying on the plastic-covered bed.

"Are you human? How can you treat an innocent—"

Something covers my face—it's blue, not heavy, feels like a towel. I open my eyes. The red ceiling is gone, and the world has turned blue. There's something around my ankles, knees, chest—rope or twine, it has a hard feel to it. These men are good at tying me up, and as they work, they talk as if nothing is out of the ordinary.

"Where'd you put the radio?"

"Don't know. I haven't seen your precious radio since the day before yesterday. Maybe Section Chief Kim took it to his room?"

"No, it's somewhere here; I brought it in—oh, there it is."

"Put the kettle here. I'll handle it."

"Make sure you got him on that side of the head."

"For God's sake quit worrying. We'll make sure your suit stays nice and clean—not that it cost you all that much in the first place." A chuckle.

I'm shivering. It's cold. Teeth clattering together. I grit them. *I can take it. Got to take it. Won't let them make me look bad. Got to stand tall.* Promises to myself, chantlike. But it's only a pathetic bluff. In their eyes I'm worthless, something not quite human. One summer I saw a dog get slaughtered. They put it in a sack and hung it from a branch, three men in sleeveless T-shirts, and they beat it to death with sticks and hoes. The dog was jumping around inside the sack, but finally the sack went limp. Blood was dripping out the bottom of it.

Glug-glug-glug. Water pouring down. Must be that kettle, it's up above their faces, water pouring out of it. I can't help grunting. *No, keep quiet.* My mouth opens wide, but before I can scream, water penetrates it—nostrils too. That water has no mercy. I swallow, I swallow again, and again. My throat's going to burst. The water has a smell. A nauseating stink that's rust-like, fishy, heavy like metal. I'm sick to my stomach, I'm retching. Waterfall, the gush of water, the rust smell, lightning flashes inside my eyes, and then it's dark. I grunt. *Stop, stop it.* My chest is about to explode. *Don't do that*, I tell myself. *Please.* My body wants to thrash around. But they're holding me down; they're too heavy. Inside my eyes it's yellow now. *Tied down, can't move.*

"Mr. Shin, how long have you been acting—quite some time now, isn't it? Just how many years has it been?" A woman's voice.

"Well, this year would be nineteen—I think." A man's voice.

"Gracious, almost twenty years. It seems like only a few years to me." The woman laughs.

"Well, that may seem long to some people, but I still feel like I did when I started out. That was when I was twenty-four, fresh out of the army . . ."

Where are those voices coming from? Who are they? *The radio.* Water pouring into my nose again. "My, my, spoken so humbly. To my eyes anyway, your face isn't much different from back then—you still look like a young man in your twenties." A giggle. "Well, thank you. My wife would be pleased to hear that." Chuckling. "No, I mean it. Oh yes, your good wife is the famous fashion designer Ŏm Mi-ran— correct? And not too long ago she had a show at the Lotte Hotel that was a huge success, I believe. And that's probably why everyone says you have such good taste in clothing. . . ." *Can't breathe. Can't take any more.* The inside of my nose is hot, burning. I see sparks shooting up, dying out, shooting up, dying out. My throat hurts, like I've swallowed fire. *Don't swallow the water.* I've got to keep my mouth closed. *Come on, take it. Got to endure. Just a little.* I'm groaning. *A little more. You can do it.* I squirm like a madman. But I can't move. The pressure's enormous, all over me. A waterfall. I hear myself groaning. I'm under the waterfall and I'm sinking; I'm upside down, I'm sinking, I'm sinking, I'm sinking. My body . . . my neck, my throat . . . it's going to burst. A giggle. "I imagine you have a number of die-hard fans among the good housewives listening in today. At the height of your popularity, whenever and wherever you appeared, the ladies turned out in droves—isn't that so? And if the truth be told, I was one of them." "Well, this is indeed an honor. . . ." I'm going to squirm free or die trying. I feel like a minnow flopping helplessly on the sand. Like a toad that kids catch out in the paddies, when it's hotter than hell, and they throw it to the ground trying to kill it. There it lies, round white belly heaving. "Oh, Section Chief Yi, you had a call." "Me? Who was it?" "Got me. It was a woman—your wife, maybe? Had a silky tone of voice. Hey, I bet it was Madam O from Emperor Chin's Palace." Chuckling. "Don't play dumb, dammit. Of course it was her. You know why she's after me—I ran up a tab there, and yesterday was payday." "Of all the lucky SOBs. I can't afford a tab. What with all the deductions from my measly pay, I'm afraid to show the wife what's left. Hey, hold him tight—I'm getting splashed, for God's sake! Guy's holding up pretty well—he's a tough breed. The more I think about it, fuck, why don't I quit this job and go into business for myself? We're supposed to get a bonus this month. Hell, what's the use of a bonus when you've got jack shit to begin with? Take out the school loan for the kids and whatnot, and there's nothing left. These days you can hardly afford to get a kid through high school—no joke. Almost the same as putting him through college. . . ." My arms and legs are getting tired. I can't even squirm. . . . I feel like I'm drifting. Sinking into a sea of mud. Ankles . . . knees . . . thighs . . . waist . . . and now I'm in up to my chest, deeper and deeper I go. Water . . . dribbling . . . pouring. The mud's up to my chin. Wheels, metal. The treads of a tank. A black, heavy weight that's going to push me down into the sea of mud. Rolling toward me. I've got to get out of here. Before it's too late. *Open the window, the window, oh oh, hey hey. I wait outside your window, all through the moonlit night, oh oh, hey hey.* Man beside my head humming along with that song. *Oh oh, I pray outside your window, all through the moonlit night, oh oh, hey hey.* I hear myself groaning again. The human race can go to hell for all I care. They've stripped me naked, they've thrown me into a waterfall, I'm sinking, sinking, sinking. I hate this world. Everything that lives in it can go to hell. That means you, Sŏ Chŏng-min, and you, Yi Sang-jun; you two are the reason I'm here . . . and you men, laughing while you take me apart . . . and that huge tank that's rolling toward me, that's going to crush me—I hate you with a mad passion, everyone and everything, and you can all go to hell. I want to kill all of you. Every one of you . . . I want to strangle every last one of you. I'm groaning. I'll kill you all; I'll kill you before you can take me apart. . . . More water. The pressure of that waterfall, it's too much. My throat's tearing open. The water's dark, it's polluted and black, and it's in my nose, my mouth, my throat. *Open your window, oh oh, open your window for me, oh oh, hey hey.* Groaning. I'm dying. Look at me, I'm dying. *Oh oh, hey hey.* It's so stupid to die like this, a pathetic mess . . . dying for no reason. *Hey hey.* The water . . . the song . . . the humming. *Hey hey, oh oh.* . . .

No more water. No more waterfall. The rumbling of that huge tank, the sea of mud—all gone. It's over. The end. *I want to live*—a desire so fierce I can't believe myself at first. *I want to live. I've got to live. I can't die.* I'm groaning. Panting. Eyes snap open. A shout rips from my throat: "Don't kill me! I'll talk; I'll tell you everything you want, everything!"

The blue cover is gone from my face. The men look down at me, expressionless. The one in the leather jacket grabs my hair and pulls my head up. He's grinning.

"Look at this guy, still out of it—listen, you, it's not 'everything we want'; just tell us the truth, spill it out."

"All right, all right, I'll talk, I'll tell you the truth, I'll confess. Just don't kill me, I'm begging you!"

A faint smile of satisfaction on the man's face. I'm retching. But nothing comes up. I'm saturated with water and sweat. The man lets go of my hair, my head falls back, my eyes close.

"What did I tell you? You come clean with us, and we can avoid this unpleasantness." *Tsk-tsk.* "We already know everything, see? Now, what about O Sŏng-su? Your uncle—your father's elder brother. We had a look at your family history, and guess what, he went north around the time of the war. Seems he was quite the big shot among the Reds. How does that grab you?"

My heart drops. I feel like a huge hole is opening inside it, and within that hole is pitch darkness. That hole is unfathomable, a huge trap of blackness, and if any of us in this severed land of ours gets pulled in, it opens wide its maw and he can never get out again. I have a hunch it's all over now. I slowly open my eyes, and there it is, that monochrome cascade, filling every space about me, that blood-red world. My eyes have filled with tears, but I don't know exactly why.

Six

The instant I fed him the name of his uncle who went north, his face
turned white. *See? With these guys, it does the trick every time. At first
glance all you notice is the naive face and the "Who-me?" attitude, but
with the majority of this type, you root around beneath the surface, and
you'll find there's a problem with their family background. After all,
once you plant a red bean, it's not going to grow into a black bean. You
grow up in a family with an unsound ideology, and you're bound to go
off on a tangent. And so it looks like this guy has come to the end of the
line. Now we've taken the wind out of his sails, he won't even think of resisting or trying to twist his words around. I bet he'll do anything to save
his skin. I've got him where I want him now.* I could feel a big grin coming on as I looked at his pale face.

*Guy looks like a rag doll—must be worn out. Well, he ought to be.
Force-feed them water, and they turn into jelly—amazing how the
human body works. Well, hell, I'm tired too. And I'm sick of this job,
having to keep after these guys night and day and never getting a decent night's sleep. Sometimes I get this urge to take off the "uniform"
for good, but when I get right down to it, it's not like I've come up with
a brilliant alternative, and so that urge always remains just a thought.
The kids are growing, and the wife, now she knows the smell of money,
is always griping about something at home. The biggest headache is
Mother. Think about it—I'm trying to get through life, and something or
somebody is always holding me back—it's a damn shame I have to live
like this. I wonder if other men with family responsibilities feel like I do.
When I'm having it out, day in and day out, like I am right now, with
these guys who are a cancer on our society, the little woman is probably
watching a soap opera on TV, and my senile mother is plopped down
in the middle of her own shit, playing with it and making a nice mess,
smearing it all over the floor and the walls. As for the kids, I can't really
pick on them for anything, but now that they're growing and you add
up the school fees, spending money, money for clothes, they're like a bottomless hole. All right, you two, the first thing you've got to do is study
hard. Number one, you're a girl, so you'll do fine going to school in
the provinces, getting a degree in pharmacy, and marrying a guy with
money. And son, make sure you get into one of the service academies,*

the military academy—that's the only way poor slobs like me and you get ahead in the world. *That's how I drill it into them when I come home after a few drinks and I'm in a good mood. They always kneel down and lower their heads, nice and respectful, during this lecture, and they're so cute and adorable, I get so choked up I want to give them a big hug and kiss.*

"All right, Mr. O, what's this heaven-on-earth stuff all about? Yi Sang-jun talked about it with you." I indicated part of his statement as I asked him this.

"Oh, that. . . . How can I say it, . . . we were thinking there ought to be a world fit for people to live in   it was something like that."

The guy was so timid, speaking slowly, fumbling for words.

"A world fit for people to live in." I snorted. "Isn't heaven-on-earth something that stands for paradise?"

"Well, what we meant was . . . not paradise, which is an existence after death, something that exists only in people's minds. We were talking about how our own society eventually has to be made into a place that's on a level with heaven."

"Yi Sang-jun insists he's a Christian—how about you, Mr. O?"

"No, I'm not, but I didn't feel that Yi Sang-jun as a Christian was wrong in his thoughts about society. So—"

I snorted again. "If that's the case, then what is this ideal society you're thinking about? Must be what you mean by a world that's fit for people to live in."

"Well, I guess you could say that. . . . In other words, it's a society where everyone cares for each other and helps each other out, . . . where everybody gets along together and there aren't any poor people or people who are treated unfairly."

"Oho, now I got it—just what I thought! A socialist state. What you fine gentlemen are proposing is to uproot the system, and you're not afraid to use violence to do it. So you're conspiring to gather together all the impure elements you can find and launch a socialist revolution—right?"

I banged the table in triumph. This was the moment I'd been waiting for.

There was fear all over the guy's face—he didn't know what to say.

"Equality for all, is that it? A world without any poor slobs, nobody gets the shit end of the stick, nobody's exploited—everybody lives the same. And that's heaven-on-earth? What a crock, Mr. O. What you're saying is ridiculous. What's going to happen when these evil bastards throw their weight around in this heaven-on-earth of yours? Tell me, what happens when we have all these evil bastards swarming around like cockroaches? Do we let them be, leave everything to chance—and then the world is going to turn into a paradise all by itself? That's the stupidest thing I ever heard. Those evil bastards have to stand before God's judgment. Those little snakes have to be stamped out, every last one of them. The Bible makes it very clear. On the day of the last judgment the whole world turns into a plague of hell, and God sends down shafts of fiery lightning to burn this corrupt world. All of Satan's offspring have to be rooted out and burned up, every last one of them. Only the offspring of the righteous may enter heaven-on-earth. But listen to you—a world where everyone lives equally, good and evil alike, where everybody gets treated nice? That's what you want?"

"No, that's not what I meant. I can't believe you're talking about socialism—"

Rather than listen to this guy make excuses, I banged the table to get his attention back.

"It's ridiculous—doesn't make sense and you know it! The way you get equality and peace is through judgment and punishment. We all know that Jesus taught us to love our enemies, but he was referring to something completely different. He was teaching us to love our enemies who show repentance, remorse, penitence—he didn't mean the offspring of Satan. And it's guys like you who are the offspring of Satan. Actually you're worse than that—you're Satan himself. Dreaming of the socialist revolution. Communists, Reds, the wickedest people on earth—you're like poison mushrooms. We've got to root out those mushrooms and kill them, spores and all, make sure they never sprout again, wipe them all out, every last one. The day all of you poison mushrooms and germs go extinct, that'll be the day when we achieve a paradise. And this is why we have to go through all this shit, day in and day out; it's why we never get a good night's sleep. Somebody has to do it. You understand?"

I felt a little better getting that off my chest. At church once I got up and gave a prayer along those lines during the time when members of the congregation get to offer their own special prayers. And I have to admit, I did a fantastic job. So fantastic that in the benediction, to my embarrassment, the minister quoted me. *Truly a moving prayer from Deacon Ch'oe. It's thanks to gentlemen like you, Deacon Ch'oe, struggling day and night against the forces of evil in this degenerate world of ours, that we in this country are able to enjoy such prosperity and stability today. It's time for those of us in this congregation to pray ceaselessly, to fight tenaciously, to more actively and bravely spread the gospel.* After the service the minister kept telling me how wonderful my prayer was, and my wife couldn't stop sighing in admiration.

There was a knock on the door, and Miss Chŏng hesitantly stuck her head inside.

"Uh, Section Chief Ch'oe, I brought the meal, sir."

"Okay, come on in."

Miss Chŏng placed the newspaper-covered tray on the desk and left.

I removed the newspaper and pushed the tray toward the guy.

"Go on, eat. Don't let the soup get cold, or else it gets all greasy on top." I made a point of softening my tone. *Yeah, you've got to eat. Now we're getting started, you need a good meal under your belt, build up your energy, and then the confession will tumble off your lips.* I was feeling pretty satisfied with myself as I watched him.

The guy reluctantly picked up his chopsticks and after a moment's hesitation began slowly to eat. Now that we'd knocked all the starch out of him, he looked kind of pitiful as he worked the chopsticks. When you get right down to it, there's something wretched and servile about the act of eating, whether it's a person or an animal who's doing it. I took a look at the sheet of newspaper that had been covering the tray. Yesterday's morning edition. Baseball teams getting worked up over the new prospects. People flocking to the theaters to see an American movie called *Rambo*. Immature college kids still running around— when were they ever going to learn? And all the money wasted on the tear gas we had to use on them—so what's new? *Hell—what a shit life I have. Why can't I have time on my hands and camp out in front of movie theaters? Damn!* I cleared my throat, spat on the floor, rubbed it out with my shoe.

Another knock on the door. This time it was Pak whose head appeared.

"Section Chief Ch'oe, sir, a call from home."

I put down the newspaper, rose, and left. *Goddammit, what's she calling for?* The phone was upstairs, and it was damned aggravating having to go up and down every time you got a call.

"Dear, it's me—put me out of my misery, please!"

No preliminaries. Whining and blubbering from the moment I picked up.

"What the fuck is it now?!"

"It's your mother—she made another mess. I had to make a quick trip to the grocery store, and somehow she crawled out to the living room and peed all over the sofa. What am I going to do? I've scrubbed with rags and sprayed scent all around, and I can't get rid of the stink. The minister and the people from church are going to be here soon— what am I going to do?"

Her sniffling made it sound worse than it was. I felt a surge of irritation and couldn't do anything about it. If I was at home, at least I could destroy the damn telephone.

"Anyway, dear, you do remember that the minister's coming today? They're coming at one-thirty. And you know, the minister has something to tell you, so please be here then; you don't have to stay long."

I slammed the telephone down. Pak and Miss Chŏng were looking through some magazines, but when they realized how angry I was, they quickly looked the other way. I went outside for a smoke. There was quite a bit of snow in the yard, and the wind was swirling around my feet. The snow had begun accumulating the previous morning, and it was up to my ankles now. There seemed to be a temporary lull, but I'd heard on the news this morning that there had been much more snow so far this winter than in previous years. Hunched up, I sat on the brick wall of the flower garden. A lone Japanese maple stood there, bare of leaves, only its skeleton of branches remaining.

Dear, we need to decide what to do about your mother. How much

*longer do we all have to live like hell, just on account of one person?
What about that prayer house I found? The facilities are better than
some, and I think we can trust the director since he's a Christian. Can we
please send your mother there? I don't see what other choice we have—
we need to take care of ourselves while we're still healthy. And it's for
your mother's own good. Everybody knows what our situation is, and
they're not going to think badly of us for sending a parent to a prayer
house.* For some time now my wife had been bringing this up—and
always looking anxious about it. It's not as if I wasn't considering that
possibility myself. Actually it had been nagging at me for a while. She
didn't know about this, but not long after she brought up the idea, I
went on my own to take a look at that prayer house. My first impression was that it was more of a mental institution than a prayer house.
It looked like one of those unlicensed inns—a lot of rooms crammed
into a small space; a lock on the outside of each door; and apart from a
barred window so small you could barely poke your head out, no ven-
tilation that I could see. There were seven or eight people to a room,
and I gathered that apart from being fed, they got nothing in the way
of services. I was told that most of them were either mentally ill or had
gone senile in their old age. And that some of them had seizures and
occasionally were chained at the ankles as a restraint. I didn't see any
visitors, but I did see a dozen or so dogs, roaming the grounds and
snarling. My insides churned and I had a splitting headache at the
thought of abandoning my mother to that awful place, and I ran down
the hill to my car.

But now I was no longer sure I could put up with it anymore. What
was I going to do? Did I have any option other than sending her there?
I puffed away on my cigarette as I tried to suppress my aggravation.
Was I going to give her up? And to a place like that. . . ? Again I cleared
my throat and spat. The yellowish gob of mucus looked like pus on the
white snow. Suddenly I thought of my father.

Father met his end on the railroad tracks; he was drunk. No last
words, no last outcry; he closed his eyes for the last time, a gruesome, grotesque death. I've never been able to get rid of the sight of
his dark red blood splashed senselessly in the vicinity of the tracks.

His mangled corpse looked like a rag. It was barely covered by an old straw sack. I ran there when I got the news, but for the life of me the tears wouldn't come. All I could do was stand there, shuddering with blind hostility and hatred: everything was ugly to me, and so I hated everything.

Who made Father that way? I asked myself then. Who had destroyed him like this, turning him into a hideous mess of a carcass that trailed shreds of flesh and glops of blood? I tried to figure out who was responsible. This much I knew: it had been late at night, he was drunk, he was on his way home, and in a moment of insanity he had jumped in front of a train. But to simply chalk up his death to an accident or suicide was too much for me—it was so unfair. I had to assign responsibility for his death. I told myself I had to find out who or what was responsible.

After Father was relieved of his job, he became an alcoholic. *Talshik*, he would tell me, *you have to kill those Red sons of bitches. They're your enemies, all of them. They spill your blood, you spill theirs. You can pay off those who are kind to you in a generation, but when it comes to your enemies, they remain enemies for hundreds, thousands of years. Your dad has the grudge and resentment of his whole family to settle, and you have to settle what I can't. Only then can your grandparents and the families of your uncles close their eyes in peace—they should still be alive, but dammit, they're lying dead in the ground. Unless we get rid of the seed of those Red sons of bitches, peace and unification will never come to this land of ours. Your generation has to do everything it can to unify North and South.* I was still young at the time, and he would put his hands on my shoulders to make sure I understood, and at times the tears would stream from his eyes.

"Destroy Communism," "Down with Communism," "On Guard against Spies"—I always had these slogans on the wall behind my desk. I could always count on Father getting emotional when he saw them. And he would tell me, *Don't trust people. You can't trust anyone in this world except your blood relations. Humans are a cunning and evil breed. When you have them in front of you, they smile and make a big show of being friendly—as if they're the kindest and most affection-*

ate people you'd ever want to meet—but deep down inside they're like a sharp knife, and the minute you turn away, they'll stick you in the back. That's exactly what the Reds are like. Your grandfather turned his back on them, and that's how he passed. And it's the ones who are closest to you who are the animals that take your kindness and then become your enemy. Father pounded home this message as I was growing up, but the fact was, his words didn't have that much of an emotional impact on me.

But the moment I saw before me, scattered across the railroad tracks, the clumps of flesh and the clots of blood that used to be my father, I felt for the first time that I understood him. That's when I realized with absolute clarity that the crimson blood of my father flowed through me like a curse. It was the blood of grudge and vengeance, of curse and hatred, and it had been flowing through me ever since the slaughter of my grandparents and other relatives. Their blood had become one within my father, and my father's blood in turn now coursed through me, the absolute master of my heart and blood vessels.

And it was at the railroad tracks that I realized I had finally found my mortal enemies. They had been there all along, and they had inflicted a miserable death upon my grandparents, my relatives, my father—they were all the same. Those enemies, I knew, would attack me and choke the life out of me, and then, before long, they would set their sights on my son, my daughters, my wife, I was sure of it, and after that they would try to harm my grandchildren and their children and all their many descendants. Those enemies of mine were hidden everywhere. Like poison mushrooms, those abominations lurked in this free land of ours, poisonous centipedes vigilant for any opening, ready to crawl out and have their way with us. Those abominations— the offspring of Satan, conniving to throw the state into chaos, to overturn a peaceful world, and finally to create a den of darkness and blood—they were the Reds.

Slowly I rose. I breathed out toward the sky. Fresh cold air crept into my lungs. I guess I was feeling a little better. I checked my watch—it was almost noon. And I was almost done with this guy. Maybe I'd be able to go out drinking with the others at the Abang Palace in the evening. And then I remembered I had to drop by our house for lunch—the minister was coming. I'd feel less blue when we sang a hymn and prayed. There was something about religious faith—a power that was deep and mysterious. It was so peaceful, that feeling of warmth and grace that came over me when we got down on our knees before the Lord, closed our eyes, and prayed—it was such an amazing experience, it was difficult to describe in words. *The moment that your heart weakens and your courage falters, seek out God. At such times God will accept you, Deacon Ch'oe, in his embrace. Esteemed individuals such as you, Deacon Ch'oe, are the most valuable, the most precious of God's keepers of this world; may God grant you the valor of David and the wisdom of Solomon.* The minister would probably tell me something uplifting like that in his prayer today. *Yeah. I'm not living my life just for myself. Isn't it my duty to protect my community, my nation, against the forces of wickedness and evil? I've got to keep my courage up. Yes I do.*

I went back inside and started down the steps to the basement. It sounded like the others were hard at work. The rooms were alive with shouting and moaning. Humming a tune, I turned toward the Red Room.

Seven

I bury myself in the cushy sofa, but when I try to lift my arms, it's too much for me—they hurt. I pass my hand along the soft, chocolate-colored fabric. I can't figure it out—the look and touch of it are new and different, as if I've never experienced this object in my life. Can something this soft be real?

Can I really believe what he said about going home? I think about this as I try to rub away the ache in my knees. Since evening I've had a hunch that things are somehow different. They were gone for a while, and when they came back after lunch, I noticed a change in their attitude. There was something relaxed about them, they were talking more respectfully to me—it was obvious they were trying to project a gentler tone. And then early in the evening several of them looked me all over, and they were plainly relieved when they didn't see any visible injuries. And the man in the leather jacket said something. *Looks like you had yourself a sweet dream last night, Mr. O—dreamed you were going home.* But nothing really surprised me anymore.

I look up at the TV. A man and a woman are walking along a riverbank. "Sŏng-gi, we never should have met. It's so miserable having to break up like this and turn our backs on each other." "Ŭn-hye—you don't really mean that, do you?" What's going on with those two? And what kind of people are watching this couple on the television at this moment, following their childish words and actions? I bite down on my lip, feeling I've been taken in by an elaborate deception.

Through the window I see snow falling silently through the darkness. Light from inside slants across the ground; everything beyond is dim and featureless. I wonder where I am. The room is furnished like a plain old living room in a single-family home; you'd have a hard time believing there's such a big basement down below. But judging from the lack of headlights or noise from traffic, I'm in a building that sits all by itself in some foothills or a flat area away from the city.

I watch the snow accumulate outside the window, and it all still feels like a dream, something vague and insubstantial, a dream from which I can't easily awaken. The scene outside is so peaceful, so imbued with feeling, and yet it's incredibly unreal and absurd. How did I end up like this?

"Mr. O, you probably hold a grudge against me, but once you know the facts, you ought to be thanking me. Who do you think's arranged for your release?" The man chuckles.

I direct my unfocused eyes outside and consider. All through the night that man was asking me questions in the Red Room, but now I can't even remember what they were all about. Except for the fact that I was forced like a sleepwalker to repeat fragmented words that had nothing to do with me, that I didn't even understand, and to speak words that I was told to speak.

The man and the woman in the television show burst into laughter —it sounds fake to me. I want to shut my eyes and never open them again. I'm shaking with an anger I don't understand, an anger I don't know where to direct.

"I tell you what, Mr. O, let's forget this ever happened and just go our happy way. I didn't intend for our little business to work out like it did, but when you try to do things for your country and your people, things happen—you know that. After you're back home, just be careful what you say—though I'm sure you know better, since you're a sensible man. A word to the wise is sufficient, right?" The man chuckles. "All right, let's shake and say good-bye. And with a smile—that way, we won't feel awkward if we run into each other in the future." He chuckles again. This man in the leather jacket is asking me to shake hands with him. All I can do is look stupidly at his face. God only knows how many faces he has. Are any of them the face of a human being? What is the true character of the human race anyway? I still feel like I'm drifting in a horrible, drawn-out nightmare. The man sticks out his hand. When he sees I'm not taking it, he pulls it back without a hint of embarrassment.

A car arrives outside. Two men come in. The same men who brought me here.

"So long, Mr. O," says the man in the leather jacket as I'm leaving. "My name is Ch'oe Tal-shik, by the way. And for your own good, remember what I said just now. And so . . ."

I'm placed in the back seat. The car sets into motion. Ch'oe Tal-shik? Why would he tell me his name? When we're outside the iron gate, one of the men removes his suit jacket and puts it over my head. From this point on it's a rewind of when they brought me here.

The car clunks along a dirt road, and finally the rattling stops and the ride is smooth and gentle. The radio comes on. It's the news. The stock market continues bullish. Heavy snow in the Sŏrak Mountain area has brought traffic to a standstill. The UN Combined Forces Command has announced a minor skirmish in the DMZ, brought about by a North Korean provocation. In Seoul an armed man entered an apartment and strangled a housewife and her daughter before escaping. A city in Iran is burning after Iraqi bombing that leaves several hundred dead. In Pusan a Korean boxer defended his world title with a KO. And finally an announcement of the names of individuals and organiza-

tions that have taken part in a fund-raising campaign for children
with heart disease.

I keep feeling like I'm going to break into a grin. Here I am, head
down, covered by a suit jacket, listening to a news announcer tell
me what I've missed during the last few days. One morning I'm led
off without leaving a trace and locked up in a basement room that's
painted a grotesque color, and yet nobody has noticed, no one shows
the slightest concern. I disappear, my existence goes up in smoke, and
yet the world keeps turning, time keeps passing, nothing has changed.
And now I'm returning and still nobody notices. I grin, chuckling to
myself. *Don't hold a grudge against me. You don't know how lucky you
are to be going home in one piece.* So says that man Ch'oe Tal-shik.

Sure. Maybe I shouldn't be concerned. Somehow I fell into a poor
excuse for a trap, floundered around for a bit, and managed to get
out—that's all. I wonder how many other people are undergoing
terrible suffering in a secret room or a hidden basement at this very
moment—while the rest of us go on with our lives, relaxed and
nonchalant, without the slightest clue that they're missing. That was
me not so long ago—especially me. That was me as I solved a math
problem on the blackboard, walked innocently down the street,
drained a beer with the other teachers after school, lay on my
stomach, chin in hand, watching baseball on TV, with nary a thought
that somewhere in this land of ours there existed that bizarre,
grotesque Red Room.

Suddenly the jacket is removed from my head.

"Okay, you can sit up now."

Light from streetlights sweeps by outside. I recognize this area
with its shop signs and the people hunched over as they hurry home.
Oh oh, I like the way you look, oh oh, you look so cute to me. Now it's a
song from the radio. And then the car stops, and the driver jumps out
and opens the door for me.

"Here we are. You can walk the rest of the way. Don't forget this."

The man hands me my briefcase. I take it in my arms, and without
saying anything I get out. I stand there like a bump on a log and watch

the car recede into the distance. Snow has accumulated on the street, and it reflects the light from the streetlights. I look about. There, the alley, the same one where the men took me and put me in the car, how many days ago—I haven't yet figured out how many days and nights I've been away.

I start to walk. My legs wobble. A couple of steps, and I have to lean against a utility pole for support. Off in the distance the fifteen-story apartment building sticks up into the gloom of the night. That's where home is. My wife waits anxiously for me, our daughter in her arms. One, two, three, four. . . . My gaze fixes on a column of windows, and I go up a floor at a time. But before I arrive at my ninth-floor apartment, my field of vision is hopelessly confused by the dense cluster of lights—it's like a henhouse. Tears well up in my eyes. I'm back. Back home. Home where my wife and daughter wait. . . . But it's impossible for me to move quickly. What could be the reason? I'm not quite sure that this human form standing in the snow and looking toward my home belongs to me. For sure I'm no longer who I was before. That me has been taken away, is lost forever. That me was shredded, body and soul, during those days and nights in the Red Room. And then those men bring home that human form, shredded with a hatred and a disgust that would sicken the world and everyone in it, dump it here, and walk away whistling, never to be seen again.

Something is rising inside me, something hot and burning. It's spreading hot throughout me, building an enormous heat—it's my rage. I start for home again. Someone is coming toward me. Before I know it I'm shouting at him.

"Excuse me! What's the date?! What day is it?!"

It's a middle-aged man I've never seen before. He looks at me in surprise.

Eight

The car left and the iron gate clanged shut.

"That guy," Pak muttered as he went inside. "He lives to tell the tale." He chuckled.

I was alone in the yard. Hands on hips, I gazed up at the night sky. The heavens were black as ink—not a glimmer to be seen. Snow was falling, a light powder that skimmed my cheeks. An empty feeling swept over me, I wasn't sure why. It's a funny thing; I spend days fighting with these guys in the Red Room, but once they're gone, I always feel like that—like the wind's been taken out of my sails—and there's a bad taste in my mouth, as if someone has cursed me in the most vicious way. What can I say? It's like the feeling you get when something precious slips through your fingers, combined with a blind hatred, a rage, and finally something poisonous starts bubbling up inside me.

I spat once and went inside. I buried myself in the living room sofa. Suddenly I noticed my reflection in the window. There I was, ugly face that looks much older than my age, lined forehead, gloomy eyes saturated with long years of hatred, rage, and suffering. _I want to get rid of you. I don't like you. I want to kill you. I want to tear you to pieces._ I wanted to yell at that monstrous face glaring at me from the window. Somehow I fought back the urge. I got up and started down the stairs to the basement.

It was damp and dim in the hallway down there—must be what an underground tomb feels like. Screams from room number three— sounded like they'd gotten down to business. Screams, gasping and all, coming out of the speakers in living stereo. I went into the room at the end of the hall. Found the switch, turned on the light. The fluorescent bulb sputtered, flickered, and came on. A blood-colored sea filled the room. . . . Being in the Red Room calms me down, settles me, always has. Red walls, red ceiling, red bed—they give rise to a giddiness that's part pleasure and part pain. Maybe that accounts for the cozy familiarity of this room.

Elbows on the desk, hands together, time to pray. Focus on a point in space to get my thoughts in order. And then human forms begin to rise from the red sea like bubbles of blood—Father, Yong-sul . . . and my son Han-su, dead from a brain hemorrhage . . . my poor boy. I closed my eyes and began to pray. _Our Lord. Our Lord who extermi-_

nates the wicked and sustains the righteous. Spare Thou this sinner and with Thy steadfast faith watch over him, lest he yield to Satan's temptation. Oh Lord. Though the sins of these sheep are many and their foolishness knows no bounds. . . . As I prayed, I felt with vivid clarity a sacred joy and benevolence envelop me with warmth, before beginning finally to fill the Red Room.

Afterword

Trauma in Contemporary Korean Fiction

BRUCE FULTON

The symptoms of what we understand today as post-traumatic stress disorder (PTSD) were identified in writing at least as early as the publication in 1920 of Sigmund Freud's *Beyond the Pleasure Principle,* part of which is devoted to trauma. But not until 1980, when the syndrome was so designated by the American Psychiatric Association, did it receive a diagnostic cachet in place of what had previously been known by such terms as "shell shock."[1] More recently PTSD has become the focus of a growing body of research on literary works dealing with trauma victims, and in particular individuals traumatized by war-related experiences.

Trauma has been a fact of life for Koreans born before the Korean War (1950–1953)—and especially for those inhabitants of Chŏlla Province who, in addition to surviving the civil war, witnessed the 1980 Kwangju Massacre, when elite paratroop forces were dispatched from their posts near the DMZ to the South Chŏlla capital of Kwangju to suppress demonstrations against the authoritarian regime of Chun Doo Hwan. Whether through uprooting from the ancestral home, life on the road as war refugees, firsthand experience of combat, or the violent deaths of loved ones, Koreans have endured a variety of horrors. Modern Korean fiction is to a large extent a literature of witness to the historical upheavals of twentieth-century Korea, and it should come as no surprise that contemporary fiction, while providing comparatively few examples of war literature, yet continues to show us how individual Koreans have been traumatized by wartime violence. Some of contemporary Korea's most important authors—among them Yun Hŭng-gil, Kim Wŏn-il, and Kong Sŏn-ok—were traumatized by events during the Korean War and/or the Kwangju Massacre, and their own trauma informs their works.[2] The extent to which trauma figures in post-1945 Korean literature may be understood by the credence given by Korean scholars—manifested in the term *division literature*—to the notion of contemporary Korean literature being in large part a literature of the division (psychological as well as physical) of the Korean peninsula.

One of the most accomplished contemporary Korean literary works that involves trauma is Ch'oe Yun's novella "There a Petal Silently Falls" (Chŏgi sori ŏpshi han chŏm kkonnip i chigo).[3] This work was inspired by the Kwangju Massacre but deals with the horrors in an elliptical and impressionistic way. What distinguishes this work of fiction from "Spirit on the Wind" and "The Red Room" in the present volume is a narrative strand in the former that represents a movement toward healing and closure. That is, although the traumatized protagonists of all three works exhibit what Cathy Caruth terms "possession by the past,"[4] it is only the traumatized girl in "There a Petal Silently Falls" for whom hope is held out for ultimate deliverance from the vicious circle of PTSD.

This volume opens with Pak Wan-sŏ's "In the Realm of the Buddha."[5] It is tempting to see much of Pak's career as a process of working through wartime trauma. She lost both an uncle (executed on an unsubstantiated allegation of treason) and a brother (forcibly conscripted by the People's Army, never to be heard from again) in the war, and the latter loss figures prominently in her debut work, the autobiographical novel *Naked Tree*.[6] Like others of her works from the 1970s and beyond, "In the Realm of the Buddha" is a dual narrative that shifts between the here-and-now and unresolved trauma of decades earlier. For the narrator trauma is viscerally alive, an undigested mass inside her that she is desperate to vomit up once and for all.

"Spirit on the Wind" is, next to the novel _The Bird_ (Sae), O Chŏng-hŭi's longest work of fiction—worthy of note for a writer whose fiction first appeared in print in 1967.[7] Unlike the first-person narrative of "In the Realm of the Buddha," the narrative of O's novella is divided between a third-person account that takes the point of view of the traumatized Ŭn-su and a first-person account by her uncomprehending husband. We thereby have both firsthand and secondhand access to Ŭn-su's uncontrollable bouts of wanderlust, but not until the end of the story does the source of Ŭn-su's trauma become apparent. In this novella we see that for Koreans trauma is not limited just to the experiences of men at war but affects women and children as well.

Im Ch'ŏr-u's "The Red Room" was first published in 1988, scarcely a year after direct presidential elections marked the democratization of the political process in South Korea.[8] And yet the subject matter of Im's story—the arbitrary detention and torture of civilians—was so sensitive that when the members of the screening committee of the annual Yi Sang Literature Prize convened to select that year's best short story or novella, they were reluctant to grant the award to "The Red Room" alone. And so for the first and only time since the launching in 1977 of this award—the most prestigious award for short fiction and novellas in South Korea—two stories shared top honors. Among the three authors represented in this volume, Im is the only one native to Chŏlla Province, site of the 1980 Kwangju Massacre and often regarded with suspicion as a hotbed of political dissidence by the Park Chung Hee (1961–1979) and Chun Doo Hwan (1980–1987) regimes. In a short essay composed upon the acceptance of his Yi Sang Prize Im wrote of the unseen apparatus of oppression wielded by those regimes and of the violence, lies, and deceit that underlay that oppression.[9] "The Red Room" is distinctive in its dual narrative, alternating between O Ki-sŏp, the victim, and Ch'oe Tal-shik, the victimizer. The latter is shown to be a victim himself, unable to dispossess himself of the trauma of witnessing fellow villagers gunned down by his constable father around the time of the civil war, and in the present day constantly reminded of that trauma by his senile, incontinent mother. At the outset of the story O Ki-sŏp is blissfully unaware of the Red Room, concealed behind the wall of violence, lies, and deceit; at the end of the story he is returned to his home, wiser and yet perhaps traumatized in his turn—a caution by the author about the vicious circle begotten by the abuse of power. Im subsequently wrote at length of the Kwangju Massacre itself in the five-volume novel *Spring Day*.[10]

Anecdotal evidence suggests that Western readers not uncommonly find modern Korean fiction both provincial and depressing. It may be salutary to approach this body of literature with an understanding of trauma. The gloominess of the literature might thereby be leavened with the empathy brought to bear on the text by any reader familiar with the historical trauma experienced by his or her own culture and society—and that would likely include most readers. In this respect modern Korean fiction may be more universal than is commonly understood.

Notes

1. See Cathy Caruth, *Unclaimed Experience: Trauma, Narrative, and History* (Baltimore: Johns Hopkins, 1996), pp. 58–59 and 130–131, n. 1.
2. See Suh Ji-moon, comp., "The Korean War in the Lives and Thoughts of Several Major Korean Writers," pp. 92–109 in *Remembering the "Forgotten War": The Korean War as Seen through Literature and Art*, ed. Philip West and Suh Ji-moon (Armonk, N.Y.: M. E. Sharpe, 2000).
3. Ch'oe Yun, "Chŏgi sori ŏpshi han chŏm kkonnip i chigo," *Munhak kwa sahoe* (Literature and society), Summer 1988; trans. by Bruce and Ju-Chan Fulton as the title story in *There a Petal Silently Falls: Three Stories by Ch'oe Yun* (New York: Columbia University Press, 2008).
4. In PTSD "the overwhelming events of the past repeatedly possess, in intrusive images and thoughts, the one who has lived through them." Cathy Caruth, "Introduction" to Part 2, "Recapturing the Past," of

Trauma: Explorations in Memory, ed. Cathy Caruth (Baltimore: Johns Hopkins, 1995), p. 151.

5. "Puch'ŏnim kŭnch'ŏ," _Hyŏndae munhak_ (Contemporary literature), July 1973.

6. Pak Wan-sŏ, _Namok_, first published serially in _Yŏsŏng tonga_ (Women's East Asia), October 1970; trans. by Yu Young-nan as _Naked Tree_ (Ithaca, N.Y.: Cornell University East Asia Series, 1995).

7. "Param ŭi nŏk," in _Param ŭi nŏk_ (Seoul: Munhak kwa chisŏng sa, 1986). _Sae_ was first published in the Spring 1995 issue of the journal _Tongsŏ munhak_ (Literature East and West); trans. by Jenny Wang Medina as _The Bird_ (London: Telegraph, 2007). The latter work concerns trauma occasioned by childhood abuse.

8. "Pulgŭn pang," _Hyŏndae munhak_, August 1988.

9. Im Ch'ŏr-u, "P'ongnyŏk kwa kŏjit kwa ŭmmo ŭi pyŏk ap e" (Confronting the wall of violence, lies, and deceit), _Yi Sang Munhak Sang susang chakp'um chip_ (Yi Sang Literature Prize anthology) (Seoul: Munhak sasang sa, 1988), pp. 496–497.

10. Im Ch'ŏr-u, _Pom nal_, 5 vols. (Seoul: Munhak kwa chisŏng sa, 1997).

About the Authors and Translators

Pak Wan-sŏ (b. 1931) is among the most important living Korean fiction writers. Some fifty volumes of her fiction and memoirs have been published, including her collected short stories in 1999. Her works, many of them autobiographical, deal with the aftermath of the Korean War and the partition of the Korean peninsula; with the transformation of Korean society that has attended Korea's development from a traditional agrarian culture to an urban-centered, high-tech economy; and with the position of women in a patriarchal society. Her empathic, colloquial narratives have endeared her to generations of readers as the "Auntie Next Door."

O Chŏng-hŭi (b. 1947) deserves major credit along with Pak Wan-sŏ for the breakthrough by Korean women fiction writers beginning in the 1970s. Her fictional oeuvre, dating from 1967 and consisting of a novel (The Bird), the novella "Spirit on the Wind," and several volumes of short fiction, is relatively small in quantity but consistently high in quality. Many of her works depict broken families as a way of highlighting the breakup of the traditional extended family in a rapidly industrializing society. She also draws on Korean folklore and history, as well as native spirituality (female shamanism), to illuminate how Koreans have responded to the post–Korean War transformation of their society.

Im Ch'ŏr-u (b. 1954) was one of the first authors to shed light on events in contemporary Korean history, such as the May 1980 Kwangju Massacre, that were suppressed owing to the anti-Communist ideology institutionalized in South Korea from 1948 until the democratization of the political process in 1987. His works deal with the legacy of ideological conflict in post-1945 Korea. Especially noteworthy among his novels is the five-volume Spring Day, which chronicles the ten days of the Kwangju Massacre. Like Pak Wan-sŏ and O Chŏng-hŭi, he has received several awards for his writing. He currently teaches creative writing at Hanshin University.

Bruce and Ju-Chan Fulton are the translators of numerous volumes of contemporary Korean fiction, including Trees on a Slope, by Hwang Sun-wŏn (University of Hawai'i Press, 2005), and The Dwarf, by Cho Se-hŭi (University of Hawai'i Press, 2006). Among their awards are the first National Endowment for the Arts Translation Fellowship ever given for a translation from the Korean and the first Banff International Literary Translation Centre residency granted for a translation from any Asian language. Bruce Fulton is the inaugural holder of the Young-Bin Min Chair in Korean Literature and Literary Translation in the Department of Asian Studies at the University of British Columbia and is the general editor of the University of Hawai`i Press Modern Korean Fiction series.

Production Notes for **Fulton** | *The Red Room*

Design and composition by University of Hawai'i Press
production department with text in Minion condensed and
display in Gill Sans and Kabel

Cover design by Julie Matsuo-Chun

Printing and binding by The Maple-Vail Book Manufacturing Group